L. W. [

Legends of Babylon and Egypt in Relation to Hebrew Tradition

in large print

L. W. King

Legends of Babylon and Egypt in Relation to Hebrew Tradition

in large print

Reproduction of the original.

1st Edition 2022 | ISBN: 978-3-36831-664-8

Verlag (Publisher): Outlook Verlag GmbH, Zeilweg 44, 60439 Frankfurt, Deutschland
Vertretungsberechtigt (Authorized to represent): E. Roepke, Zeilweg 44, 60439 Frankfurt, Deutschland
Druck (Print): Books on Demand GmbH, In de Tarpen 42, 22848 Norderstedt, Deutschland

LEGENDS OF BABYLON AND EGYPT

IN RELATION TO HEBREW TRADITION

By
Leonard W. King,
M.A., Litt.D., F.S.A.
Assistant Keeper of Egyptian and Assyrian Antiquities
in the British Museum

Professor in the University of London King's College

PREFACE

In these lectures an attempt is made, not so much to restate familiar facts, as to accommodate them to new and supplementary evidence which has been published in America since the outbreak of the war. But even without the excuse of recent discovery, no apology would be needed for any comparison or contrast of Hebrew tradition with the mythological and legendary beliefs of Babylon and Egypt. Hebrew achievements in the sphere of religion and ethics are only thrown into stronger relief when studied against their contemporary background.

The bulk of our new material is furnished by some early texts, written towards the close of the third millennium B.C. They incorporate traditions which extend in unbroken outline from their own period into the remote ages of the past, and claim to trace the history of man back to his creation. They represent the early national traditions of the Sumerian people, who preceded the Semites as the ruling race in Babylonia; and incidentally they necessitate a revision of current views with regard to the cradle of Babylonian civilization. The most remarkable of the new documents is one which relates in poetical narrative an account of the Creation, of Antediluvian history, and of the Deluge. It thus exhibits a close resemblance in structure to the corresponding Hebrew traditions, a resemblance that is not shared by the Semitic-Babylonian Versions at present known. But in matter the Sumerian tradition is more primitive than any of the Semitic versions. In spite of the fact that the text appears to have reached us in a magical setting, and to some extent in epitomized form, this early document enables us to tap the stream of tradition at a point far above any at which approach has hitherto been possible.

Though the resemblance of early Sumerian tradition to that of the Hebrews is striking, it furnishes a still closer parallel to the summaries preserved from the history of Berossus. The huge figures incorporated in the latter's chronological scheme are no longer to be treated as a product of Neo-Babylonian speculation; they reappear in their original surroundings in another of these early documents, the Sumerian Dynastic List. The sources of Berossus had inevitably been semitized by Babylon; but two of his three Antediluvian cities find their place among the five of primitive Sumerian belief, and two of his ten Antediluvian kings rejoin their Sumerian prototypes. Moreover, the recorded ages of Sumerian and Hebrew patriarchs are strangely alike. It may be added that in Egypt a new fragment of the Palermo Stele has enabled us to verify, by a very similar comparison, the accuracy of Manetho's sources for his prehistoric period, while at the same time it demonstrates the way in which possible inaccuracies in his system, deduced from independent evidence, may have arisen in remote antiquity. It is clear that both Hebrew and Hellenistic traditions were modelled on very early lines.

Thus our new material enables us to check the age, and in some measure the accuracy, of the traditions concerning the dawn of history which the Greeks reproduced from native sources, both in Babylonia and Egypt, after the conquests of

4

Alexander had brought the Near East within the range of their intimate acquaintance. The third body of tradition, that of the Hebrews, though unbacked by the prestige of secular achievement, has, through incorporation in the canons of two great religious systems, acquired an authority which the others have not enjoyed. In re-examining the sources of all three accounts, so far as they are affected by the new discoveries, it will be of interest to observe how the same problems were solved in antiquity by very different races, living under widely divergent conditions, but within easy reach of one another. Their periods of contact, ascertained in history or suggested by geographical considerations, will prompt the further question to what extent each body of belief was evolved in independence of the others. The close correspondence that has long been recognized and is now confirmed between the Hebrew and the Semitic-Babylonian systems, as compared with that of Egypt, naturally falls within the scope of our enquiry.

Excavation has provided an extraordinarily full archaeological commentary to the legends of Egypt and Babylon; and when I received the invitation to deliver the Schweich Lectures for 1916, I was reminded of the terms of the Bequest and was asked to emphasize the archaeological side of the subject. Such material illustration was also calculated to bring out, in a more vivid manner than was possible with purely literary evidence, the contrasts and parallels presented by Hebrew tradition. Thanks to a special grant for photographs from the British Academy, I was enabled to illustrate by means of lantern slides many of the

5

problems discussed in the lectures; and it was originally intended that the photographs then shown should appear as plates in this volume. But in view of the continued and increasing shortage of paper, it was afterwards felt to be only right that all illustrations should be omitted. This very necessary decision has involved a recasting of certain sections of the lectures as delivered, which in its turn has rendered possible a fuller treatment of the new literary evidence. To the consequent shifting of interest is also due a transposition of names in the title. On their literary side, and in virtue of the intimacy of their relation to Hebrew tradition, the legends of Babylon must be given precedence over those of Egypt.

For the delay in the appearance of the volume I must plead the pressure of other work, on subjects far removed from archaeological study and affording little time and few facilities for a continuance of archaeological and textual research. It is hoped that the insertion of references throughout, and the more detailed discussion of problems suggested by our new literary material, may incline the reader to add his indulgence to that already extended to me by the British Academy.

L. W. KING.

LECTURE I—EGYPT, BABYLON, AND PALESTINE, AND SOME TRADITIONAL ORIGINS OF CIVILIZATION

At the present moment most of us have little time or thought to spare for subjects not connected directly or indirectly with the war. We have put aside our own interests and studies; and after the war we shall all have a certain amount of leeway to make up in acquainting ourselves with what has been going on in countries not yet involved in the great struggle. Meanwhile the most we can do is to glance for a moment at any discovery of exceptional interest that may come to light.

The main object of these lectures will be to examine certain Hebrew traditions in the light of new evidence which has been published in America since the outbreak of the war. The evidence is furnished by some literary texts, inscribed on tablets from Nippur, one of the oldest and most sacred cities of Babylonia. They are written in Sumerian, the language spoken by the non-Semitic people whom the Semitic Babylonians conquered and displaced; and they include a very primitive version of the Deluge story and Creation myth, and some texts which throw new light on the age of Babylonian civilization and on the area within which it had its rise. In them we have recovered some of the material from which Berossus derived his dynasty of Antediluvian kings, and we are thus enabled to test the accuracy of the Greek tradition by that of the Sumerians themselves. So far then as Babylonia is concerned, these documents will necessitate a re-examination of more than one problem.

The myths and legends of ancient Egypt are also to some extent involved. The trend of much recent anthropological research has been in the direction of seeking a single place of origin for similar beliefs and practices, at least among races which were bound to one another by political or commercial ties. And we shall have occasion to test, by means of our new data, a recent theory of Egyptian influence. The Nile Valley was, of course, one the great centres from which civilization radiated throughout the ancient East; and, even when direct contact is unproved, Egyptian literature may furnish instructive parallels and contrasts in any study of Western Asiatic mythology. Moreover, by a strange coincidence, there has also been published in Egypt since the beginning of the war a record referring to the reigns of predynastic rulers in the Nile Valley. This, like some of the Nippur texts, takes us back to that dim period before the dawn of actual history, and, though the information it affords is not detailed like theirs, it provides fresh confirmation of the general accuracy of Manetho's sources, and suggests some interesting points for comparison.

But the people with whose traditions we are ultimately concerned are the Hebrews. In the first series of Schweich Lectures, delivered in the year 1908, the late Canon Driver showed how the literature of Assyria and Babylon had thrown light upon Hebrew traditions concerning the origin and early history of the world. The majority of the cuneiform documents, on which he based his comparison, date from a period no earlier than the seventh century B.C., and yet it was clear that the texts themselves, in some form or other, must have descended from a remote antiquity. He concluded his brief reference to the Creation and Deluge Tablets with these words: "The Babylonian narratives are both polytheistic, while the corresponding biblical narratives (Gen. i and vi-xi) are made the vehicle of a pure and exalted monotheism; but in spite of this fundamental difference, and also variations in detail, the resemblances are such as to leave no doubt that the Hebrew cosmogony and the Hebrew story of the Deluge are both derived ultimately from the same original as the Babylonian narratives, only transformed by the magic touch of Israel's religion, and infused by it with a new spirit."(1) Among the recently published documents from Nippur we have at last recovered one at least of those primitive originals from which the Babylonian accounts were derived, while others prove the existence of variant stories of the world's origin and early history which have not survived in the later cuneiform texts. In some of these early Sumerian records we may trace a faint but remarkable parallel with the Hebrew traditions of man's history between his Creation and the Flood. It will be our task, then, to examine the relations which the Hebrew narratives bear both to the early Sumerian and to the later Babylonian Versions, and to ascertain how far the new discoveries support or modify current views with regard to the contents of those early chapters of Genesis.

(1) Driver, *Modern Research as illustrating the Bible* (The Schweich Lectures, 1908), p. 23.

I need not remind you that Genesis is the book of Hebrew origins, and that its contents mark it off to some extent from the other books of the Hebrew Bible. The object of the Pentateuch and the Book of Joshua is to describe in their origin the fundamental institutions of the national faith and to trace from the earliest times the course of events which led to the Hebrew settlement in Palestine. Of this national history the Book of Genesis forms the introductory section. Four centuries of complete silence lie between its close and the beginning of Exodus, where we enter on the history of a nation as contrasted with that of a family.(1) While Exodus and the succeeding books contain national traditions, Genesis is largely made up of individual biography. Chapters xii-l are concerned with the immediate ancestors of the Hebrew race, beginning with Abram's migration into Canaan and closing with Joseph's death in Egypt. But the aim of the book is not confined to recounting the ancestry of Israel. It seeks also to show her relation to other peoples in the world, and probing still deeper into the past it describes how the earth itself was prepared for man's habitation. Thus the patriarchal biographies are preceded, in chapters i-xi, by an account of the original of the world, the beginnings of civilization, and the distribution of the various races of mankind. It is, of course, with certain parts of this first group of chapters that such striking parallels have long been recognized in the cuneiform texts.

(1) Cf., e.g., Skinner, *A Critical and Exegetical Commentary on Genesis* (1912), p. ii f.; Driver, *The Book*

of Genesis, 10th ed. (1916), pp. 1 ff.; Ryle, *The Book of Genesis* (1914), pp. x ff.

In approaching this particular body of Hebrew traditions, the necessity for some caution will be apparent. It is not as though we were dealing with the reported beliefs of a Malayan or Central Australian tribe. In such a case there would be no difficulty in applying a purely objective criticism, without regard to ulterior consequences. But here our own feelings are involved, having their roots deep in early associations. The ground too is well trodden; and, had there been no new material to discuss, I think I should have preferred a less contentious theme. The new material is my justification for the choice of subject, and also the fact that, whatever views we may hold, it will be necessary for us to assimilate it to them. I shall have no hesitation in giving you my own reading of the evidence; but at the same time it will be possible to indicate solutions which will probably appeal to those who view the subject from more conservative standpoints. That side of the discussion may well be postponed until after the examination of the new evidence in detail. And first of all it will be advisable to clear up some general aspects of the problem, and to define the limits within which our criticism may be applied.

It must be admitted that both Egypt and Babylon bear a bad name in Hebrew tradition. Both are synonymous with captivity, the symbols of suffering endured at the beginning and at the close of the national life. And during the struggle against Assyrian aggression, the disappointment at the failure of expected help is reflected in prophecies of the

11

period. These great crises in Hebrew history have tended to obscure in the national memory the part which both Babylon and Egypt may have played in moulding the civilization of the smaller nations with whom they came in contact. To such influence the races of Syria were, by geographical position, peculiarly subject. The country has often been compared to a bridge between the two great continents of Asia and Africa, flanked by the sea on one side and the desert on the other, a narrow causeway of highland and coastal plain connecting the valleys of the Nile and the Euphrates.(1) For, except on the frontier of Egypt, desert and sea do not meet. Farther north the Arabian plateau is separated from the Mediterranean by a double mountain chain, which runs south from the Taurus at varying elevations, and encloses in its lower course the remarkable depression of the Jordan Valley, the Dead Sea, and the 'Arabah. The Judaean hills and the mountains of Moab are merely the southward prolongation of the Lebanon and Anti-Lebanon, and their neighbourhood to the sea endows this narrow tract of habitable country with its moisture and fertility. It thus formed the natural channel of intercourse between the two earliest centres of civilization, and was later the battle-ground of their opposing empires.

(1) See G. A. Smith, *Historical Geography of the Holy Land*, pp. 5 ff., 45 ff., and Myres, *Dawn of History*, pp. 137 ff.; and cf. Hogarth, *The Nearer East*, pp. 65 ff., and Reclus, *Nouvelle Géographie universelle*, t. IX, pp. 685 ff.

The great trunk-roads of through communication run north and south, across the eastern plateaus of the Haurân and Moab, and along the coastal plains. The old highway from Egypt, which left the Delta at Pelusium, at first follows the coast, then trends eastward across the plain of Esdraelon, which breaks the coastal range, and passing under Hermon runs northward through Damascus and reaches the Euphrates at its most westerly point. Other through tracks in Palestine ran then as they do to-day, by Beesheba and Hebron, or along the 'Arabah and west of the Dead Sea, or through Edom and east of Jordan by the present Hajj route to Damascus. But the great highway from Egypt, the most westerly of the trunk-roads through Palestine, was that mainly followed, with some variant sections, by both caravans and armies, and was known by the Hebrews in its southern course as the "Way of the Philistines" and farther north as the "Way of the East".

The plain of Esraelon, where the road first trends eastward, has been the battle-ground for most invaders of Palestine from the north, and though Egyptian armies often fought in the southern coastal plain, they too have battled there when they held the southern country. Megiddo, which commands the main pass into the plain through the low Samaritan hills to the southeast of Carmel, was the site of Thothmes III's famous battle against a Syrian confederation, and it inspired the writer of the Apocalypse with his vision of an Armageddon of the future. But invading armies always followed the beaten track of caravans, and movements represented by the great campaigns were reflected in the daily passage of international commerce.

With so much through traffic continually passing within her borders, it may be matter for surprise that far more striking evidence of its cultural effect should not have been revealed by archaeological research in Palestine. Here again the explanation is mainly of a geographical character. For though the plains and plateaus could be crossed by the trunk-roads, the rest of the country is so broken up by mountain and valley that it presented few facilities either to foreign penetration or to external control. The physical barriers to local intercourse, reinforced by striking differences in soil, altitude, and climate, while they precluded Syria herself from attaining national unity, always tended to protect her separate provinces, or "kingdoms," from the full effects of foreign aggression. One city-state could be traversed, devastated, or annexed, without in the least degree affecting neighbouring areas. It is true that the population of Syria has always been predominantly Semitic, for she was on the fringe of the great breeding-ground of the Semitic race and her landward boundary was open to the Arabian nomad. Indeed, in the whole course of her history the only race that bade fair at one time to oust the Semite in Syria was the Greek. But the Greeks remained within the cities which they founded or rebuilt, and, as Robertson Smith pointed out, the death-rate in Eastern cities habitually exceeds the birth-rate; the urban population must be reinforced from the country if it is to be maintained, so that the type of population is ultimately determined by the blood of the peasantry.(1) Hence after the Arab conquest the Greek elements in Syria and Palestine tended rapidly to disappear.

The Moslem invasion was only the last of a series of similar great inroads, which have followed one another since the dawn of history, and during all that time absorption was continually taking place from desert tribes that ranged the Syrian border. As we have seen, the country of his adoption was such as to encourage the Semitic nomad's particularism, which was inherent in his tribal organization. Thus the predominance of a single racial element in the population of Palestine and Syria did little to break down or overstep the natural barriers and lines of cleavage.

(1) See Robertson Smith, *Religion of the Semites*, p. 12 f.; and cf. Smith, *Hist. Geogr.*, p. 10 f.

These facts suffice to show why the influence of both Egypt and Babylon upon the various peoples and kingdoms of Palestine was only intensified at certain periods, when ambition for extended empire dictated the reduction of her provinces in detail. But in the long intervals, during which there was no attempt to enforce political control, regular relations were maintained along the lines of trade and barter. And in any estimate of the possible effect of foreign influence upon Hebrew thought, it is important to realize that some of the channels through which in later periods it may have acted had been flowing since the dawn of history, and even perhaps in prehistoric times. It is probable that Syria formed one of the links by which we may explain the Babylonian elements that are attested in prehistoric Egyptian culture.(1) But another possible line of advance may have been by way of Arabia and across the Red Sea into Upper Egypt.

(1) Cf. *Sumer and Akkad*, pp. 322 ff.; and for a full discussion of the points of resemblance between the early Babylonian and Egyptian civilizations, see Sayce, *The Archaeology of the Cuneiform Inscriptions*, chap. iv, pp. 101 ff.

The latter line of contact is suggested by an interesting piece of evidence that has recently been obtained. A prehistoric flint knife, with a handle carved from the tooth of a hippopotamus, has been purchased lately by the Louvre,(1) and is said to have been found at Gebel el-'Arak near Naga' Hamâdi, which lies on the Nile not far below Koptos, where an ancient caravan-track leads by Wâdi Hammâmât to the Red Sea. On one side of the handle is a battle-scene including some remarkable representations of ancient boats. All the warriors are nude with the exception of a loin girdle, but, while one set of combatants have shaven heads or short hair, the others have abundant locks falling in a thick mass upon the shoulder. On the other face of the handle is carved a hunting scene, two hunters with dogs and desert animals being arranged around a central boss. But in the upper field is a very remarkable group, consisting of a personage struggling with two lions arranged symmetrically. The rest of the composition is not very unlike other examples of prehistoric Egyptian carving in low relief, but here attitude, figure, and clothing are quite un-Egyptian. The hero wears a sort of turban on his abundant hair, and a full and rounded beard descends upon his breast. A long garment clothes him from the waist and falls below the knees, his muscular calves ending in the claws of a bird of prey. There is nothing like this in prehistoric Egyptian art.

(1) See Bénédite, "Le couteau de Gebel al-'Arak", in *Foundation Eugène Piot, Mon. et. Mém.*, XXII. i. (1916).

Perhaps Monsieur Bénédite is pressing his theme too far when he compares the close-cropped warriors on the handle with the shaven Sumerians and Elamites upon steles from Telloh and Susa, for their loin-girdles are African and quite foreign to the Euphrates Valley. And his suggestion that two of the boats, flat-bottomed and with high curved ends, seem only to have navigated the Tigris and Euphrates,(1) will hardly command acceptance. But there is no doubt that the heroic personage upon the other face is represented in the familiar attitude of the Babylonian hero Gilgamesh struggling with lions, which formed so favourite a subject upon early Sumerian and Babylonian seals. His garment is Sumerian or Semitic rather than Egyptian, and the mixture of human and bird elements in the figure, though not precisely paralleled at this early period, is not out of harmony with Mesopotamian or Susan tradition. His beard, too, is quite different from that of the Libyan desert tribes which the early Egyptian kings adopted. Though the treatment of the lions is suggestive of proto-Elamite rather than of early Babylonian models, the design itself is unmistakably of Mesopotamian origin. This discovery intensifies the significance of other early parallels that have been noted between the civilizations of the Euphrates and the Nile, but its evidence, so far as it goes, does not point to Syria as the medium of prehistoric intercourse. Yet then, as later, there can have been no physical barrier to the use of the river-route from Mesopotamia into Syria and of the tracks thence southward along the land-bridge to the Nile's delta.

(1) Op. cit., p. 32.

In the early historic periods we have definite evidence that the eastern coast of the Levant exercised a strong fascination upon the rulers of both Egypt and Babylonia. It may be admitted that Syria had little to give in comparison to what she could borrow, but her local trade in wine and oil must have benefited by an increase in the through traffic which followed the working of copper in Cyprus and Sinai and of silver in the Taurus. Moreover, in the cedar forests of Lebanon and the north she possessed a product which was highly valued both in Egypt and the treeless plains of Babylonia. The cedars procured by Sneferu from Lebanon at the close of the IIIrd Dynasty were doubtless floated as rafts down the coast, and we may see in them evidence of a regular traffic in timber. It has long been known that the early Babylonian king Sharru-kin, or Sargon of Akkad, had pressed up the Euphrates to the Mediterranean, and we now have information that he too was fired by a desire for precious wood and metal. One of the recently published Nippur inscriptions contains copies of a number of his texts, collected by an ancient scribe from his statues at Nippur, and from these we gather additional details of his campaigns. We learn that after his complete subjugation of Southern Babylonia he turned his attention to the west, and that Enlil gave him the lands "from the Upper Sea to the Lower Sea", i.e. from the Mediterranean to the Persian Gulf. Fortunately this rather vague phrase, which survived in later tradition, is restated in greater detail in one of the contemporary versions, which records that Enlil "gave him the upper land, Mari, Iarmuti, and Ibla, as far as the Cedar Forest and the Silver Mountains".(1)

(1) See Poebel, *Historical Texts* (Univ. of Penns. Mus. Publ., Bab. Sect., Vol. IV, No. 1, 1914), pp. 177 f., 222 ff.

Mari was a city on the middle Euphrates, but the name may here signify the district of Mari which lay in the upper course of Sargon's march. Now we know that the later Sumerian monarch Gudea obtained his cedar beams from the Amanus range, which he names *Amanum* and describes as the "cedar mountains".(1) Doubtless he felled his trees on the eastern slopes of the mountain. But we may infer from his texts that Sargon actually reached the coast, and his "Cedar Forest" may have lain farther to the south, perhaps as far south as the Lebanon. The "Silver Mountains" can only be identified with the Taurus, where silver mines were worked in antiquity. The reference to Iarmuti is interesting, for it is clearly the same place as Iarimuta or Iarimmuta, of which we find mention in the Tell el-Amarna letters. From the references to this district in the letters of Rib-Adda, governor of Byblos, we may infer that it was a level district on the coast, capable of producing a considerable quantity of grain for export, and that it was under Egyptian control at the time of Amenophis IV. Hitherto its position has been conjecturally placed in the Nile Delta, but from Sargon's reference we must probably seek it on the North Syrian or possibly the Cilician coast. Perhaps, as Dr. Poebel suggests, it was the plain of Antioch, along the lower course and at the mouth of the Orontes. But his further suggestion that the term is used by Sargon for the whole stretch of country between the sea and the Euphrates is hardly probable. For the geographical references need not be treated as exhaustive, but as confined to the more important districts through which the expedition passed. The district of Ibla which is also mentioned by Narâm-Sin and Gudea, lay probably to the north of Iarmuti, perhaps on the southern slopes of Taurus. It, too, we may regard as a district of restricted extent rather than as a general geographical term for the extreme north of Syria.

(1) Thureau-Dangin, *Les inscriptions de Sumer de d'Akkad*, p. 108 f., Statue B, col. v. 1. 28; Germ. ed., p. 68 f.

It is significant that Sargon does not allude to any battle when describing this expedition, nor does he claim to have devastated the western countries.(1) Indeed, most of these early expeditions to the west appear to have been inspired by motives of commercial enterprise rather than of conquest. But increase of wealth was naturally followed by political expansion, and Egypt's dream of an Asiatic empire was realized by Pharaohs of the XVIIIth Dynasty. The fact that Babylonian should then have been adopted as the medium of official intercourse in Syria points to the closeness of the commercial ties which had already united the Euphrates Valley with the west. Egyptian control had passed from Canaan at the time of the Hebrew settlement, which was indeed a comparatively late episode in the early history of Syria. Whether or not we identify the Khabiri with the Hebrews, the character of the latter's incursion is strikingly illustrated by some of the Tell el-Amarna letters. We see a nomad folk pressing in upon settled peoples and gaining a foothold here and there.(2)

(1) In some versions of his new records Sargon states that "5,400 men daily eat bread before him" (see Poebel, op. cit., p. 178); though the figure may be intended to convey an idea of the size of Sargon's court, we may perhaps see in it a not inaccurate estimate of the total strength of his armed forces.

(2) See especially Professor Burney's forthcoming commentary
on Judges (passim), and his forthcoming Schweich Lectures (now delivered, in 1917).

The great change from desert life consists in the adoption of agriculture, and when once that was made by the Hebrews any further advance in economic development was dictated by their new surroundings. The same process had been going on, as we have seen, in Syria since the dawn of history, the Semitic nomad passing gradually through the stages of agricultural and village life into that of the city. The country favoured the retention of tribal exclusiveness, but ultimate survival could only be purchased at the cost of some amalgamation with their new neighbours. Below the surface of Hebrew history these two tendencies may be traced in varying action and reaction. Some sections of the race

21

engaged readily in the social and commercial life of Canaanite civilization with its rich inheritance from the past. Others, especially in the highlands of Judah and the south, at first succeeded in keeping themselves remote from foreign influence. During the later periods of the national life the country was again subjected, and in an intensified degree, to those forces of political aggression from Mesopotamia and Egypt which we have already noted as operating in Canaan. But throughout the settled Hebrew community as a whole the spark of desert fire was not extinguished, and by kindling the zeal of the Prophets it eventually affected nearly all the white races of mankind.

In his Presidential Address before the British Association at Newcastle,(1) Sir Arthur Evans emphasized the part which recent archaeology has played in proving the continuity of human culture from the most remote periods. He showed how gaps in our knowledge had been bridged, and he traced the part which each great race had taken in increasing its inheritance. We have, in fact, ample grounds for assuming an interchange, not only of commercial products, but, in a minor degree, of ideas within areas geographically connected; and it is surely not derogatory to any Hebrew writer to suggest that he may have adopted, and used for his own purposes, conceptions current among his contemporaries. In other words, the vehicle of religious ideas may well be of composite origin; and, in the course of our study of early Hebrew tradition, I suggest that we hold ourselves justified in applying the comparative method to some at any rate of the ingredients which went to form the finished product. The process is purely literary, but it finds an analogy in the study of Semitic art, especially in the later periods. And I think it will make my meaning clearer if we consider for a moment a few examples of sculpture produced by races of Semitic origin. I do not suggest that we should regard the one process as in any way proving the existence of the other. We should rather treat the comparison as illustrating in another medium the effect of forces which, it is clear, were operative at various periods upon races of the same stock from which the Hebrews themselves were descended. In such material products the eye at once detects the Semite's readiness to avail himself of foreign models. In some cases direct borrowing is obvious; in others, to adapt a metaphor from music, it is possible to trace extraneous *motifs* in the design.(2)

(1) "New Archaeological Lights on the Origins of Civilization in Europe," British Association, Newcastle-on-Tyne, 1916.

(2) The necessary omission of plates, representing the slides shown in the lectures, has involved a recasting of most passages in which points of archaeological detail were discussed; see Preface. But the following paragraphs have been retained as the majority of the monuments referred to are well known.

Some of the most famous monuments of Semitic art date from the Persian and Hellenistic periods, and if we glance at them in this connexion it is in order to illustrate during its most obvious phase a tendency of which the earlier effects are less pronounced. In the sarcophagus of the Sidonian king Eshmu-'azar II, which is preserved in the Louvre,(1) we have indeed a monument to which no Semitic sculptor can lay claim. Workmanship and material are Egyptian, and there is no doubt that it was sculptured in Egypt and transported to Sidon by sea. But the king's own engravers added the long Phoenician inscription, in which he adjures princes and men not to open his resting-place since there are no jewels therein, concluding with some potent curses against any violation of his tomb. One of the latter implores the holy gods to deliver such violators up "to a mighty prince who shall rule over them", and was probably suggested by Alexander's recent occupation of Sidon in 332 B.C. after his reduction and drastic punishment of Tyre. King Eshmun-'zar was not unique in his choice of burial in an Egyptian coffin, for he merely followed the example of his royal father, Tabnîth, "priest of 'Ashtart and king of the Sidonians", whose sarcophagus, preserved at Constantinople, still bears in addition to his own epitaph that of its former occupant, a certain Egyptian general Penptah. But more instructive than these borrowed memorials is a genuine example of Phoenician work, the stele set up by Yehaw-milk, king of Byblos, and dating from the fourth or fifth century B.C.(2) In the sculptured panel at the head of the stele the king is represented in the Persian dress of the period standing in the presence of 'Ashtart or Astarte, his "Lady, Mistress of Byblos". There is no doubt that the stele is of native workmanship, but the influence of Egypt may be seen in the technique of the carving, in the winged disk above the figures, and still more in the representation of the goddess in her character as the Egyptian Hathor, with disk and horns, vulture head-dress and papyrus-sceptre. The inscription records the dedication of an altar and shrine to the goddess, and these too we may conjecture were fashioned on Egyptian lines.

(1) *Corp. Inscr. Semit.*, I. i, tab. II.

(2) *C.I.S.*, I. i, tab. I.

The representation of Semitic deities under Egyptian forms and with Egyptian attributes was encouraged by the introduction of their cults into Egypt itself. In addition to Astarte of Byblos, Ba'al, Anath, and Reshef were all borrowed from Syria in comparatively early times and given Egyptian characters. The conical Syrian helmet of Reshef, a god of war and thunder, gradually gave place to the white Egyptian crown, so that as Reshpu he was represented as a royal warrior; and Qadesh, another form of Astarte, becoming popular with Egyptian women as a patroness of love and fecundity, was also sometimes modelled on Hathor.(1)

(1) See W. Max Müller, *Egyptological Researches*, I, p. 32 f., pl. 41, and S. A. Cook, *Religion of Ancient Palestine*, pp. 83 ff.

Semitic colonists on the Egyptian border were ever ready to adopt Egyptian symbolism in delineating the native gods to whom they owed allegiance, and a particularly striking example of this may be seen on a stele of the Persian period preserved in the Cairo Museum.(1) It was found at Tell

Defenneh, on the right bank of the Pelusiac branch of the Nile, close to the old Egyptian highway into Syria, a site which may be identified with that of the biblical Tahpanhes and the Daphnae of the Greeks. Here it was that the Jewish fugitives, fleeing with Jeremiah after the fall of Jerusalem, founded a Jewish colony beside a flourishing Phoenician and Aramaean settlement. One of the local gods of Tahpanhes is represented on the Cairo monument, an Egyptian stele in the form of a naos with the winged solar disk upon its frieze. He stands on the back of a lion and is clothed in Asiatic costume with the high Syrian tiara crowning his abundant hair. The Syrian workmanship is obvious, and the Syrian character of the cult may be recognized in such details as the small brazen fire-altar before the god, and the sacred pillar which is being anointed by the officiating priest. But the god holds in his left hand a purely Egyptian sceptre and in his right an emblem as purely Babylonian, the weapon of Marduk and Gilgamesh which was also wielded by early Sumerian kings.

(1) Müller, op. cit., p. 30 f., pl. 40. Numismatic evidence exhibits a similar readiness on the part of local Syrian cults to adopt the veneer of Hellenistic civilization while retaining in great measure their own individuality; see Hill, "Some Palestinian Cults in the Graeco-Roman Age", in *Proceedings of the British Academy*, Vol. V (1912).

The Elephantine papyri have shown that the early Jews of the Diaspora, though untrammeled by the orthodoxy of Jerusalem, maintained the purity of their local cult in the face of considerable difficulties. Hence the gravestones of their Aramaean contemporaries, which have been found in

Egypt, can only be cited to illustrate the temptations to which they were exposed.(1) Such was the memorial erected by Abseli to the memory of his parents, Abbâ and Ahatbû, in the fourth year of Xerxes, 481 B.C.(2) They had evidently adopted the religion of Osiris, and were buried at Saqqârah in accordance with the Egyptian rites. The upper scene engraved upon the stele represents Abbâ and his wife in the presence of Osiris, who is attended by Isis and Nephthys; and in the lower panel is the funeral scene, in which all the mourners with one exception are Asiatics. Certain details of the rites that are represented, and mistakes in the hieroglyphic version of the text, prove that the work is Aramaean throughout.(3)

(1) It may be admitted that the Greek platonized cult of Isis and Osiris had its origin in the fusion of Greeks and Egyptians which took place in Ptolemaic times (cf. Scott-Moncrieff, *Paganism and Christianity in Egypt*, p. 33 f.). But we may assume that already in the Persian period the Osiris cult had begun to acquire a tinge of mysticism, which, though it did not affect the mechanical reproduction of the native texts, appealed to the Oriental mind as well as to certain elements in Greek religion. Persian influence probably prepared the way for the Platonic exegesis of the Osiris and Isis legends which we find in Plutarch; and the latter may have been in great measure a development, and not, as is often assumed, a complete misunderstanding of the later Egyptian cult.

(2) *C.I.S.*, II. i, tab. XI, No. 122.

(3) A very similar monument is the Carpentras Stele
(*C.I.S.*, II., i, tab. XIII, No. 141), commemorating Taba,
daughter of Tahapi, an Aramaean lady who was also a convert
to Osiris. It is rather later than that of Abbâ and his
wife, since the Aramaic characters are transitional from the
archaic to the square alphabet; see Driver, *Notes on the
Hebrew Text of the Books of Samuel*, pp. xviii ff., and
Cooke, *North Semitic Inscriptions*, p. 205 f. The Vatican
Stele (op. cit. tab. XIV. No. 142), which dates from the
fourth century, represents inferior work.

If our examples of Semitic art were confined to the Persian
and later periods, they could only be employed to throw
light on their own epoch, when through communication had
been organized, and there was consequently a certain
pooling of commercial and artistic products throughout the
empire.(1) It is true that under the Great King the various
petty states and provinces were encouraged to manage their
own affairs so long as they paid the required tribute, but
their horizon naturally expanded with increase of commerce
and the necessity for service in the king's armies. At this
time Aramaic was the speech of Syria, and the population,
especially in the cities, was still largely Aramaean. As early
as the thirteenth century sections of this interesting Semitic
race had begun to press into Northern Syria from the middle
Euphrates, and they absorbed not only the old Canaanite
population but also the Hittite immigrants from Cappadocia.

The latter indeed may for a time have furnished rulers to the vigorous North Syrian principalities which resulted from this racial combination, but the Aramaean element, thanks to continual reinforcement, was numerically dominant, and their art may legitimately be regarded as in great measure a Semitic product. Fortunately we have recovered examples of sculpture which prove that tendencies already noted in the Persian period were at work, though in a minor degree, under the later Assyrian empire. The discoveries made at Zenjirli, for example, illustrate the gradually increasing effect of Assyrian influence upon the artistic output of a small North Syrian state.

(1) Cf. Bevan, *House of Seleucus*, Vol. I, pp. 5, 260 f.

The artistic influence of Mesopotamia was even more widely
spread than that of Egypt during the Persian period. This is
suggested, for example, by the famous lion-weight discovered
at Abydos in Mysia, the town on the Hellespont famed for the
loves of Hero and Leander. The letters of its Aramaic
inscription (*C.I.S.*, II. i, tab. VII, No. 108) prove by
their form that it dates from the Persian period, and its
provenance is sufficiently attested. Its weight moreover
suggests that it was not merely a Babylonian or Persian
importation, but cast for local use, yet in design and
technique it is scarcely distinguishable from the best
Assyrian work of the seventh century.

This village in north-western Syria, on the road between Antioch and Mar'ash, marks the site of a town which lay near the southern border or just within the Syrian district of Sam'al. The latter is first mentioned in the Assyrian inscriptions by Shalmaneser III, the son and successor of the great conqueror, Ashur-nasir-pal; and in the first half of the eighth century, though within the radius of Assyrian influence, it was still an independent kingdom. It is to this period that we must assign the earliest of the inscribed monuments discovered at Zenjirli and its neighbourhood. At Gerjin, not far to the north-west, was found the colossal statue of Hadad, chief god of the Aramaeans, which was fashioned and set up in his honour by Panammu I, son of Qaral and king of Ya'di.[1] In the long Aramaic inscription engraved upon the statue Panammu records the prosperity of his reign, which he ascribes to the support he has received from Hadad and his other gods, El, Reshef, Rekub-el, and Shamash. He had evidently been left in peace by Assyria, and the monument he erected to his god is of Aramaean workmanship and design. But the influence of Assyria may be traced in Hadad's beard and in his horned head-dress, modelled on that worn by Babylonian and Assyrian gods as the symbol of divine power.

(1) See F. von Luschan, *Sendschirli*, I. (1893), pp. 49 ff., pl. vi; and cf. Cooke, *North Sem. Inscr.*, pp. 159 ff. The characters of the inscription on the statue are of the same archaic type as those of the Moabite Stone, though unlike them they are engraved in relief; so too are the inscriptions of Panammu's later successor Bar-rekub (see

below). Gerjin was certainly in Ya'di, and Winckler's suggestion that Zenjirli itself also lay in that district but near the border of Sam'al may be provisionally accepted;
the occurrence of the names in the inscriptions can be explained in more than one way (see Cooke, op. cit., p. 183).

The political changes introduced into Ya'di and Sam'al by Tiglath-pileser IV are reflected in the inscriptions and monuments of Bar-rekub, a later king of the district. Internal strife had brought disaster upon Ya'di and the throne had been secured by Panammu II, son of Bar-sur, whose claims received Assyrian support. In the words of his son Bar-rekub, "he laid hold of the skirt of his lord, the king of Assyria", who was gracious to him; and it was probably at this time, and as a reward for his loyalty, that Ya'di was united with the neighbouring district of Sam'al. But Panammu's devotion to his foreign master led to his death, for he died at the siege of Damascus, in 733 or 732 B.C., "in the camp, while following his lord, Tiglath-pileser, king of Assyria". His kinsfolk and the whole camp bewailed him, and his body was sent back to Ya'di, where it was interred by his son, who set up an inscribed statue to his memory. Bar-rekub followed in his father's footsteps, as he leads us to infer in his palace-inscription found at Zenjirli: "I ran at the wheel of my lord, the king of Assyria, in the midst of mighty kings, possessors of silver and possessors of gold." It is not strange therefore that his art should reflect Assyrian influence far more strikingly than that of Panammu I. The

31

figure of himself which he caused to be carved in relief on the left side of the palace-inscription is in the Assyrian style,(1) and so too is another of his reliefs from Zenjirli. On the latter Bar-rekub is represented seated upon his throne with eunuch and scribe in attendance, while in the field is the emblem of full moon and crescent, here ascribed to "Ba'al of Harran", the famous centre of moon-worship in Northern Mesopotamia.(2)

(1) *Sendschirli*, IV (1911), pl. lxvii. Attitude and treatment of robes are both Assyrian, and so is the arrangement of divine symbols in the upper field, though some of the latter are given under unfamiliar forms. The king's close-fitting peaked cap was evidently the royal headdress of Sam'al; see the royal figure on a smaller stele of inferior design, op. cit., pl. lxvi.

(2) Op. cit. pp. 257, 346 ff., and pl. lx. The general style of the sculpture and much of the detail are obviously Assyrian. Assyrian influence is particularly noticeable in Bar-rekub's throne; the details of its decoration are precisely similar to those of an Assyrian bronze throne in the British Museum. The full moon and crescent are not of the familiar form, but are mounted on a standard with tassels.

The detailed history and artistic development of Sam'al and Ya'di convey a very vivid impression of the social and material effects upon the native population of Syria, which followed the westward advance of Assyria in the eighth century. We realize not only the readiness of one party in the state to defeat its rival with the help of Assyrian support, but also the manner in which the life and activities of the nation as a whole were unavoidably affected by their action. Other Hittite-Aramaean and Phoenician monuments, as yet undocumented with literary records, exhibit a strange but not unpleasing mixture of foreign *motifs*, such as we see on the stele from Amrith(1) in the inland district of Arvad. But perhaps the most remarkable example of Syrian art we possess is the king's gate recently discovered at Carchemish.(2) The presence of the hieroglyphic inscriptions points to the survival of Hittite tradition, but the figures represented in the reliefs are of Aramaean, not Hittite, type. Here the king is seen leading his eldest son by the hand in some stately ceremonial, and ranged in registers behind them are the younger members of the royal family, whose ages are indicated by their occupations.(3) The employment of basalt in place of limestone does not disguise the sculptor's debt to Assyria. But the design is entirely his own, and the combined dignity and homeliness of the composition are refreshingly superior to the arrogant spirit and hard execution which mar so much Assyrian work. This example is particularly instructive, as it shows how a borrowed art may be developed in skilled hands and made to serve a purpose in complete harmony with its new environment.

(1) *Collection de Clercq*, t. II, pl. xxxvi. The stele is sculptured in relief with the figure of a North Syrian god. Here the winged disk is Egyptian, as well as the god's helmet with uraeus, and his loin-cloth; his attitude and his

supporting lion are Hittite; and the lozenge-mountains, on which the lion stands, and the technique of the carving are Assyrian. But in spite of its composite character the design is quite successful and not in the least incongruous.

(2) Hogarth, *Carchemish*, Pt. I (1914), pl. B. 7 f.

(3) Two of the older boys play at knuckle-bones, others whip
spinning-tops, and a little naked girl runs behind supporting herself with a stick, on the head of which is carved a bird. The procession is brought up by the queen-mother, who carries the youngest baby and leads a pet lamb.

Such monuments surely illustrate the adaptability of the Semitic craftsman among men of Phoenician and Aramaean strain. Excavation in Palestine has failed to furnish examples of Hebrew work. But Hebrew tradition itself justifies us in regarding this *trait* as of more general application, or at any rate as not repugnant to Hebrew thought, when it relates that Solomon employed Tyrian craftsmen for work upon the Temple and its furniture; for Phoenician art was essentially Egyptian in its origin and general character. Even Eshmun-'zar's desire for burial in an Egyptian sarcophagus may be paralleled in Hebrew tradition of a much earlier period, when, in the last verse of Genesis,(1) it is recorded that Joseph died, "and they embalmed him, and he was put in a coffin in Egypt". Since it formed the subject of prophetic denunciation, I refrain for the moment from citing the notorious adoption of Assyrian customs at certain periods of the later Judaean monarchy. The two records I have referred to will suffice, for we have in them cherished traditions, of which the Hebrews themselves were proud, concerning the most famous example of Hebrew religious architecture and the burial of one of the patriarchs of the race. A similar readiness to make use of the best available resources, even of foreign origin, may on analogy be regarded as at least possible in the composition of Hebrew literature.

(1) Gen. l. 26, assigned by critics to E.

We shall see that the problems we have to face concern the possible influence of Babylon, rather than of Egypt, upon Hebrew tradition. And one last example, drawn from the later period, will serve to demonstrate how Babylonian influence penetrated the ancient world and has even left some trace upon modern civilization. It is a fact, though one perhaps not generally realized, that the twelve divisions on the dials of our clocks and watches have a Babylonian, and ultimately a Sumerian, ancestry. For why is it we divide the day into twenty-four hours? We have a decimal system of reckoning, we count by tens; why then should we divide the day and night into twelve hours each, instead of into ten or some multiple of ten? The reason is that the Babylonians divided the day into twelve double-hours; and the Greeks took over their ancient system of time-division along with their knowledge of astronomy and passed it on to us. So if we ourselves, after more than two thousand years, are making use of an old custom from Babylon, it would not be surprising if the Hebrews, a contemporary race, should have fallen under her influence even before they were carried away as captives and settled forcibly upon her river-banks.

We may pass on, then, to the site from which our new material has been obtained—the ancient city of Nippur, in central Babylonia. Though the place has been deserted for at least nine hundred years, its ancient name still lingers on in local tradition, and to this day *Niffer* or *Nuffar* is the name the Arabs give the mounds which cover its extensive ruins. No modern town or village has been built upon them or in their immediate neighbourhood. The nearest considerable town is Dîwânîyah, on the left bank of the Hillah branch of the Euphrates, twenty miles to the south-west; but some four miles to the south of the ruins is the village of Sûq el-'Afej, on the eastern edge of the 'Afej marshes, which begin to the south of Nippur and stretch away westward. Protected by its swamps, the region contains a few primitive settlements of the wild 'Afej tribesmen, each a group of reed-huts clustering around the mud fort of its ruling sheikh. Their chief enemies are the Shammâr, who dispute with them possession of the pastures. In summer the marshes near the mounds are merely pools of water connected by channels through the reed-beds, but in spring the flood-water converts them into a vast lagoon, and all that meets the eye are a few small hamlets built on rising knolls above the water-level. Thus Nippur may be almost isolated during the floods, but the mounds are protected from the waters' encroachment by an outer ring of former habitation which has slightly raised the level of the encircling area. The ruins of the city stand from thirty to seventy feet above the plain, and in the north-eastern corner there rose, before the excavations, a conical mound, known by the Arabs as *Bint el-Emîr* or "The Princess". This prominent landmark represents the temple-tower of Enlil's famous sanctuary, and even after excavation it is still the first object that the approaching traveller sees on the horizon. When he has climbed its summit he enjoys an uninterrupted view over desert and swamp.

The cause of Nippur's present desolation is to be traced to the change in the bed of the Euphrates, which now lies far to the west. But in antiquity the stream flowed through the centre of the city, along the dry bed of the Shatt en-Nîl, which divides the mounds into an eastern and a western group. The latter covers the remains of the city proper and was occupied in part by the great business-houses and bazaars. Here more than thirty thousand contracts and accounts, dating from the fourth millennium to the fifth century B.C., were found in houses along the former river-bank. In the eastern half of the city was Enlil's great temple Ekur, with its temple-tower Imkharsag rising in successive stages beside it. The huge temple-enclosure contained not only the sacrificial shrines, but also the priests' apartments, store-chambers, and temple-magazines. Outside its enclosing wall, to the south-west, a large triangular mound, christened "Tablet Hill" by the excavators, yielded a further supply of records. In addition to business-documents of the First Dynasty of Babylon and of the later Assyrian, Neo-Babylonian, and Persian periods, between two and three thousand literary texts and fragments were discovered here, many of them dating from the Sumerian period. And it is possible that some of the early literary texts that have been published were obtained in other parts of the city.

No less than twenty-one different strata, representing separate periods of occupation, have been noted by the American excavators at various levels within the Nippur mounds,(1) the earliest descending to virgin soil some twenty feet below the present level of the surrounding plain. The remote date of Nippur's foundation as a city and cult-centre is attested by the fact that the pavement laid by Narâm-Sin in the south-eastern temple-court lies thirty feet above virgin soil, while only thirty-six feet of superimposed *débris* represent the succeeding millennia of occupation down to Sassanian and early Arab times. In the period of the Hebrew captivity the city still ranked as a great commercial market and as one of the most sacred repositories of Babylonian religious tradition. We know that not far off was Tel-abib, the seat of one of the colonies of Jewish exiles, for that lay "by the river of Chebar",(2) which we may identify with the Kabaru Canal in Nippur's immediate neighbourhood. It was "among the captives by the river Chebar" that Ezekiel lived and prophesied, and it was on Chebar's banks that he saw his first vision of the Cherubim.(3) He and other of the Jewish exiles may perhaps have mingled with the motley crowd that once thronged the streets of Nippur, and they may often have gazed on the huge temple-tower which rose above the city's flat roofs. We know that the later population of Nippur itself included a considerable Jewish element, for the upper strata of the mounds have yielded numerous clay bowls with Hebrew, Mandaean, and Syriac magical inscriptions;(4) and not the least interesting of the objects recovered was the wooden box of a Jewish scribe, containing his pen and ink-vessel and a little scrap of crumbling parchment inscribed with a few Hebrew characters.(5)

(1) See Hilprecht, *Explorations in Bible Lands*, pp. 289 ff., 540 ff.; and Fisher, *Excavations at Nippur*, Pt. I (1905), Pt. II (1906).

(2) Ezek. iii. 15.

(3) Ezek. i. 1, 3; iii. 23; and cf. x. 15, 20, 22, and xliii. 3.

(4) See J. A. Montgomery, *Aramaic Incantation Texts from Nippur*, 1913

(5) Hilprecht, *Explorations*, p. 555 f.

Of the many thousands of inscribed clay tablets which were found in the course of the expeditions, some were kept at Constantinople, while others were presented by the Sultan Abdul Hamid to the excavators, who had them conveyed to America. Since that time a large number have been published. The work was necessarily slow, for many of the texts were found to be in an extremely bad state of preservation. So it happened that a great number of the boxes containing tablets remained until recently still packed up in the store-rooms of the Pennsylvania Museum. But under the present energetic Director of the Museum, Dr. G. B. Gordon, the process of arranging and publishing the mass of literary material has been "speeded up". A staff of skilled workmen has been employed on the laborious task of cleaning the broken tablets and fitting the fragments together. At the same time the help of several Assyriologists was welcomed in the further task of running over and sorting the collections as they were prepared for study. Professor Clay, Professor Barton, Dr. Langdon, Dr. Edward Chiera, and Dr. Arno Poebel have all participated in the work. But the lion's share has fallen to the last-named scholar, who was given leave of absence by John Hopkins University in order to take up a temporary appointment at the Pennsylvania Museum. The result of his labours was published by the Museum at the end of 1914.(1) The texts thus made available for study are of very varied interest. A great body of them are grammatical and represent compilations made by Semitic scribes of the period of Hammurabi's dynasty for their study of the old Sumerian tongue. Containing, as most of them do, Semitic renderings of the Sumerian words and expressions collected, they are as great a help to us in our study of Sumerian language as they were to their compilers; in particular they have thrown much new light on the paradigms of the demonstrative and personal pronouns and on Sumerian verbal forms. But literary texts are also included in the recent publications.

(1) Poebel, *Historical Texts* and *Historical and Grammatical Texts* (Univ. of Penns. Mus. Publ., Bab. Sect., Vol. IV, No. 1, and Vol. V), Philadelphia, 1914.

When the Pennsylvania Museum sent out its first expedition, lively hopes were entertained that the site selected would yield material of interest from the biblical standpoint. The city of Nippur, as we have seen, was one of the most sacred and most ancient religious centres in the country, and Enlil, its city-god, was the head of the Babylonian pantheon. On such a site it seemed likely that we might find versions of the Babylonian legends which were current at the dawn of history before the city of Babylonia and its Semitic inhabitants came upon the scene. This expectation has proved to be not unfounded, for the literary texts include the Sumerian Deluge Version and Creation myth to which I referred at the beginning of the lecture. Other texts of almost equal interest consist of early though fragmentary lists of historical and semi-mythical rulers. They prove that Berossus and the later Babylonians depended on material of quite early origin in compiling their dynasties of semi-mythical kings. In them we obtain a glimpse of ages more remote than any on which excavation in Babylonia has yet thrown light, and for the first time we have recovered genuine native tradition of early date with regard to the cradle of Babylonian culture. Before we approach the Sumerian legends themselves, it will be as well to-day to trace back in this tradition the gradual merging of history into legend and myth, comparing at the same time the ancient Egyptian's picture of his own remote past. We will also ascertain whether any new light is thrown by our inquiry upon Hebrew traditions concerning the earliest history of the human race and the origins of civilization.

41

In the study of both Egyptian and Babylonian chronology there has been a tendency of late years to reduce the very early dates that were formerly in fashion. But in Egypt, while the dynasties of Manetho have been telescoped in places, excavation has thrown light on predynastic periods, and we can now trace the history of culture in the Nile Valley back, through an unbroken sequence, to its neolithic stage. Quite recently, too, as I mentioned just now, a fresh literary record of these early predynastic periods has been recovered, on a fragment of the famous Palermo Stele, our most valuable monument for early Egyptian history and chronology. Egypt presents a striking contrast to Babylonia in the comparatively small number of written records which have survived for the reconstruction of her history. We might well spare much of her religious literature, enshrined in endless temple-inscriptions and papyri, if we could but exchange it for some of the royal annals of Egyptian Pharaohs. That historical records of this character were compiled by the Egyptian scribes, and that they were as detailed and precise in their information as those we have recovered from Assyrian sources, is clear from the few extracts from the annals of Thothmes III's wars which are engraved on the walls of the temple at Karnak.(1) As in Babylonia and Assyria, such records must have formed the foundation on which summaries of chronicles of past Egyptian history were based. In the Palermo Stele it is recognized that we possess a primitive chronicle of this character.

(1) See Breasted, *Ancient Records*, I, p. 4, II, pp. 163 ff.

Drawn up as early as the Vth Dynasty, its historical summary proves that from the beginning of the dynastic age onward a yearly record was kept of the most important achievements of the reigning Pharaoh. In this fragmentary but invaluable epitome, recording in outline much of the history of the Old Kingdom,(1) some interesting parallels have long been noted with Babylonian usage. The early system of time-reckoning, for example, was the same in both countries, each year being given an official title from the chief event that occurred in it. And although in Babylonia we are still without material for tracing the process by which this cumbrous method gave place to that of reckoning by regnal years, the Palermo Stele demonstrates the way in which the latter system was evolved in Egypt. For the events from which the year was named came gradually to be confined to the fiscal "numberings" of cattle and land. And when these, which at first had taken place at comparatively long intervals, had become annual events, the numbered sequence of their occurrence corresponded precisely to the years of the king's reign. On the stele, during the dynastic period, each regnal year is allotted its own space or rectangle,(2) arranged in horizontal sequence below the name and titles of the ruling king.

(1) Op. cit., I, pp. 57 ff.

(2) The spaces are not strictly rectangles, as each is divided vertically from the next by the Egyptian hieroglyph for "year".

The text, which is engraved on both sides of a great block of black basalt, takes its name from the fact that the fragment hitherto known has been preserved since 1877 at the Museum of Palermo. Five other fragments of the text have now been published, of which one undoubtedly belongs to the same monument as the Palermo fragment, while the others may represent parts of one or more duplicate copies of that famous text. One of the four Cairo fragments(1) was found by a digger for *sebakh* at Mitrahîneh (Memphis); the other three, which were purchased from a dealer, are said to have come from Minieh, while the fifth fragment, at University College, is also said to have come from Upper Egypt,(2) though it was purchased by Professor Petrie while at Memphis. These reports suggest that a number of duplicate copies were engraved and set up in different Egyptian towns, and it is possible that the whole of the text may eventually be recovered. The choice of basalt for the records was obviously dictated by a desire for their preservation, but it has had the contrary effect; for the blocks of this hard and precious stone have been cut up and reused in later times. The largest and most interesting of the new fragments has evidently been employed as a door-sill, with the result that its surface is much rubbed and parts of its text are unfortunately almost undecipherable. We shall see that the earliest section of its record has an important bearing on our knowledge of Egyptian predynastic history and on the traditions of that remote period which have come down to us from the history of Manetho.

(1) See Gautier, *Le Musée Égyptien*, III (1915), pp. 29 ff., pl. xxiv ff., and Foucart, *Bulletin de l'Institut Français d'Archéologie Orientale*, XII, ii (1916), pp. 161 ff.; and cf.

Gardiner, *Journ. of Egypt. Arch.*, III, pp. 143 ff., and Petrie, *Ancient Egypt*, 1916, Pt. III, pp. 114 ff.

(2) Cf. Petrie, op. cit., pp. 115, 120.

From the fragment of the stele preserved at Palermo we already knew that its record went back beyond the Ist Dynasty into predynastic times. For part of the top band of the inscription, which is there preserved, contains nine names borne by kings of Lower Egypt or the Delta, which, it had been conjectured, must follow the gods of Manetho and precede the "Worshippers of Horus", the immediate predecessors of the Egyptian dynasties.(1) But of contemporary rulers of Upper Egypt we had hitherto no knowledge, since the supposed royal names discovered at Abydos and assigned to the time of the "Worshippers of Horus" are probably not royal names at all.(2) With the possible exception of two very archaic slate palettes, the first historical memorials recovered from the south do not date from an earlier period than the beginning of the Ist Dynasty. The largest of the Cairo fragments now helps us to fill in this gap in our knowledge.

(1) See Breasted, *Anc. Rec.*, I, pp. 52, 57.

(2) Cf. Hall, *Ancient History of the Near East*, p. 99 f.

On the top of the new fragment(1) we meet the same band of rectangles as at Palermo,(2) but here their upper portions are broken away, and there only remains at the base of each of them the outlined figure of a royal personage, seated in the same attitude as those on the Palermo stone. The remarkable fact about these figures is that, with the apparent exception of the third figure from the right,(3) each wears, not the Crown of the North, as at Palermo, but the Crown of the South. We have then to do with kings of Upper Egypt, not the Delta, and it is no longer possible to suppose that the predynastic rulers of the Palermo Stele were confined to those of Lower Egypt, as reflecting northern tradition. Rulers of both halves of the country are represented, and Monsieur Gautier has shown,(4) from data on the reverse of the inscription, that the kings of the Delta were arranged on the original stone before the rulers of the south who are outlined upon our new fragment. Moreover, we have now recovered definite proof that this band of the inscription is concerned with predynastic Egyptian princes; for the cartouche of the king, whose years are enumerated in the second band immediately below the kings of the south, reads Athet, a name we may with certainty identify with Athothes, the second successor of Menes, founder of the Ist Dynasty, which is already given under the form Ateth in the Abydos List of Kings.(5) It is thus quite certain that the first band of the inscription relates to the earlier periods before the two halves of the country were brought together under a single ruler.

(1) Cairo No. 1; see Gautier, *Mus. Égypt.*, III, pl. xxiv f.

(2) In this upper band the spaces are true rectangles, being separated by vertical lines, not by the hieroglyph for "year" as in the lower bands; and each rectangle is assigned to a separate king, and not, as in the other bands, to a

year of a king's reign.

(3) The difference in the crown worn by this figure is probably only apparent and not intentional; M. Foucart, after a careful examination of the fragment, concludes that it is due to subsequent damage or to an original defect in the stone; cf. *Bulletin*, XII, ii, p. 162.

(4) Op. cit., p. 32 f.

(5) In Manetho's list he corresponds to {Kenkenos}, the second successor of Menes according to both Africanus and Eusebius, who assign the name Athothis to the second ruler of the dynasty only, the Teta of the Abydos List. The form Athothes is preserved by Eratosthenes for both of Menes' immediate successors.

Though the tradition of these remote times is here recorded on a monument of the Vth Dynasty, there is no reason to doubt its general accuracy, or to suppose that we are dealing with purely mythological personages. It is perhaps possible, as Monsieur Foucart suggests, that missing portions of the text may have carried the record back through purely mythical periods to Ptah and the Creation. In that case we should have, as we shall see, a striking parallel to early Sumerian tradition. But in the first extant portions of the Palermo text we are already in the realm of genuine tradition. The names preserved appear to be those of individuals, not of mythological creations, and we may assume that their owners really existed. For though the invention of writing had not at that time been achieved, its place was probably taken by oral tradition. We know that with certain tribes of Africa at the present day, who possess no knowledge of writing, there are functionaries charged with the duty of preserving tribal traditions, who transmit orally to their successors a remembrance of past chiefs and some details of events that occurred centuries before.(1) The predynastic Egyptians may well have adopted similar means for preserving a remembrance of their past history.

(1) M. Foucart illustrates this point by citing the case of the Bushongos, who have in this way preserved a list of no less than a hundred and twenty-one of their past kings; op. cit., p. 182, and cf. Tordey and Joyce, "Les Bushongos", in *Annales du Musée du Congo Belge*, sér. III, t. II, fasc. i (Brussels, 1911).

Moreover, the new text furnishes fresh proof of the general accuracy of Manetho, even when dealing with traditions of this prehistoric age. On the stele there is no definite indication that these two sets of predynastic kings were contemporaneous rulers of Lower and Upper Egypt respectively; and since elsewhere the lists assign a single sovereign to each epoch, it has been suggested that we should regard them as successive representatives of the legitimate kingdom.(1) Now Manetho, after his dynasties of gods and demi-gods, states that thirty Memphite kings reigned for 1,790 years, and were followed by ten Thinite kings whose reigns covered a period of 350 years. Neglecting the figures as obviously erroneous, we may well admit that the Greek historian here alludes to our two pre-Menite dynasties. But the fact that he should regard them as ruling consecutively does not preclude the other alternative. The modern convention of arranging lines of contemporaneous rulers in parallel columns had not been evolved in antiquity, and without some such method of distinction contemporaneous rulers, when enumerated in a list, can only be registered consecutively. It would be natural to assume that, before the unification of Egypt by the founder of the Ist Dynasty, the rulers of North and South were independent princes, possessing no traditions of a united throne on which any claim to hegemony could be based. On the assumption that this was so, their arrangement in a consecutive series would not have deceived their immediate successors. But it would undoubtedly tend in course of time to obliterate the tradition of their true order, which even at the period of the Vth Dynasty may have been completely forgotten. Manetho would thus have introduced no strange or novel confusion; and this explanation would of course apply to other sections of his system where the dynasties he enumerates appear to be too many for their period. But his reproduction of two lines of predynastic rulers, supported as it now is by the early evidence of the Palermo text, only serves to increase our confidence in the general accuracy of his sources, while at the same time it illustrates very effectively the way in which possible inaccuracies, deduced from independent data, may have arisen in quite early times.

(1) Foucart, loc. cit.

In contrast to the dynasties of Manetho, those of Berossus are so imperfectly preserved that they have never formed the basis of Babylonian chronology.(1) But here too, in the chronological scheme, a similar process of reduction has taken place. Certain dynasties, recovered from native sources and at one time regarded as consecutive, were proved to have been contemporaneous; and archaeological evidence suggested that some of the great gaps, so freely assumed in the royal sequence, had no right to be there. As a result, the succession of known rulers was thrown into truer perspective, and such gaps as remained were being partially filled by later discoveries. Among the latter the most important find was that of an early list of kings, recently published by Père Scheil(2) and subsequently purchased by the British Museum shortly before the war. This had helped us to fill in the gap between the famous Sargon of Akkad and the later dynasties, but it did not carry us far beyond Sargon's own time. Our archaeological evidence also comes suddenly to an end. Thus the earliest picture we have hitherto obtained of the Sumerians has been that of a race employing an advanced system of writing and possessed of a knowledge of metal. We have found, in short, abundant remains of a bronze-age culture, but no traces of preceding ages of development such as meet us on early Egyptian sites. It was a natural inference that the advent of the Sumerians in the Euphrates Valley was sudden, and that they had brought their highly developed culture with them from some region of Central or Southern Asia.

(1) While the evidence of Herodotus is extraordinarily valuable for the details he gives of the civilizations of both Egypt and Babylonia, and is especially full in the case

of the former, it is of little practical use for the chronology. In Egypt his report of the early history is confused, and he hardly attempts one for Babylonia. It is probable that on such subjects he sometimes misunderstood
his informants, the priests, whose traditions were more accurately reproduced by the later native writers Manetho and Berossus. For a detailed comparison of classical authorities in relation to both countries, see Griffith in Hogarth's *Authority and Archaeology*, pp. 161 ff.

(2) See *Comptes rendus*, 1911 (Oct.), pp. 606 ff., and *Rev. d'Assyr.*, IX (1912), p. 69.

The newly published Nippur documents will cause us to modify that view. The lists of early kings were themselves drawn up under the Dynasty of Nîsin in the twenty-second century B.C., and they give us traces of possibly ten and at least eight other "kingdoms" before the earliest dynasty of the known lists.(1) One of their novel features is that they include summaries at the end, in which it is stated how often a city or district enjoyed the privilege of being the seat of supreme authority in Babylonia. The earliest of their sections lie within the legendary period, and though in the third dynasty preserved we begin to note signs of a firmer historical tradition, the great break that then occurs in the text is at present only bridged by titles of various "kingdoms" which the summaries give; a few even of these are missing and the relative order of the rest is not assured. But in spite of their imperfect state of preservation, these documents are of great historical value and will furnish a framework for future chronological schemes. Meanwhile we may attribute to some of the later dynasties titles in complete agreement with Sumerian tradition. The dynasty of Ur-Engur, for example, which preceded that of Nîsin, becomes, if we like, the Third Dynasty of Ur. Another important fact which strikes us after a scrutiny of the early royal names recovered is that, while two or three are Semitic,(2) the great majority of those borne by the earliest rulers of Kish, Erech, and Ur are as obviously Sumerian.

(1) See Poebel, *Historical Texts*, pp. 73 ff. and *Historical and Grammatical Texts*, pl. ii-iv, Nos. 2-5. The best preserved of the lists is No. 2; Nos. 3 and 4 are comparatively small fragments; and of No. 5 the obverse only is here published for the first time, the contents of the reverse having been made known some years ago by Hilprecht (cf. *Mathematical, Metrological, and Chronological Tablets*, p. 46 f., pl. 30, No. 47). The fragments belong to separate copies of the Sumerian dynastic record, and it happens that the extant portions of their text in some places cover the same period and are duplicates of one another.

(2) Cf., e.g., two of the earliest kings of Kish, Galumum and Zugagib. The former is probably the Semitic-Babylonian word *kalumum*, "young animal, lamb," the latter *zukakîbum*, "scorpion"; cf. Poebel, *Hist. Texts*, p. 111.

The occurrence of these names points to Semitic infiltration into Northern Babylonia since the dawn of history, a state of things we should naturally expect. It is improbable that on this point Sumerian tradition should have merely reflected the conditions of a later period.

It is clear that in native tradition, current among the Sumerians themselves before the close of the third millennium, their race was regarded as in possession of Babylonia since the dawn of history. This at any rate proves that their advent was not sudden nor comparatively recent, and it further suggests that Babylonia itself was the cradle of their civilization. It will be the province of future archaeological research to fill out the missing dynasties and to determine at what points in the list their strictly historical basis disappears. Some, which are fortunately preserved near the beginning, bear on their face their legendary character. But for our purpose they are none the worse for that.

In the first two dynasties, which had their seats at the cities of Kish and Erech, we see gods mingling with men upon the earth. Tammuz, the god of vegetation, for whose annual death Ezekiel saw women weeping beside the Temple at Jerusalem, is here an earthly monarch. He appears to be described as "a hunter", a phrase which recalls the death of Adonis in Greek mythology. According to our Sumerian text he reigned in Erech for a hundred years.

Another attractive Babylonian legend is that of Etana, the prototype of Icarus and hero of the earliest dream of human flight.(1) Clinging to the pinions of his friend the Eagle he beheld the world and its encircling stream recede beneath him; and he flew through the gate of heaven, only to fall headlong back to earth. He is here duly entered in the list, where we read that "Etana, the shepherd who ascended to heaven, who subdued all lands", ruled in the city of Kish for 635 years.

(1) The Egyptian conception of the deceased Pharaoh ascending to heaven as a falcon and becoming merged into the
sun, which first occurs in the Pyramid texts (see Gardiner in Cumont's *Études Syriennes*, pp. 109 ff.), belongs to a different range of ideas. But it may well have been combined with the Etana tradition to produce the funerary eagle employed so commonly in Roman Syria in representations of
the emperor's apotheosis (cf. Cumont, op. cit., pp. 37 ff., 115).

The god Lugal-banda is another hero of legend. When the hearts of the other gods failed them, he alone recovered the Tablets of Fate, stolen by the bird-god Zû from Enlil's palace. He is here recorded to have reigned in Erech for 1,200 years.

Tradition already told us that Erech was the native city of Gilgamesh, the hero of the national epic, to whom his ancestor Ut-napishtim related the story of the Flood. Gilgamesh too is in our list, as king of Erech for 126 years.

We have here in fact recovered traditions of Post-diluvian kings. Unfortunately our list goes no farther back than that, but it is probable that in its original form it presented a general correspondence to the system preserved from

54

Berossus, which enumerates ten Antediluvian kings, the last of them Xisuthros, the hero of the Deluge. Indeed, for the dynastic period, the agreement of these old Sumerian lists with the chronological system of Berossus is striking. The latter, according to Syncellus, gives 34,090 or 34,080 years as the total duration of the historical period, apart from his preceding mythical ages, while the figure as preserved by Eusebius is 33,091 years.(1) The compiler of one of our new lists,(2) writing some 1,900 years earlier, reckons that the dynastic period in his day had lasted for 32,243 years. Of course all these figures are mythical, and even at the time of the Sumerian Dynasty of Nîsin variant traditions were current with regard to the number of historical and semi-mythical kings of Babylonia and the duration of their rule. For the earlier writer of another of our lists,(3) separated from the one already quoted by an interval of only sixty-seven years, gives 28,876(4) years as the total duration of the dynasties at his time. But in spite of these discrepancies, the general resemblance presented by the huge totals in the variant copies of the list to the alternative figures of Berossus, if we ignore his mythical period, is remarkable. They indicate a far closer correspondence of the Greek tradition with that of the early Sumerians themselves than was formerly suspected.

(1) The figure 34,090 is that given by Syncellus (ed. Dindorf, p. 147); but it is 34,080 in the equivalent which is added in "sars", &c. The discrepancy is explained by some as due to an intentional omission of the units in the second reckoning; others would regard 34,080 as the correct figure

(cf. *Hist. of Bab.*, p. 114 f.). The reading of ninety against eighty is supported by the 33,091 of Eusebius (*Chron. lib. pri.*, ed. Schoene, col. 25).

(2) No. 4.

(3) No. 2.

(4) The figures are broken, but the reading given may be accepted with some confidence; see Poebel, *Hist. Inscr.*, p. 103.

Further proof of this correspondence may be seen in the fact that the new Sumerian Version of the Deluge Story, which I propose to discuss in the second lecture, gives us a connected account of the world's history down to that point. The Deluge hero is there a Sumerian king named Ziusudu, ruling in one of the newly created cities of Babylonia and ministering at the shrine of his city-god. He is continually given the royal title, and the foundation of the Babylonian "kingdom" is treated as an essential part of Creation. We may therefore assume that an Antediluvian period existed in Sumerian tradition as in Berossus.(1) And I think Dr. Poebel is right in assuming that the Nippur copies of the Dynastic List begin with the Post-diluvian period.(2)

(1) Of course it does not necessarily follow that the figure assigned to the duration of the Antediluvian or mythical period by the Sumerians would show so close a resemblance to

that of Berossus as we have already noted in their estimates of the dynastic or historical period. But there is no need to assume that Berossus' huge total of a hundred and twenty "sars" (432,000 years) is entirely a product of Neo-Babylonian speculation; the total 432,000 is explained as representing ten months of a cosmic year, each month consisting of twelve "sars", i.e. 12 x 3600 = 43,200 years. The Sumerians themselves had no difficulty in picturing two of their dynastic rulers as each reigning for two "ners" (1,200 years), and it would not be unlikely that "sars" were distributed among still earlier rulers; the numbers were easily written. For the unequal distribution of his hundred and twenty "sars" by Berossus among his ten Antediluvian kings, see Appendix II.

(2) The exclusion of the Antediluvian period from the list may perhaps be explained on the assumption that its compiler
confined his record to "kingdoms", and that the mythical rulers who preceded them did not form a "kingdom" within his
definition of the term. In any case we have a clear indication that an earlier period was included before the true "kingdoms", or dynasties, in an Assyrian copy of the list, a fragment of which is preserved in the British Museum from the Library of Ashur-bani-pal at Nineveh; see *Chron. conc. Early Bab. Kings* (Studies in East. Hist., II f.), Vol. I, pp. 182 ff., Vol. II, pp. 48 ff., 143 f. There we find traces of an extra column of text preceding that in which the first Kingdom of Kish was recorded. It would

seem
almost certain that this extra column was devoted to
Antediluvian kings. The only alternative explanation would
be that it was inscribed with the summaries which conclude
the Sumerian copies of our list. But later scribes do not so
transpose their material, and the proper place for summaries
is at the close, not at the beginning, of a list. In the
Assyrian copy the Dynastic List is brought up to date, and
extends down to the later Assyrian period. Formerly its
compiler could only be credited with incorporating
traditions of earlier times. But the correspondence of the
small fragment preserved of its Second Column with part of
the First Column of the Nippur texts (including the name of
"Enmennunna") proves that the Assyrian scribe reproduced an
actual copy of the Sumerian document.

Though Professor Barton, on the other hand, holds that
the Dynastic List had no concern with the Deluge, his
suggestion that the early names preserved by it may have
been the original source of Berossus' Antediluvian rulers(1)
may yet be accepted in a modified form. In coming to his
conclusion he may have been influenced by what seems to
me an undoubted correspondence between one of the rulers
in our list and the sixth Antediluvian king of Berossus. I think
few will be disposed to dispute the equation

{Daonos poimon} = Etana, a shepherd.

Each list preserves the hero's shepherd origin and the
correspondence of the names is very close, Daonos merely

transposing the initial vowel of Etana.(2) That Berossus should have translated a Post-diluvian ruler into the Antediluvian dynasty would not be at all surprising in view of the absence of detailed correspondence between his later dynasties and those we know actually occupied the Babylonian throne. Moreover, the inclusion of Babylon in his list of Antediluvian cities should make us hesitate to regard all the rulers he assigns to his earliest dynasty as necessarily retaining in his list their original order in Sumerian tradition. Thus we may with a clear conscience seek equations between the names of Berossus' Antediluvian rulers and those preserved in the early part of our Dynastic List, although we may regard the latter as equally Post-diluvian in Sumerian belief.

(1) See the brief statement he makes in the course of a review of Dr. Poebel's volumes in the *American Journal of Semitic Languages and Literature*, XXXI, April 1915, p. 225. He does not compare any of the names, but he promises a study of those preserved and a comparison of the list with Berossus and with Gen. iv and v. It is possible that Professor Barton has already fulfilled his promise of further discussion, perhaps in his *Archaeology and the Bible*, to the publication of which I have seen a reference in another connexion (cf. *Journ. Amer. Or. Soc.*, Vol. XXXVI, p. 291); but I have not yet been able to obtain sight of a copy.

(2) The variant form {Daos} is evidently a mere contraction, and any claim it may have had to represent more closely the

original form of the name is to be disregarded in view of our new equation.

This reflection, and the result already obtained, encourage us to accept the following further equation, which is yielded by a renewed scrutiny of the lists:

{'Ammenon} = Enmenunna.

Here Ammenon, the fourth of Berossus' Antediluvian kings, presents a wonderfully close transcription of the Sumerian name. The n of the first syllable has been assimilated to the following consonant in accordance with a recognized law of euphony, and the resultant doubling of the m is faithfully preserved in the Greek. Precisely the same initial component, *Enme*, occurs in the name Enmeduranki, borne by a mythical king of Sippar, who has long been recognized as the original of Berossus' seventh Antediluvian king, {Euedorakhos}.(1) There too the original n has been assimilated, but the Greek form retains no doubling of the m and points to its further weakening.

(1) Var. {Euedoreskhos}; the second half of the original name, Enmeduranki, is more closely preserved in *Edoranchus*, the form given by the Armenian translator of Eusebius.

I do not propose to detain you with a detailed discussion of Sumerian royal names and their possible Greek equivalents. I will merely point out that the two suggested equations, which I venture to think we may regard as established, throw the study of Berossus' mythological personages upon a new plane. No equivalent has hitherto been suggested for {Daonos}; but {'Ammenon} has been confidently explained as the equivalent of a conjectured Babylonian original, Ummânu, lit. "Workman". The fact that we should now have recovered the Sumerian original of the name, which proves to have no connexion in form or meaning with the previously suggested Semitic equivalent, tends to cast doubt on other Semitic equations proposed. Perhaps {'Amelon} or {'Amillaros} may after all not prove to be the equivalent of Amêlu, "Man", nor {'Amempsinos} that of Amêl-Sin. Both may find their true equivalents in some of the missing royal names at the head of the Sumerian Dynastic List. There too we may provisionally seek {'Aloros}, the "first king", whose equation with Aruru, the Babylonian mother-goddess, never appeared a very happy suggestion.(1) The ingenious proposal,(2) on the other hand, that his successor, {'Alaparos}, represents a miscopied {'Adaparos}, a Greek rendering of the name of Adapa, may still hold good in view of Etana's presence in the Sumerian dynastic record. Ut-napishtim's title, Khasisatra or Atrakhasis, "the Very Wise", still of course remains the established equivalent of {Xisouthros}; but for {'Otiartes} (? {'Opartes}), a rival to Ubar-Tutu, Ut-napishtim's father, may perhaps appear. The new identifications do not of course dispose of the old ones, except in the case of Ummânu; but they open up a new line of approach and provide a fresh field for conjecture.(3) Semitic, and possibly contracted, originals are still possible for unidentified mythical kings of Berossus; but such equations will inspire greater confidence, should we be able to establish Sumerian originals for the

Semitic renderings, from new material already in hand or to be obtained in the future.

(1) Dr. Poebel (*Hist Inscr.*, p. 42, n. 1) makes the interesting suggestion that {'Aloros} may represent an abbreviated and corrupt form of the name Lal-ur-alimma, which has come down to us as that of an early and mythical king of Nippur; see Rawlinson, *W.A.I.*, IV, 60 (67), V, 47 and 44, and cf. *Sev. Tabl. of Creat.*, Vol. I, p. 217, No. 32574, Rev., l. 2 f. It may be added that the sufferings with which the latter is associated in the tradition are perhaps such as might have attached themselves to the first human ruler of the world; but the suggested equation, though
tempting by reason of the remote parallel it would thus furnish to Adam's fate, can at present hardly be accepted in view of the possibility that a closer equation to {'Aloros} may be forthcoming.

(2) Hommel, *Proc. Soc. Bibl. Arch.*, Vol. XV (1893), p. 243.

(3) See further Appendix II.

But it is time I read you extracts from the earlier extant portions of the Sumerian Dynastic List, in order to illustrate the class of document with which we are dealing. From them it will be seen that the record is not a tabular list of names like the well-known King's Lists of the Neo-Babylonian period. It is cast in the form of an epitomized chronicle and gives under set formulae the length of each king's reign, and his father's name in cases of direct succession to father or brother. Short phrases are also sometimes added, or inserted in the sentence referring to a king, in order to indicate his humble origin or the achievement which made his name famous in tradition. The head of the First Column of the text is wanting, and the first royal name that is completely preserved is that of Galumum, the ninth or tenth ruler of the earliest "kingdom", or dynasty, of Kish. The text then runs on connectedly for several lines:

Galumum ruled for nine hundred years.
Zugagib ruled for eight hundred and forty years.
Arpi, son of a man of the people, ruled for seven hundred and
twenty
years.
Etana, the shepherd who ascended to heaven, who subdued all lands,
ruled for six hundred and thirty-five years.(1)
Pili . . ., son of Etana, ruled for four hundred and ten years.
Enmenunna ruled for six hundred and eleven years.
Melamkish, son of Enmenunna, ruled for nine hundred years.
Barsalnunna, son of Enmenunna, ruled for twelve hundred years.
Mesza(. . .), son of Barsalnunna, ruled for (. . .) years.
(. . .), son of Barsalnunna, ruled for (. . .) years.

(1) Possibly 625 years.

63

A small gap then occurs in the text, but we know that the last two representatives of this dynasty of twenty-three kings are related to have ruled for nine hundred years and six hundred and twenty-five years respectively. In the Second Column of the text the lines are also fortunately preserved which record the passing of the first hegemony of Kish to the "Kingdom of Eanna", the latter taking its name from the famous temple of Anu and Ishtar in the old city of Erech. The text continues:

The kingdom of Kish passed to Eanna.

In Eanna, Meskingasher, son of the Sun-god, ruled as high priest and king for three hundred and twenty-five years. Meskingasher entered into(1) (. . .) and ascended to (. . .).

Enmerkar, son of Meskingasher, the king of Erech who built (. . .) with the people of Erech,(2) ruled as king for four hundred and twenty years.

Lugalbanda, the shepherd, ruled for twelve hundred years.

Dumuzi,(3), the hunter(?), whose city was . . ., ruled for a hundred years.

Gishbilgames,(4) whose father was A,(5) the high priest of Kullab, ruled for one hundred and twenty-six(6) years.

(. . .)lugal, son of Gishbilgames, ruled for (. . .) years.

(1) The verb may also imply descent into.

(2) The phrase appears to have been imperfectly copied by the scribe. As it stands the subordinate sentence reads "the king of Erech who built with the people of Erech". Either the object governed by the verb has been omitted, in which case we might restore some such phrase as "the city"; or, perhaps, by a slight transposition, we should read "the king who built Erech with the people of Erech". In any case the first building of the city of Erech, as distinguished from its ancient cult-centre Eanna, appears to be recorded here in the tradition. This is the first reference to Erech in the text; and Enmerkar's father was high priest as well as king.

(3) i.e. Tammuz.

(4) i.e. Gilgamesh.

(5) The name of the father of Gilgamesh is rather strangely expressed by the single sign for the vowel a and must apparently be read as A. As there is a small break in the text at the end of this line, Dr. Poebel not unnaturally assumed that A was merely the first syllable of the name, of which the end was wanting. But it has now been shown that the complete name was A; see Förtsch, *Orient. Lit.-Zeit.*, Vol. XVIII, No. 12 (Dec., 1915), col. 367 ff. The reading is deduced from the following entry in an Assyrian

explanatory
list of gods (*Cun. Texts in the Brit. Mus.*, Pt. XXIV, pl.
25, ll. 29-31): "The god A, who is also equated to the god
Dubbisaguri (i.e. 'Scribe of Ur'), is the priest of Kullab;
his wife is the goddess Ninguesirka (i.e. 'Lady of the edge
of the street')." A, the priest of Kullab and the husband of
a goddess, is clearly to be identified with A, the priest of
Kullab and father of Gilgamesh, for we know from the
Gilgamesh Epic that the hero's mother was the goddess
Ninsun. Whether Ninguesirka was a title of Ninsun, or
represents a variant tradition with regard to the parentage
of Gilgamesh on the mother's side, we have in any case
confirmation of his descent from priest and goddess. It was
natural that A should be subsequently deified. This was not
the case at the time our text was inscribed, as the name is
written without the divine determinative.

(6) Possibly 186 years.

This group of early kings of Erech is of exceptional
interest. Apart from its inclusion of Gilgamesh and the gods
Tammuz and Lugalbanda, its record of Meskingasher's reign
possibly refers to one of the lost legends of Erech. Like him
Melchizedek, who comes to us in a chapter of Genesis
reflecting the troubled times of Babylon's First Dynasty,(1)
was priest as well as king.(2) Tradition appears to have
credited Meskingasher's son and successor, Enmerkar, with
the building of Erech as a city around the first settlement
Eanna, which had already given its name to the "kingdom". If
so, Sumerian tradition confirms the assumption of modern

research that the great cities of Babylonia arose around the still more ancient cult-centres of the land. We shall have occasion to revert to the traditions here recorded concerning the parentage of Meskingasher, the founder of this line of kings, and that of its most famous member, Gilgamesh. Meanwhile we may note that the closing rulers of the "Kingdom of Eanna" are wanting. When the text is again preserved, we read of the hegemony passing from Erech to Ur and thence to Awan:

The k(ingdom of Erech(3) passed to) Ur.
In Ur Mesannipada became king and ruled for eighty years.
Meskiagunna, son of Mesannipada, ruled for thirty years.
Elu(...) ruled for twenty-five years.
Balu(...) ruled for thirty-six years.
Four kings (thus) ruled for a hundred and seventy-one years.
The kingdom of Ur passed to Awan.
In Awan . . .

(1) Cf. *Hist. of Bab.*, p. 159 f.

(2) Gen. xiv. 18.

(3) The restoration of Erech here, in place of Eanna, is based on the absence of the latter name in the summary; after the building of Erech by Enmerkar, the kingdom was probably reckoned as that of Erech.

With the "Kingdom of Ur" we appear to be approaching a firmer historical tradition, for the reigns of its rulers are recorded in decades, not hundreds of years. But we find in the summary, which concludes the main copy of our Dynastic List, that the kingdom of Awan, though it consisted of but three rulers, is credited with a total duration of three hundred and fifty-six years, implying that we are not yet out of the legendary stratum. Since Awan is proved by newly published historical inscriptions from Nippur to have been an important deity of Elam at the time of the Dynasty of Akkad,(1) we gather that the "Kingdom of Awan" represented in Sumerian tradition the first occasion on which the country passed for a time under Elamite rule. At this point a great gap occurs in the text, and when the detailed dynastic succession in Babylonia is again assured, we have passed definitely from the realm of myth and legend into that of history.(2)

(1) Poebel, *Hist. Inscr.*, p. 128.

(2) See further, Appendix II.

What new light, then, do these old Sumerian records throw on Hebrew traditions concerning the early ages of mankind? I think it will be admitted that there is something strangely familiar about some of those Sumerian extracts I read just now. We seem to hear in them the faint echo of another narrative, like them but not quite the same.

And all the days that Adam lived were nine hundred and thirty years; and he died.

And Seth lived an hundred and five years, and begat Enosh: and Seth lived after he begat Enosh eight hundred and seven

68

years, and begat sons and daughters: and all the days of Seth were nine hundred and twelve years: and he died.

... and all the days of Enosh were nine hundred and five years: and he died.

... and all the days of Kenan were nine hundred and ten years: and he died. ... and all the days of Mahalalel were eight hundred ninety and five years: and he died.

... and all the days of Jared were nine hundred sixty and two years: and he died.

... and all the days of Enoch were three hundred sixty and five years: and Enoch walked with God: and he was not; for God took him.

... and all the days of Methuselah were nine hundred sixty and nine years: and he died.

... and all the days of Lamech were seven hundred seventy and seven years: and he died.

And Noah was five hundred years old: and Noah begat Shem,
Ham, and Japheth.

Throughout these extracts from "the book of the generations of Adam",(1) Galumum's nine hundred years(2) seem to run almost like a refrain; and Methuselah's great age, the recognized symbol for longevity, is even exceeded by two of the Sumerian patriarchs. The names in the two lists are not the same,(3) but in both we are moving in the same atmosphere and along similar lines of thought. Though each list adheres to its own set formulae, it estimates the length of human life in the early ages of the world on much the same gigantic scale as the other. Our Sumerian records are not quite so formal in their structure as the Hebrew narrative, but the short notes which here and there relieve their stiff monotony may be paralleled in the Cainite genealogy of the preceding chapter in Genesis.(4) There Cain's city-building, for example, may pair with that of Enmerkar; and though our new records may afford no precise equivalents to Jabal's patronage of nomad life, or to the invention of music and metal-working ascribed to Jubal and Tubal-cain, these too are quite in the spirit of Sumerian and Babylonian tradition, in their attempt to picture the beginnings of civilization. Thus Enmeduranki, the prototype of the seventh Antediluvian patriarch of Berossus, was traditionally revered as the first exponent of divination.(5) It is in the chronological and general setting, rather than in the Hebrew names and details, that an echo seems here to reach us from Sumer through Babylon.

(1) Gen. v. 1 ff. (P).

(2) The same length of reign is credited to Melamkish and to one and perhaps two other rulers of that first Sumerian "kingdom".

(3) The possibility of the Babylonian origin of some of the Hebrew names in this geneaology and its Cainite parallel has long been canvassed; and considerable ingenuity has been expended in obtaining equations between Hebrew names and those of the Antediluvian kings of Berossus by tracing a common meaning for each suggested pair. It is unfortunate that our new identification of {'Ammenon} with the Sumerian *Enmenunna* should dispose of one of the best parallels obtained, viz. {'Ammenon} = Bab. *ummânu*, "workman" || Cain, Kenan = "smith". Another satisfactory pair suggested is {'Amelon} = Bab. *amêlu*, "man" || Enosh = "man"; but the resemblance of the former to *amêlu* may prove to be fortuitous, in view of the possibility of descent from a quite different Sumerian original. The alternative may perhaps have to be faced that the Hebrew parallels to Sumerian and Babylonian traditions are here confined to chronological structure and general contents, and do not extend to Hebrew renderings of Babylonian names. It may be added that such correspondence between personal names in different languages is not very significant by itself. The name of Zugagib of Kish, for example, is paralleled by the title borne by one of the earliest kings of the Ist Dynasty of Egypt, Narmer, whose carved slate palettes have been found at Kierakonpolis; he too was known as "the Scorpion."

71

(4) Gen. iv. 17 ff. (J).

(5) It may be noted that an account of the origin of divination is included in his description of the descendents of Noah by the writer of the Biblical Antiquities of Philo, a product of the same school as the Fourth Book of Esdras and the Apocalypse of Baruch; see James, *The Biblical Antiquities of Philo*, p. 86.

I may add that a parallel is provided by the new Sumerian records to the circumstances preceding the birth of the Nephilim at the beginning of the sixth chapter of Genesis.(1) For in them also great prowess or distinction is ascribed to the progeny of human and divine unions. We have already noted that, according to the traditions the records embody, the Sumerians looked back to a time when gods lived upon the earth with men, and we have seen such deities as Tammuz and Lugalbanda figuring as rulers of cities in the dynastic sequence. As in later periods, their names are there preceded by the determinative for divinity. But more significant still is the fact that we read of two Sumerian heroes, also rulers of cities, who were divine on the father's or mother's side but not on both. Meskingasher is entered in the list as "son of the Sun-god",(2) and no divine parentage is recorded on the mother's side. On the other hand, the human father of Gilgamesh is described as the high priest of Kullab, and we know from other sources that his mother was the goddess Ninsun.(3) That this is not a fanciful interpretation is proved by a passage in the Gilgamesh Epic itself,(4) in which its hero is described as two-thirds god and one-third man. We again find ourselves back in the same stratum of tradition with which the Hebrew narratives have made us so familiar.

(1) Gen. vi. 1-4 (J).

(2) The phrase recalls the familiar Egyptian royal designation "son of the Sun," and it is possible that we may connect with this same idea the Palermo Stele's inclusion of the mother's and omission of the father's name in its record of the early dynastic Pharaohs. This suggestion does not exclude the possibility of the prevalence of matrilineal (and perhaps originally also of matrilocal and matripotestal) conditions among the earliest inhabitants of Egypt. Indeed the early existence of some form of mother-right may have originated, and would certainly have encouraged, the growth of a tradition of solar parentage for the head of the state.

(3) Poebel, *Hist. Inscr.*, p. 124 f.

(4) Tablet I, Col. ii, l. 1; and cf. Tablet IX, Col. ii. l. 16.

What light then does our new material throw upon traditional origins of civilization? We have seen that in Egypt a new fragment of the Palermo Stele has confirmed in a remarkable way the tradition of the predynastic period which was incorporated in his history by Manetho. It has long been recognized that in Babylonia the sources of

Berossus must have been refracted by the political atmosphere of that country during the preceding nineteen hundred years. This inference our new material supports; but when due allowance has been made for a resulting disturbance of vision, the Sumerian origin of the remainder of his evidence is notably confirmed. Two of his ten Antediluvian kings rejoin their Sumerian prototypes, and we shall see that two of his three Antediluvian cities find their place among the five of primitive Sumerian belief. It is clear that in Babylonia, as in Egypt, the local traditions of the dawn of history, current in the Hellenistic period, were modelled on very early lines. Both countries were the seats of ancient civilizations, and it is natural that each should stage its picture of beginnings upon its own soil and embellish it with local colouring.

It is a tribute to the historical accuracy of Hebrew tradition to recognize that it never represented Palestine as the cradle of the human race. It looked to the East rather than to the South for evidence of man's earliest history and first progress in the arts of life. And it is in the East, in the soil of Babylonia, that we may legitimately seek material in which to verify the sources of that traditional belief.

The new parallels I have to-day attempted to trace between some of the Hebrew traditions, preserved in Gen. iv-vi, and those of the early Sumerians, as presented by their great Dynastic List, are essentially general in character and do not apply to details of narrative or to proper names. If they stood alone, we should still have to consider whether they are such as to suggest cultural influence or independent origin. But fortunately they do not exhaust the evidence we have lately recovered from the site of Nippur, and we will postpone formulating our conclusions with regard to them until the whole field has been surveyed. From the biblical standpoint by far the most valuable of our new documents is one that incorporates a Sumerian version of the Deluge story. We shall see that it presents a variant and more primitive picture of that great catastrophe than those of the Babylonian and Hebrew versions. And what is of even greater interest, it connects the narrative of the Flood with that of Creation, and supplies a brief but intermediate account of the Antediluvian period. How then are we to explain this striking literary resemblance to the structure of the narrative in Genesis, a resemblance that is completely wanting in the Babylonian versions? But that is a problem we must reserve for the next lecture.

LECTURE II — DELUGE STORIES AND THE NEW SUMERIAN VERSION

In the first lecture we saw how, both in Babylonia and Egypt, recent discoveries had thrown light upon periods regarded as prehistoric, and how we had lately recovered traditions concerning very early rulers both in the Nile Valley and along the lower Euphrates. On the strength of the latter discovery we noted the possibility that future excavation in Babylonia would lay bare stages of primitive culture similar to those we have already recovered in Egyptian soil. Meanwhile the documents from Nippur had shown us what the early Sumerians themselves believed about their own origin, and we traced in their tradition the gradual blending of history with legend and myth. We saw that the new Dynastic List took us back in the legendary sequence at least to the beginning of the Post-diluvian period. Now one of the newly published literary texts fills in the gap beyond, for it gives us a Sumerian account of the history of the world from the Creation to the Deluge, at about which point, as we saw, the extant portions of the Dynastic List take up the story. I propose to devote my lecture to-day to this early version of the Flood and to the effect of its discovery upon some current theories.

The Babylonian account of the Deluge, which was discovered by George Smith in 1872 on tablets from the Royal Library at Nineveh, is, as you know, embedded in a long epic of twelve Books recounting the adventures of the Old Babylonian hero Gilgamesh. Towards the end of this composite tale, Gilgamesh, desiring immortality, crosses the Waters of Death in order to beg the secret from his ancestor Ut-napishtim, who in the past had escaped the Deluge and had been granted immortality by the gods. The Eleventh Tablet, or Book, of the epic contains the account of the Deluge which Ut-napishtim related to his kinsman Gilgamesh. The close correspondence of this Babylonian story with that contained in Genesis is recognized by every one and need not detain us. You will remember that in some passages the accounts tally even in minute details, such, for example, as the device of sending out birds to test the abatement of the waters. It is true that in the Babylonian version a dove, a swallow, and a raven are sent forth in that order, instead of a raven and the dove three times. But such slight discrepancies only emphasize the general resemblance of the narratives.

In any comparison it is usually admitted that two accounts have been combined in the Hebrew narrative. I should like to point out that this assumption may be made by any one, whatever his views may be with regard to the textual problems of the Hebrew Bible and the traditional authorship of the Pentateuch. And for our purpose at the moment it is immaterial whether we identify the compiler of these Hebrew narratives with Moses himself, or with some later Jewish historian whose name has not come down to us. Whoever he was, he has scrupulously preserved his two texts and, even when they differ, he has given each as he found it. Thanks to this fact, any one by a careful examination of the narrative can disentangle the two versions for himself. He will find each gives a consistent story. One of them appears to be simpler and more primitive than the other, and I will refer to them as the earlier and the later Hebrew Versions.(1) The Babylonian text in the Epic of Gilgamesh contains several peculiarities of each of the Hebrew versions, though the points of resemblance are more detailed in the earlier of the two.

(1) In the combined account in Gen. vi. 5-ix. 17, if the following passages be marked in the margin or underlined, and then read consecutively, it will be seen that they give a consistent and almost complete account of the Deluge: Gen.

vi. 9-22; vii. 6, 11, 13-16 (down to "as God commanded him"), 17 (to "upon the earth"), 18-21, 24; viii. 1, 2 (to "were stopped"), 3 (from "and after")-5, 13 (to "from off the earth"), 14-19; and ix. 1-17. The marked passages represent the "later Hebrew Version." If the remaining passages be then read consecutively, they will be seen to give a different version of the same events, though not so completely preserved as the other; these passages substantially represent the "earlier Hebrew Version". In commentaries on the Hebrew text they are, of course, usually referred to under the convenient symbols J and P, representing respectively the earlier and the later versions. For further details, see any of the modern commentaries on Genesis, e.g. Driver, *Book of Genesis*, pp. 85 ff.; Skinner, *Genesis*, pp. 147 ff.; Ryle, *Genesis*, p. 96 f.

Now the tablets from the Royal Library at Nineveh inscribed with the Gilgamesh Epic do not date from an earlier period than the seventh century B.C. But archaeological evidence has long shown that the traditions themselves were current during all periods of Babylonian history; for Gilgamesh and his half-human friend Enkidu were favourite subjects for the seal-engraver, whether he lived in Sumerian times or under the Achaemenian kings of Persia. We have also, for some years now, possessed two early fragments of the Deluge narrative, proving that the story was known to the Semitic inhabitants of the country at the time of Hammurabi's dynasty.(1) Our newly discovered text from Nippur was also written at about that period, probably before 2100 B.C. But the composition itself, apart from the tablet on which it is inscribed, must go back very much earlier than that. For instead of being composed in Semitic Babylonian, the text is in Sumerian, the language of the earliest known inhabitants of Babylonia, whom the Semites eventually displaced. This people, it is now recognized, were the originators of the Babylonian civilization, and we saw in the first lecture that, according to their own traditions, they had occupied that country since the dawn of history.

(1) The earlier of the two fragments is dated in the eleventh year of Ammizaduga, the tenth king of Hammurabi's
dynasty, i.e. in 1967 B.C.; it was published by Scheil, *Recueil de travaux*, Vol. XX, pp. 55 ff. Here the Deluge story does not form part of the Gilgamesh Epic, but is

recounted in the second tablet of a different work; its hero bears the name Atrakhasis, as in the variant version of the Deluge from the Nineveh library. The other and smaller fragment, which must be dated by its script, was published by Hilprecht (*Babylonian Expedition*, series D, Vol. V, Fasc. 1, pp. 33 ff.), who assigned it to about the same period; but it is probably of a considerably later date. The most convenient translations of the legends that were known

before the publication of the Nippur texts are those given by Rogers, *Cuneiform Parallels to the Old Testament* (Oxford, 1912), and Dhorme, *Choix de textes religieux Assyro-Babyloniens* (Paris, 1907).

The Semites as a ruling race came later, though the occurrence of Semitic names in the Sumerian Dynastic List suggests very early infiltration from Arabia. After a long struggle the immigrants succeeded in dominating the settled race; and in the process they in turn became civilized. They learnt and adopted the cuneiform writing, they took over the Sumerian literature. Towards the close of the third millennium, when our tablet was written, the Sumerians as a race had almost ceased to exist. They had been absorbed in the Semitic population and their language was no longer the general language of the country. But their ancient literature and sacred texts were carefully preserved and continued to be studied by the Semitic priests and scribes. So the fact that the tablet is written in the old Sumerian tongue proves that the story it tells had come down from a very much earlier period. This inference is not affected by certain small differences in idiom which its language presents when compared with that of Sumerian building-inscriptions. Such would naturally occur in the course of transmission, especially in a text which, as we shall see, had been employed for a practical purpose after being subjected to a process of reduction to suit it to its new setting.

When we turn to the text itself, it will be obvious that the story also is very primitive. But before doing so we will inquire whether this very early version is likely to cast any light on the origin of Deluge stories such as are often met with in other parts of the world. Our inquiry will have an interest apart from the question itself, as it will illustrate the views of two divergent schools among students of primitive literature and tradition. According to one of these views, in its most extreme form, the tales which early or primitive man tells about his gods and the origin of the world he sees around him are never to be regarded as simple stories, but are to be consistently interpreted as symbolizing natural phenomena. It is, of course, quite certain that, both in Egypt and Babylonia, mythology in later periods received a strong astrological colouring; and it is equally clear that some legends derive their origin from nature myths. But the theory in the hands of its more enthusiastic adherents goes further than that. For them a complete absence of astrological colouring is no deterrent from an astrological interpretation; and, where such colouring does occur, the possibility of later embellishment is discounted, and it is treated without further proof as the base on which the original story rests. One such interpretation of the Deluge narrative in Babylonia, particularly favoured by recent German writers, would regard it as reflecting the passage of the Sun through a portion of the ecliptic. It is assumed that the primitive Babylonians were aware that in the course of ages the spring equinox must traverse the southern or watery region of the zodiac. This, on their system, signified a submergence of the whole universe in water, and the Deluge myth would symbolize the safe passage of the vernal Sun-god through that part of the ecliptic. But we need not spend time over that view, as its underlying conception is undoubtedly quite a late development of Babylonian astrology.

More attractive is the simpler astrological theory that the voyage of any Deluge hero in his boat or ark represents the daily journey of the Sun-god across the heavenly ocean, a conception which is so often represented in Egyptian sculpture and painting. It used to be assumed by holders of the theory that this idea of the Sun as "the god in the boat" was common among primitive races, and that that would account for the widespread occurrence of Deluge-stories among scattered races of the world. But this view has recently undergone some modification in accordance with the general trend of other lines of research. In recent years there has been an increased readiness among archaeologists to recognize evidence of contact between the great civilizations of antiquity. This has been particularly the case in the area of the Eastern Mediterranean; but the possibility has also been mooted of the early use of land-routes running from the Near East to Central and Southern Asia. The discovery in Chinese Turkestan, to the east of the Caspian, of a prehistoric culture resembling that of Elam has now been followed by the finding of similar remains by Sir Aurel Stein in the course of the journey from which he has lately returned.(1) They were discovered in an old basin of the Helmand River in Persian Seistan, where they had been laid bare by wind-erosion. But more interesting still, and an incentive to further exploration in that region, is another of his discoveries last year, also made near the Afghan border. At two sites in the Helmand Delta, well above the level of inundation, he came across fragments of pottery inscribed in early Aramaic characters,(2) though, for obvious reasons, he has left them with all his other collections in India. This unexpected find, by the way, suggests for our problem possibilities of wide transmission in comparatively early times.

(1) See his "Expedition in Central Asia", in *The Geographical Journal*, Vol. XLVII (Jan.-June, 1916), pp. 358 ff.

(2) Op. cit., p. 363.

The synthetic tendency among archaeologists has been reflected in anthropological research, which has begun to question the separate and independent origin, not only of the more useful arts and crafts, but also of many primitive customs and beliefs. It is suggested that too much stress has been laid on environment; and, though it is readily admitted that similar needs and experiences may in some cases have given rise to similar expedients and explanations, it is urged that man is an imitative animal and that inventive genius is far from common.(1) Consequently the wide dispersion of many beliefs and practices, which used generally to be explained as due to the similar and independent working of the human mind under like conditions, is now often provisionally registered as evidence of migratory movement or of cultural drift. Much good work has recently been done in tabulating the occurrence of many customs and beliefs, in order to ascertain their lines of distribution. Workers are as yet in the collecting stage, and it is hardly necessary to say that explanatory theories are still to be regarded as purely tentative and provisional. At the meetings of the British Association during the last few years, the most breezy discussions in the Anthropological Section have undoubtedly centred around this subject. There are several works in the field, but the most comprehensive theory as yet put forward is one that concerns us, as it has given a new lease of life to the old solar interpretation of the Deluge story.

(1) See, e.g. Marett, *Anthropology* (2nd ed., 1914), Chap. iv, "Environment," pp. 122 ff.; and for earlier tendencies, particularly in the sphere of mythological exegesis, see S. Reinach, *Cultes, Mythes et Religions*, t. IV (1912), pp. 1 ff.

In a land such as Egypt, where there is little rain and the sky is always clear, the sun in its splendour tended from the earliest period to dominate the national consciousness. As intercourse increased along the Nile Valley, centres of Sun-worship ceased to be merely local, and the political rise of a city determined the fortunes of its cult. From the proto-dynastic period onward, the "King of the two Lands" had borne the title of "Horus" as the lineal descendant of the great Sun-god of Edfu, and the rise of Ra in the Vth Dynasty, through the priesthood of Heliopolis, was confirmed in the solar theology of the Middle Kingdom. Thus it was that other deities assumed a solar character as forms of Ra. Amen, the local god of Thebes, becomes Amen-Ra with the political rise of his city, and even the old Crocodile-god, Sebek, soars into the sky as Sebek-Ra. The only other movement in the religion of ancient Egypt, comparable in importance to this solar development, was the popular cult of Osiris as God of the Dead, and with it the official religion had to come to terms. Horus is reborn as the posthumous son of Osiris, and Ra gladdens his abode during his nightly journey through the Underworld. The theory with which we are concerned suggests that this dominant trait in Egyptian religion passed, with other elements of culture, beyond the bounds of the Nile Valley and influenced the practice and beliefs of distant races.

This suggestion has been gradually elaborated by its author, Professor Elliot Smith, who has devoted much attention to the anatomical study of Egyptian mummification. Beginning with a scrutiny of megalithic building and sun-worship,[1] he has subsequently deduced, from evidence of common distribution, the existence of a culture-complex, including in addition to these two elements the varied practices of tattooing, circumcision, ear-piercing, that quaint custom known as couvade, head-deformation, and the prevalence of serpent-cults, myths of petrifaction and the Deluge, and finally of mummification. The last ingredient was added after an examination of Papuan mummies had disclosed their apparent resemblance in points of detail to Egyptian mummies of the XXIst Dynasty. As a result he assumes the existence of an early cultural movement, for which the descriptive title "heliolithic" has been coined.(2) Starting with Egypt as its centre, one of the principal lines of its advance is said to have lain through Syria and Mesopotamia and thence along the coastlands of Asia to the Far East. The method of distribution and the suggested part played by the Phoenicians have been already criticized sufficiently. But in a modified form the theory has found considerable support, especially among ethnologists interested in Indonesia. I do not propose to examine in detail the evidence for or against it. It will suffice to note that the Deluge story and its alleged Egyptian origin in solar worship form one of the prominent strands in its composition.

(1) Cf. Elliot Smith, *The Ancient Egyptians*, 1911.

(2) See in particular his monograph "On the significance of the Geographical Distribution of the Practice of Mummification" in the *Memoirs of the Manchester Literary and Philosophical Society*, 1915.

One weakness of this particular strand is that the Egyptians themselves possessed no tradition of the Deluge. Indeed the annual inundation of the Nile is not such as would give rise to a legend of world-destruction; and in this respect it presents a striking contrast to the Tigris and Euphrates. The ancient Egyptian's conception of his own

86

gentle river is reflected in the form he gave the Nile-god, for Hapi is represented as no fierce warrior or monster. He is given a woman's breasts as a sign of his fecundity. The nearest Egyptian parallel to the Deluge story is the "Legend of the Destruction of Mankind", which is engraved on the walls of a chamber in the tomb of Seti I.(1) The late Sir Gaston Maspero indeed called it "a dry deluge myth", but his paradox was intended to emphasize the difference as much as the parallelism presented. It is true that in the Egyptian myth the Sun-god causes mankind to be slain because of their impiety, and he eventually pardons the survivors. The narrative thus betrays undoubted parallelism to the Babylonian and Hebrew stories, so far as concerns the attempted annihilation of mankind by the offended god, but there the resemblance ends. For water has no part in man's destruction, and the essential element of a Deluge story is thus absent.(2) Our new Sumerian document, on the other hand, contains what is by far the earliest example yet recovered of a genuine Deluge tale; and we may thus use it incidentally to test this theory of Egyptian influence, and also to ascertain whether it furnishes any positive evidence on the origin of Deluge stories in general.

(1) It was first published by Monsieur Naville, *Tranc. Soc. Bibl. Arch.*, IV (1874), pp. 1 ff. The myth may be most conveniently studied in Dr. Budge's edition in *Egyptian Literature*, Vol. I, "Legends of the Gods" (1912), pp. 14 ff., where the hieroglyphic text and translation are printed on opposite pages; cf. the summary, op. cit., pp. xxiii ff., where the principal literature is also cited. See also his

Gods of the Egyptians, Vol. I, chap. xii, pp. 388 ff.

(2) The undoubted points of resemblance, as well as the equally striking points of divergence, presented by the Egyptian myth when compared with the Babylonian and Hebrew stories of a Deluge may be briefly indicated. The impiety of men in complaining of the age of Ra finds a parallel in the wickedness of man upon the earth (J) and the corruption of all flesh (P) of the Hebrew Versions. The summoning by Ra of the great Heliopolitan cosmic gods in council, including his personified Eye, the primaeval pair Shu and Tefnut, Keb the god of the earth and his consort Nut the sky-goddess, and Nu the primaeval water-god and originally Nut's male counterpart, is paralleled by the *puhur ilâni*, or "assembly of the gods", in the Babylonian Version (see Gilg. Epic. XI. l. 120 f., and cf. ll. 10 ff.); and they meet in "the Great House", or Sun-temple at Heliopolis, as the Babylonian gods deliberate in Shuruppak. Egyptian, Babylonian, and Hebrew narratives all agree in the divine determination to destroy mankind and in man's ultimate survival. But the close of the Egyptian story diverges into another sphere. The slaughter of men by the Eye of Ra in the form of the goddess Hathor, who during the night wades in their blood, is suggestive of Africa; and so too is her drinking of men's blood mixed with the narcotic mandrake and

with seven thousand vessels of beer, with the result that through drunkenness she ceased from slaughter. The latter part of the narrative is directly connected with the cult-ritual and beer-drinking at the Festivals of Hathor and Ra; but the destruction of men by slaughter in place of drowning
appears to belong to the original myth. Indeed, the only suggestion of a Deluge story is suggested by the presence of Nu, the primaeval water-god, at Ra's council, and that is explicable on other grounds. In any case the points of resemblance presented by the earlier part of the Egyptian myth to Semitic Deluge stories are general, not detailed; and though they may possibly be due to reflection from Asia,
they are not such as to suggest an Egyptian origin for Deluge myths.

The tablet on which our new version of the Deluge is inscribed was excavated at Nippur during the third Babylonian expedition sent out by the University of Pennsylvania; but it was not until the summer of 1912 that its contents were identified, when the several fragments of which it was composed were assembled and put together. It is a large document, containing six columns of writing, three on each side; but unfortunately only the lower half has been recovered, so that considerable gaps occur in the text.(1) The sharp edges of the broken surface, however, suggest that it was damaged after removal from the soil, and the possibility remains that some of the missing fragments may yet be recovered either at Pennsylvania or in the Museum at

Constantinople. As it is not dated, its age must be determined mainly by the character of its script. A close examination of the writing suggests that it can hardly have been inscribed as late as the Kassite Dynasty, since two or three signs exhibit more archaic forms than occur on any tablets of that period;(2) and such linguistic corruptions as have been noted in its text may well be accounted for by the process of decay which must have already affected the Sumerian language at the time of the later kings of Nisin. Moreover, the tablet bears a close resemblance to one of the newly published copies of the Sumerian Dynastic List from Nippur;(3) for both are of the same shape and composed of the same reddish-brown clay, and both show the same peculiarities of writing. The two tablets in fact appear to have been written by the same hand, and as that copy of the Dynastic List was probably drawn up before the latter half of the First Dynasty of Babylon, we may assign the same approximate date for the writing of our text. This of course only fixes a lower limit for the age of the myth which it enshrines.

(1) The breadth of the tablet is 5 5/8 in., and it
originally measured about 7 in. in length from top to
bottom; but only about one-third of its inscribed surface is
preserved.

(2) Cf. Poebel, *Hist. Texts*, pp. 66 ff.

(3) No. 5.

That the composition is in the form of a poem may be seen at a glance from the external appearance of the tablet, the division of many of the lines and the blank spaces frequently left between the sign-groups being due to the rhythmical character of the text. The style of the poetry may be simple and abrupt, but it exhibits a familiar feature of both Semitic-Babylonian and Hebrew poetry, in its constant employment of partial repetition or paraphrase in parallel lines. The story it tells is very primitive and in many respects unlike the Babylonian Versions of the Deluge which we already possess. Perhaps its most striking peculiarity is the setting of the story, which opens with a record of the creation of man and animals, goes on to tell how the first cities were built, and ends with a version of the Deluge, which is thus recounted in its relation to the Sumerian history of the world. This literary connexion between the Creation and Deluge narratives is of unusual interest, in view of the age of our text. In the Babylonian Versions hitherto known they are included in separate epics with quite different contexts. Here they are recounted together in a single document, much as they probably were in the history of Berossus and as we find them in the present form of the Book of Genesis. This fact will open up some interesting problems when we attempt to trace the literary descent of the tradition.

But one important point about the text should be emphasized at once, since it will affect our understanding of some very obscure passages, of which no satisfactory explanation has yet been given. The assumption has hitherto been made that the text is an epic pure and simple. It is quite true that the greater part of it is a myth, recounted as a narrative in poetical form, but there appear to me to be clear indications that the myth was really embedded in an incantation. If this was so, the mythological portion was recited for a magical purpose, with the object of invoking the aid of the chief deities whose actions in the past are there described, and of increasing by that means the potency of the spell.(1) In the third lecture I propose to treat in more detail the employment and significance of myth in magic, and we shall have occasion to refer to other instances, Sumerian, Babylonian, and Egyptian, in which a myth has reached us in a magical setting.

(1) It will be seen that the subject-matter of any myth
treated in this way has a close connexion with the object
for which the incantation was performed.

In the present case the inference of magical use is drawn from certain passages in the text itself, which appear to be explicable only on that hypothesis. In magical compositions of the later period intended for recitation, the sign for "Incantation" is usually prefixed. Unfortunately the beginning of our text is wanting; but its opening words are given in the colophon, or title, which is engraved on the left-hand edge of the tablet, and it is possible that the traces of the first sign there are to be read as EN, "Incantation".(1) Should a re-examination of the tablet establish this reading of the word, we should have definite proof of the suggested magical setting of the narrative. But even if we assume its absence, that would not invalidate the arguments that can be adduced in favour of recognizing the existence of a magical element, for they are based on internal evidence and enable us to explain certain features which are inexplicable on Dr. Poebel's hypothesis. Moreover, we shall later on examine another of the newly published Sumerian compositions from Nippur, which is not only semi-epical in character, but is of precisely the same shape, script, and period as our text, and is very probably a tablet of the same series. There also the opening signs of the text are wanting, but far more of its contents are preserved and they present unmistakable traces of magical use. Its evidence, as that of a parallel text, may therefore be cited in support of the present contention. It may be added that in Sumerian magical compositions of this early period, of which we have not yet recovered many quite obvious examples, it is possible that the prefix "Incantation" was not so invariable as in the later magical literature.

(1) Cf. Poebel, *Hist. Texts*, p. 63, and *Hist. and Gram. Texts*, pl. i. In the photographic reproduction of the edges of the tablet given in the latter volume, pl. lxxxix, the traces of the sign suggest the reading EN (= Sem. *siptu*, "incantation"). But the sign may very possibly be read AN. In the latter case we may read, in the traces of the two sign-groups at the beginning of the text, the names of both Anu and Enlil, who appear so frequently as the two presiding deities in the myth.

It has already been remarked that only the lower half of our tablet has been recovered, and that consequently a number of gaps occur in the text. On the obverse the upper portion of each of the first three columns is missing, while of the remaining three columns, which are inscribed upon the reverse, the upper portions only are preserved. This difference in the relative positions of the textual fragments recovered is due to the fact that Sumerian scribes, like their later Babylonian and Assyrian imitators, when they had finished writing the obverse of a tablet, turned it over from bottom to top—not, as we should turn a sheet of paper, from right to left. But in spite of the lacunae, the sequence of events related in the mythological narrative may be followed without difficulty, since the main outline of the story is already familiar enough from the versions of the Semitic-Babylonian scribes and of Berossus. Some uncertainties naturally remain as to what exactly was included in the missing portions of the tablet; but the more important episodes are fortunately recounted in the extant fragments, and these suffice for a definition of the distinctive character of the Sumerian Version. In view of its literary importance it may be advisable to attempt a somewhat detailed discussion of its contents, column by column;(1) and the analysis may be most conveniently divided into numbered sections, each of which refers to one of the six columns of the tablet. The description of the First Column will serve to establish the general character of the text. Through the analysis of the tablet parallels and contrasts will be noted with the Babylonian and Hebrew Versions. It will then be possible to summarise, on a surer foundation, the literary history of the traditions, and finally to estimate the effect of our new evidence upon current theories as to the origin and wide dispersion of Deluge stories.

(1) In the lecture as delivered the contents of each column were necessarily summarized rather briefly, and conclusions were given without discussion of the evidence.

The following headings, under which the six numbered sections may be arranged, indicate the contents of each column and show at a glance the main features of the Sumerian Version:

I. Introduction to the Myth, and account of Creation.

II. The Antediluvian Cities.

III. The Council of the Gods, and Ziusudu's piety.

IV. The Dream-Warning.

V. The Deluge, the Escape of the Great Boat, and the Sacrifice to the Sun-god.

VI. The Propitiation of the Angry Gods, and Ziusudu's Immortality.

I. INTRODUCTION TO THE MYTH, AND ACCOUNT OF CREATION

The beginning of the text is wanting, and the earliest lines preserved of the First Column open with the closing sentences of a speech, probably by the chief of the four creating deities, who are later on referred to by name. In it

95

there is a reference to a future destruction of mankind, but the context is broken; the lines in question begin:

"As for my human race, from (*or* in) its destruction will I cause it to be (...),

For Nintu my creatures (...) will I (...)."

From the reference to "my human race" it is clear that the speaker is a creating deity; and since the expression is exactly parallel to the term "my people" used by Ishtar, or Bêlit-ili, "the Lady of the gods", in the Babylonian Version of the Deluge story when she bewails the destruction of mankind, Dr. Poebel assigns the speech to Ninkharsagga, or Nintu,(1) the goddess who later in the column is associated with Anu, Enlil, and Enki in man's creation. But the mention of Nintu in her own speech is hardly consistent with that supposition,(2) if we assume with Dr. Poebel, as we are probably justified in doing, that the title Nintu is employed here and elsewhere in the narrative merely as a synonym of Ninkharsagga.(3) It appears to me far more probable that one of the two supreme gods, Anu or Enlil, is the speaker,(4) and additional grounds will be cited later in support of this view. It is indeed possible, in spite of the verbs and suffixes in the singular, that the speech is to be assigned to both Anu and Enlil, for in the last column, as we shall see, we find verb in the singular following references to both these deities. In any case one of the two chief gods may be regarded as speaking and acting on behalf of both, though it may be that the inclusion of the second name in the narrative was not original but simply due to a combination of variant traditions. Such a conflate use of Anu-Enlil would present a striking parallel to the Hebrew combination Yahweh-Elohim, though of course in the case of the former pair the subsequent stage of identification was never attained. But the evidence furnished by the text is not conclusive, and it is preferable here and elsewhere in the narrative to regard either Anu or Enlil as speaking and acting both on his own behalf and as the other's representative.

(1) Op. cit., p. 21 f.; and cf. Jastrow, *Hebrew and Babylonian Traditions*, p. 336.

(2) It necessitates the taking of (*dingir*) *Nin-tu-ra* as a genitive, not a dative, and the very awkward rendering "my, Nintu's, creations".

(3) Another of the recently published Sumerian mythological
compositions from Nippur includes a number of myths in which
Enki is associated first with Ninella, referred to also as Nintu, "the Goddess of Birth", then with Ninshar, referred to also as Ninkurra, and finally with Ninkharsagga. This text exhibits the process by which separate traditions with regard to goddesses originally distinct were combined together, with the result that their heroines were subsequently often identified with one another. There the myths that have not been subjected to a very severe process of editing, and in consequence the welding is not so complete as in the Sumerian Version of the Deluge.

97

(4) If Enlil's name should prove to be the first word of the composition, we should naturally regard him as the speaker here and as the protagonist of the gods throughout the text, a *rôle* he also plays in the Semitic-Babylonian Version.

This reference to the Deluge, which occurs so early in the text, suggests the probability that the account of the Creation and of the founding of Antediluvian cities, included in the first two columns, is to be taken merely as summarizing the events that led up to the Deluge. And an almost certain proof of this may be seen in the opening words of the composition, which are preserved in its colophon or title on the left-hand edge of the tablet. We have already noted that the first two words are there to be read, either as the prefix "Incantation" followed by the name "Enlil", or as the two divine names "Anu (and) Enlil". Now the signs which follow the traces of Enlil's name are quite certain; they represent "Ziusudu", which, as we shall see in the Third Column, is the name of the Deluge hero in our Sumerian Version. He is thus mentioned in the opening words of the text, in some relation to one or both of the two chief gods of the subsequent narrative. But the natural place for his first introduction into the story is in the Third Column, where it is related that "at that time Ziusudu, the king" did so-and-so. The prominence given him at the beginning of the text, at nearly a column's interval before the lines which record the creation of man, is sufficient proof that the Deluge story is the writer's main interest, and that preceding episodes are merely introductory to it.

98

What subject then may we conjecture was treated in the missing lines of this column, which precede the account of Creation and close with the speech of the chief creating deity? Now the Deluge narrative practically ends with the last lines of the tablet that are preserved, and the lower half of the Sixth Column is entirely wanting. We shall see reason to believe that the missing end of the tablet was not left blank and uninscribed, but contained an incantation, the magical efficacy of which was ensured by the preceding recitation of the Deluge myth. If that were so, it would be natural enough that the text should open with its main subject. The cause of the catastrophe and the reason for man's rescue from it might well be referred to by one of the creating deities in virtue of the analogy these aspects of the myth would present to the circumstances for which the incantation was designed. A brief account of the Creation and of Antediluvian history would then form a natural transition to the narrative of the Deluge itself. And even if the text contained no incantation, the narrative may well have been introduced in the manner suggested, since this explanation in any case fits in with what is still preserved of the First Column. For after his reference to the destruction of mankind, the deity proceeds to fix the chief duty of man, either as a preliminary to his creation, or as a reassertion of that duty after his rescue from destruction by the Flood. It is noteworthy that this duty consists in the building of temples to the gods "in a clean spot", that is to say "in hallowed places". The passage may be given in full, including the two opening lines already discussed:

"As for my human race, from (*or* in) its destruction will I cause it to be (. . .), For Nintu my creatures (. . .) will I (. . .).

The people will I cause to . . . in their settlements,

Cities . . . shall (man) build, in there protection will I cause him to rest,

That he may lay the brick of our houses in a clean spot,

That in a clean spot he may establish our . . . !"

In the reason here given for man's creation, or for his rescue from the Flood, we have an interesting parallel to the Sixth Tablet of the Semitic-Babylonian Creation Series. At the opening of that tablet Marduk, in response to "the word of the gods", is urged by his heart to devise a cunning plan which he imparts to Ea, namely the creation of man from his own divine blood and from bone which he will fashion. And the reason he gives for his proposal is precisely that which, as we have seen, prompted the Sumerian deity to create or preserve the human race. For Marduk continues:

"I will create man who shall inhabit (. . .),

That the service of the gods may be established and that their shrines may be built."(1)

(1) See *The Seven Tablets of Creation*, Vol. I, pp. 86 ff.

100

We shall see later, from the remainder of Marduk's speech, that the Semitic Version has been elaborated at this point in order to reconcile it with other ingredients in its narrative, which were entirely absent from the simpler Sumerian tradition. It will suffice here to note that, in both, the reason given for man's existence is the same, namely, that the gods themselves may have worshippers.(1) The conception is in full agreement with early Sumerian thought, and reflects the theocratic constitution of the earliest Sumerian communities. The idea was naturally not repugnant to the Semites, and it need not surprise us to find the very words of the principal Sumerian Creator put into the mouth of Marduk, the city-god of Babylon.

(1) It may be added that this is also the reason given for man's creation in the introduction to a text which celebrates the founding or rebuilding of a temple.

The deity's speech perhaps comes to an end with the declaration of his purpose in creating mankind or in sanctioning their survival of the Deluge; and the following three lines appear to relate his establishment of the divine laws in accordance with which his intention was carried out. The passage includes a refrain, which is repeated in the Second Column:

The sublime decrees he made perfect for it.

It may probably be assumed that the refrain is employed in relation to the same deity in both passages. In the Second Column it precedes the foundation of the Babylonian kingdom and the building of the Antediluvian cities. In that passage there can be little doubt that the subject of the verb is the chief Sumerian deity, and we are therefore the more inclined to assign to him also the opening speech of the First Column, rather than to regard it as spoken by the Sumerian goddess whose share in the creation would justify her in claiming mankind as her own. In the last four lines of the column we have a brief record of the Creation itself. It was carried out by the three greatest gods of the Sumerian pantheon, Anu, Enlil and Enki, with the help of the goddess Ninkharsagga; the passage reads:

When Anu, Enlil, Enki and Ninkharsagga
Created the blackheaded (i.e. mankind),
The *niggil(ma)* of the earth they caused the earth to
produce(?),
The animals, the four-legged creatures of the field, they
artfully called into existence.

The interpretation of the third line is obscure, but there is no doubt that it records the creation of something which is represented as having taken place between the creation of mankind and that of animals. This object, which is written as *nig-gil* or *nig-gil-ma*, is referred to again in the Sixth Column, where the Sumerian hero of the Deluge assigns to it the honorific title, "Preserver of the Seed of Mankind". It must therefore have played an important part in man's preservation from the Flood; and the subsequent bestowal of the title may be paralleled in the early Semitic Deluge fragment from Nippur, where the boat in which Ut-napishtim escapes is assigned the very similar title "Preserver of Life".(1) But *niggilma* is not the word used in the Sumerian Version of Ziusudu's boat, and I am inclined to suggest a meaning for it in connexion with the magical element in the text, of the existence of which there is other evidence. On that assumption, the prominence given to its creation may be paralleled in the introduction to a later magical text, which described, probably in connexion with an incantation, the creation of two small creatures, one white and one black, by Nin-igi-azag, "The Lord of Clear Vision", one of the titles borne by Enki or Ea. The time of their creation is indicated as after that of "cattle, beasts of the field and creatures of the city", and the composition opens in a way which is very like the opening of the present passage in our text.(2) In neither text is there any idea of giving a complete account of the creation of the world, only so much of the original myth being included in each case as suffices for the writer's purpose. Here we may assume that the creation of mankind and of animals is recorded because they were to be saved from the Flood, and that of the *niggilma* because of the part it played in ensuring their survival.

(1) See Hilprecht, *Babylonian Expedition*, Series D, Vol. V, Fasc. 1, plate, Rev., l. 8; the photographic reproduction clearly shows, as Dr. Poebel suggests (*Hist. Texts*, p. 61 n 3), that the line should read: *((isu)elippu) si-i lu (isu)ma-gur-gur-ma sum-sa lu na-si-rat na-pis-tim*, "That ship shall be a *magurgurru* (giant boat), and its name shall be 'Preserver of Life' (lit. 'She that preserves life')."

(2) See *Seven Tablets of Creation*, Vol. I, pp. 122 ff. The

103

text opens with the words "When the gods in their assembly had made (the world), and had created the heavens, and had formed the earth, and had brought living creatures into being . . .", the lines forming an introduction to the special act of creation with which the composition was concerned.

The discussion of the meaning of *niggilma* may best be postponed till the Sixth Column, where we find other references to the word. Meanwhile it may be noted that in the present passage the creation of man precedes that of animals, as it did in the earlier Hebrew Version of Creation, and probably also in the Babylonian version, though not in the later Hebrew Version. It may be added that in another Sumerian account of the Creation(1) the same order, of man before animals, is followed.

(1) Cf. *Sev. Tabl.*, Vol. I, p. 134 f.; but the text has been subjected to editing, and some of its episodes are obviously displaced.

II. THE ANTEDILUVIAN CITIES

As we saw was the case with the First Column of the text, the earliest part preserved of the Second Column contains the close of a speech by a deity, in which he proclaims an act he is about to perform. Here we may assume with some confidence that the speaker is Anu or Enlil, preferably the latter, since it would be natural to ascribe the political constitution of Babylonia, the foundation of which is foreshadowed, to the head of the Sumerian pantheon. It would appear that a beginning had already been made in the establishment of "the kingdom", and, before proceeding to his further work of founding the Antediluvian cities, he follows the example of the speaker in the First Column of the text and lays down the divine enactments by which his purpose was accomplished. The same refrain is repeated:

The sub(lime decrees) he made perfect for it.

The text then relates the founding by the god of five cities, probably "in clean places", that is to say on hallowed ground. He calls each by its name and assigns it to its own divine patron or city-god:

(In clean place)s he founded (five) cit(ies).

And after he had called their names and they had been allotted to divine rulers(?),—

The ... of these cities, Eridu, he gave to the leader, Nu-dimmud,

Secondly, to Nugira(?) he gave Bad-...,(1)

Thirdly, Larak he gave to Pabilkharsag,

Fourthly, Sippar he gave to the hero, the Sun-god,

Fifthly, Shuruppak he gave to "the God of Shuruppak",—

After he had called the names of these cities, and they had been allotted to divine rulers(?),

(1) In Semitic-Babylonian the first component of this city-name would read "Dûr".

The completion of the sentence, in the last two lines of the column, cannot be rendered with any certainty, but the passage appears to have related the creation of small rivers and pools. It will be noted that the lines which contain the names of the five cities and their patron gods(1) form a long explanatory parenthesis, the preceding line being repeated after their enumeration.

(1) The precise meaning of the sign-group here provisionally rendered "divine ruler" is not yet ascertained.

As the first of the series of five cities of Eridu, the seat of Nudimmud or Enki, who was the third of the creating deities, it has been urged that the upper part of the Second Column must have included an account of the founding of Erech, the city of Anu, and of Nippur, Enlil's city.(1) But the numbered sequence of the cities would be difficult to reconcile with the earlier creation of other cities in the text, and the mention of Eridu as the first city to be created would be quite in accord with its great age and peculiarly sacred character as a cult-centre. Moreover the evidence of the Sumerian Dynastic List is definitely against any claim of Erech to Antediluvian existence. For when the hegemony passed from the first Post-diluvian "kingdom" to the second, it went not to Erech but to the shrine Eanna, which gave its name to the second "kingdom"; and the city itself was apparently not founded before the reign of Enmerkar, the second occupant of the throne, who is the first to be given the title "King of Erech". This conclusion with regard to Erech incidentally disposes of the arguments for Nippur's Antediluvian rank in primitive Sumerian tradition, which have been founded on the order of the cities mentioned at the beginning of the later Sumerian myth of Creation.(2) The evidence we thus obtain that the early Sumerians themselves regarded Eridu as the first city in the world to be created, increases the hope that future excavation at Abu Shahrain may reveal Sumerian remains of periods which, from an archaeological standpoint, must still be regarded as prehistoric.

(1) Cf. Poebel, op. cit., p. 41.

(2) The city of Nippur does not occur among the first four "kingdoms" of the Sumerian Dynastic List; but we may probably assume that it was the seat of at least one early "kingdom", in consequence of which Enlil, its city-god, attained his later pre-eminent rank in the Sumerian pantheon.

It is noteworthy that no human rulers are mentioned in connexion with Eridu and the other four Antediluvian cities; and Ziusudu, the hero of the story, is apparently the only mortal whose name occurred in our text. But its author's principal subject is the Deluge, and the preceding history of the world is clearly not given in detail, but is merely summarized. In view of the obviously abbreviated form of the narrative, of which we have already noted striking evidence in its account of the Creation, we may conclude that in the fuller form of the tradition the cities were also assigned human rulers, each one the representative of his city-god. These would correspond to the Antediluvian dynasty of Berossus, the last member of which was Xisuthros, the later counterpart of Ziusudu.

In support of the exclusion of Nippur and Erech from the myth, it will be noted that the second city in the list is not Adab,(1) which was probably the principal seat of the goddess Ninkharsagga, the fourth of the creating deities. The names of both deity and city in that line are strange to us. Larak, the third city in the series, is of greater interest, for it is clearly Larankha, which according to Berossus was the seat of the eighth and ninth of his Antediluvian kings. In commercial documents of the Persian period, which have been found during the excavations at Nippur, Larak is described as lying "on the bank of the old Tigris", a phrase which must be taken as referring to the Shatt el-Hai, in view of the situation of Lagash and other early cities upon it or in its immediate neighbourhood. The site of the city should perhaps be sought on the upper course of the stream, where it tends to approach Nippur. It would thus have lain in the neighbourhood of Bismâya, the site of Adab. Like Adab, Lagash, Shuruppak, and other early Sumerian cities, it was probably destroyed and deserted at a very early period, though it was reoccupied under its old name in Neo-Babylonian or Persian times. Its early disappearance from Babylonian history perhaps in part accounts for our own unfamiliarity with Pabilkharsag, its city-god, unless we may regard the name as a variant from of Pabilsag; but it is hardly likely that the two should be identified.

(1) The site of Adab, now marked by the mounds of Bismâya, was partially excavated by an expedition sent out in 1903 by the University of Chicago, and has provided valuable material for the study of the earliest Sumerian period; see *Reports of the Expedition of the Oriental Exploration Fund* (Babylonian Section of the University of Chicago), and Banks, *Bismya* (1912). On grounds of antiquity alone we might perhaps have expected its inclusion in the myth.

In Sibbar, the fourth of the Antediluvian cities in our series, we again have a parallel to Berossus. It has long been recognized that Pantibiblon, or Pantibiblia, from which the third, fourth, fifth, sixth, and seventh of his Antediluvian kings all came, was the city of Sippar in Northern Babylonia. For the seventh of these rulers, {Euedorakhos}, is clearly Enmeduranki, the mythical king of Sippar, who in Babylonian tradition was regarded as the founder of divination. In a fragmentary composition that has come down to us he is described, not only as king of Sippar, but as "beloved of Anu, Enlil, and Enki", the three creating gods of our text; and it is there recounted how the patron deities of divination, Shamash and Adad, themselves taught him to practise their art.(1) Moreover, Berossus directly implies the existence of Sippar before the Deluge, for in the summary of his version that has been preserved Xisuthros, under divine instruction, buries the sacred writings concerning the origin of the world in "Sispara", the city of the Sun-god, so that after the Deluge they might be dug up and transmitted to mankind. Ebabbar, the great Sun-temple, was at Sippar, and it is to the Sun-god that the city is naturally allotted in the new Sumerian Version.

(1) Cf. Zimmern, *Beiträge zur Kenntniss der Bab. Relig.*, pp. 116 ff.

The last of the five Antediluvian cities in our list is Shuruppak, in which dwelt Ut-napishtim, the hero of the Babylonian version of the Deluge. Its site has been identified with the mounds of Fâra, in the neighbourhood of the Shatt el-Kâr, the former bed of the Euphrates; and the excavations that were conducted there in 1902 have been most productive of remains dating from the prehistoric period of Sumerian culture.(1) Since our text is concerned mainly with the Deluge, it is natural to assume that the foundation of the city from which the Deluge-hero came would be recorded last, in order to lead up to the central episode of the text. The city of Ziusudu, the hero of the Sumerian story, is unfortunately not given in the Third Column, but, in view of Shuruppak's place in the list of Antediluvian cities, it is not improbable that on this point the Sumerian and Babylonian Versions agreed. In the Gilgamesh Epic Shuruppak is the only Antediluvian city referred to, while in the Hebrew accounts no city at all is mentioned in connexion with Noah. The city of Xisuthros, too, is not recorded, but as his father came from Larankha or Larak, we may regard that city as his in the Greek Version. Besides Larankha, the only Antediluvian cities according to Berossus were Babylon and Sippar, and the influence of Babylonian theology, of which we here have evidence, would be sufficient to account for a disturbance of the original traditions. At the same time it is not excluded that Larak was also the scene of the Deluge in our text, though, as we have noted, the position of Shuruppak at the close of the Sumerian list points to it as the more probable of the two. It may be added that we cannot yet read the name of the deity to whom Shuruppak was allotted, but as it is expressed by the city's name preceded by the divine determinative, the rendering "the God of Shuruppak" will meanwhile serve.

(1) See *Hist. of Sum. and Akk.*, pp. 24 ff.

The creation of small rivers and pools, which seems to have followed the foundation of the five sacred cities, is best explained on the assumption that they were intended for the supply of water to the cities and to the temples of their five patron gods. The creation of the Euphrates and the Tigris, if recorded in our text at all, or in its logical order, must have occurred in the upper portion of the column. The fact that in the later Sumerian account their creation is related between that of mankind and the building of Nippur and Erech cannot be cited in support of this suggestion, in view of the absence of those cities from our text and of the process of editing to which the later version has been subjected, with a consequent disarrangement of its episodes.

III. THE COUNCIL OF THE GODS, AND ZIUSUDU'S PIETY

From the lower part of the Third Column, where its text is first preserved, it is clear that the gods had already decided to send a Deluge, for the goddess Nintu or Ninkharsagga, here referred to also as "the holy Innanna", wails aloud for the intended destruction of "her people". That this decision has been decreed by the gods in council is clear from a passage in the Fourth Column, where it is stated that the sending of a flood to destroy mankind was "the word of the assembly (of the gods)". The first lines preserved in the present column describe the effect of the decision on the various gods concerned and their action at the close of the council.

In the lines which described the Council of the Gods, broken references to "the people" and "a flood" are preserved, after which the text continues:

At that time Nintu (. . .) like a (. . .),
 The holy Innanna lament(ed) on account of her people.
 Enki in his own heart (held) counsel;
 Anu, Enlil, Enki and Ninkharsagga (. . .).
 The gods of heaven and earth in(voked) the name of Anu and Enlil.

It is unfortunate that the ends of all the lines in this column are wanting, but enough remains to show a close correspondence of the first two lines quoted with a passage in the Gilgamesh Epic where Ishtar is described as lamenting

112

the destruction of mankind.(1) This will be seen more clearly by printing the two couplets in parallel columns:

SUMERIAN VERSION SEMITIC VERSION

At that time Nintu (...)	Ishtar cried aloud like a woman
like a (...), in travail,	
The holy Innanna lament(ed)	Bêlit-ili lamented with a loud
on account of her people.	voice.

(1) Gilg. Epic, XI, l. 117 f.

The expression Bêlit-ili, "the Lady of the Gods", is attested as a title borne both by the Semitic goddess Ishtar and by the Sumerian goddess Nintu or Ninkharsagga. In the passage in the Babylonian Version, "the Lady of the Gods" has always been treated as a synonym of Ishtar, the second half of the couplet being regarded as a restatement of the first, according to a recognized law of Babylonian poetry. We may probably assume that this interpretation is correct, and we may conclude by analogy that "the holy Innanna" in the second half of the Sumerian couplet is there merely employed as a synonym of Nintu.(1) When the Sumerian myth was recast in accordance with Semitic ideas, the *rôle* of creatress of mankind, which had been played by the old Sumerian goddess Ninkharsagga or Nintu, was naturally transferred to the Semitic Ishtar. And as Innanna was one of Ishtar's designations, it was possible to make the change by a simple transcription of the lines, the name Nintu being replaced by the synonymous title Bêlit-ili, which was also shared by Ishtar. Difficulties are at once introduced if we

113

assume with Dr. Poebel that in each version two separate goddesses are represented as lamenting, Nintu or Bêlit-ili and Innanna or Ishtar. For Innanna as a separate goddess had no share in the Sumerian Creation, and the reference to "her people" is there only applicable to Nintu. Dr. Poebel has to assume that the Sumerian names should be reversed in order to restore them to their original order, which he suggests the Babylonian Version has preserved. But no such textual emendation is necessary. In the Semitic Version Ishtar definitely displaces Nintu as the mother of men, as is proved by a later passage in her speech where she refers to her own bearing of mankind.(2) The necessity for the substitution of her name in the later version is thus obvious, and we have already noted how simply this was effected.

(1) Cf. also Jastrow, *Hebr. and Bab. Trad.*, p. 336.

(2) Gilg. Epic, XI, l. 123.

Another feature in which the two versions differ is that in the Sumerian text the lamentation of the goddess precedes the sending of the Deluge, while in the Gilgamesh Epic it is occasioned by the actual advent of the storm. Since our text is not completely preserved, it is just possible that the couplet was repeated at the end of the Fourth Column after mankind's destruction had taken place. But a further apparent difference has been noted. While in the Sumerian Version the goddess at once deplores the divine decision, it is clear from Ishtar's words in the Gilgamesh Epic that in the assembly of the gods she had at any rate concurred in it.(1) On the other hand, in Bêlit-ili's later speech in the Epic, after

114

Ut-napishtim's sacrifice upon the mountain, she appears to subscribe the decision to Enlil alone.(2) The passages in the Gilgamesh Epic are not really contradictory, for they can be interpreted as implying that, while Enlil forced his will upon the other gods against Bêlit-ili's protest, the goddess at first reproached herself with her concurrence, and later stigmatized Enlil as the real author of the catastrophe. The Semitic narrative thus does not appear, as has been suggested, to betray traces of two variant traditions which have been skilfully combined, though it may perhaps exhibit an expansion of the Sumerian story. On the other hand, most of the apparent discrepancies between the Sumerian and Babylonian Versions disappear, on the recognition that our text gives in many passages only an epitome of the original Sumerian Version.

(1) Cf. l. 121 f., "Since I commanded evil in the assembly of the gods, (and) commanded battle for the destruction of my people".

(2) Cf. ll. 165 ff., "Ye gods that are here! So long as I forget not the (jewels of) lapis lazuli upon my neck, I will keep these days in my memory, never will I forget them! Let the gods come to the offering, but let not Enlil come to the offering, since he took not counsel but sent the deluge and surrendered my people to destruction."

The lament of the goddess is followed by a brief account of the action taken by the other chief figures in the drama. Enki holds counsel with his own heart, evidently devising the project, which he afterwards carried into effect, of preserving the seed of mankind from destruction. Since the verb in the following line is wanting, we do not know what action is there recorded of the four creating deities; but the fact that the gods of heaven and earth invoked the name of Anu and Enlil suggests that it was their will which had been forced upon the other gods. We shall see that throughout the text Anu and Enlil are the ultimate rulers of both gods and men.

The narrative then introduces the human hero of the Deluge story:

At that time Ziusudu, the king, ... priest of the god (...),

Made a very great ..., (...).

In humility he prostrates himself, in reverence (...),

Daily he stands in attendance (...).

A dream,(1) such as had not been before, comes forth(2) ... (...),

By the Name of Heaven and Earth he conjures (...).

(1) The word may also be rendered "dreams".

(2) For this rendering of the verb *e-de*, for which Dr. Poebel does not hazard a translation, see Rawlinson, *W.A.I.*, IV, pl. 26, l. 24 f.(a), *nu-e-de* = Sem. *la us-su-u* (Pres.); and cf. Brünnow, *Classified List*, p. 327.

An alternative rendering "is created" is also possible, and would give equally good sense; cf. *nu-e-de* = Sem. *la su-pu-u*, *W.A.I.*, IV, pl. 2, l. 5 (a), and Brünnow, op. cit., p. 328.

The name of the hero, Ziusudu, is the fuller Sumerian equivalent of Ut-napishtim (or Uta-napishtim), the abbreviated Semitic form which we find in the Gilgamesh Epic. For not only are the first two elements of the Sumerian name identical with those of the Semitic Ut-napishtim, but the names themselves are equated in a later Babylonian syllabary or explanatory list of words.[1] We there find "Ut-napishte" given as the equivalent of the Sumerian "Zisuda", evidently an abbreviated form of the name Ziusudu;[2] and it is significant that the names occur in the syllabary between those of Gilgamesh and Enkidu, evidently in consequence of the association of the Deluge story by the Babylonians with their national epic of Gilgamesh. The name Ziusudu may be rendered "He who lengthened the day of life" or "He who made life long of days",[3] which in the Semitic form is abbreviated by the omission of the verb. The reference is probably to the immortality bestowed upon Ziusudu at the close of the story, and not to the prolongation of mankind's existence in which he was instrumental. It is scarcely necessary to add that the name has no linguistic connexion with the Hebrew name Noah, to which it also presents no parallel in meaning.

(1) Cf. *Cun. Texts in the Brit. Mus.*, Pt. XVIII, pl. 30, l. 9 (a).

(2) The name in the Sumerian Version is read by Dr. Poebel as Ziugiddu, but there is much in favour of Prof. Zimmern's suggestion, based on the form Zisuda, that the third syllable of the name should be read as *su*. On a fragment of another Nippur text, No. 4611, Dr. Langdon reads the name

as *Zi-u-sud-du* (cf. Univ. of Penns. Mus. Publ., Bab. Sec., Vol. X, No. 1, p. 90, pl. iv a); the presence of the phonetic complement *du* may be cited in favour of this reading, but it does not appear to be supported by the photographic reproductions of the name in the Sumerian Deluge Version given by Dr. Poebel (*Hist. and Gramm. Texts*, pl. lxxxviii f.). It may be added that, on either alternative, the meaning of the name is the same.

(3) The meaning of the Sumerian element *u* in the name, rendered as *utu* in the Semitic form, is rather obscure, and Dr. Poebel left it unexplained. It is very probable, as suggested by Dr. Langdon (cf. *Proc. Soc. Bibl. Arch.*, XXXVI, 1914, p. 190), that we should connect it with the Semitic *uddu*; in that case, in place of "breath", the rending he suggests, I should be inclined to render it here as "day", for *uddu* as the meaning "dawn" and the sign UD is employed both for *urru*, "day-light", and *ûmu*, "day".

It is an interesting fact that Ziusudu should be described simply as "the king", without any indication of the city or area he ruled; and in three of the five other passages in the text in which his name is mentioned it is followed by the same title without qualification. In most cases Berossus tells us the cities from which his Antediluvian rulers came; and if the end of the line had been preserved it might have been possible to determine definitely Ziusudu's city, and incidentally the scene of the Deluge in the Sumerian Version, by the name of the deity in whose service he acted as priest. We have already noted some grounds for believing that his city may have been Shuruppak, as in the Babylonian Version; and if that were so, the divine name reads as "the God of Shurrupak" should probably be restored at the end of the line.(1)

(1) The remains that are preserved of the determinative, which is not combined with the sign EN, proves that Enki's name is not to be restored. Hence Ziusudu was not priest of Enki, and his city was probably not Eridu, the seat of his divine friend and counsellor, and the first of the Antediluvian cities. Sufficient reason for Enki's intervention on Ziusudu's behalf is furnished by the fact that, as God of the Deep, he was concerned in the proposed method of man's destruction. His rivalry of Enlil, the God of the Earth, is implied in the Babylonian Version (cf. Gilg. Epic. XI, ll. 39-42), and in the Sumerian Version this would naturally extend to Anu, the God of Heaven.

The employment of the royal title by itself accords with the tradition from Berossus that before the Deluge, as in later periods, the land was governed by a succession of supreme rulers, and that the hero of the Deluge was the last of them. In the Gilgamesh Epic, on the other hand, Ut-napishtim is given no royal nor any other title. He is merely referred to as a "man of Shuruppak, son of Ubar-Tutu", and he appears in the guise of an ancient hero or patriarch not invested with royal power. On this point Berossus evidently preserves the original Sumerian traditions, while the Hebrew Versions resemble the Semitic-Babylonian narrative. The Sumerian conception of a series of supreme Antediluvian rulers is of course merely a reflection from the historical period, when the hegemony in Babylonia was contested among the city-states. The growth of the tradition may have been encouraged by the early use of *lugal*, "king", which, though always a term of secular character, was not very sharply distinguished from that of *patesi* and other religious titles, until, in accordance with political development, it was required to connote a wider dominion. In Sumer, at the time of the composition of our text, Ziusudu was still only one in a long line of Babylonian rulers, mainly historical but gradually receding into the realms of legend and myth. At the time of the later Semites there had been more than one complete break in the tradition and the historical setting of the old story had become dim. The fact that Hebrew tradition should range itself in this matter with Babylon rather than with Sumer is important as a clue in tracing the literary history of our texts.

The rest of the column may be taken as descriptive of Ziusudu's activities. One line records his making of some very great object or the erection of a huge building;(1) and since the following lines are concerned solely with religious activities, the reference is possibly to a temple or some other structure of a sacred character. Its foundation may have been recorded as striking evidence of his devotion to his god; or, since the verb in this sentence depends on the words "at that time" in the preceding line, we may perhaps regard his action as directly connected with the revelation to be made to him. His personal piety is then described: daily he occupied himself in his god's service, prostrating himself in humility and constant in his attendance at the shrine. A dream (or possibly dreams), "such as had not been before", appears to him and he seems to be further described as conjuring "by the Name of Heaven and Earth"; but as the ends of all these lines are broken, the exact connexion of the phrases is not quite certain.

(1) The element *gur-gur*, "very large" or "huge", which occurs in the name of this great object or building, *an- sag- gur-gur*, is employed later in the term for the "huge boat", *(gish)ma-gur-gur*, in which Ziusudu rode out the storm. There was, of course, even at this early period a natural tendency to picture on a superhuman scale the lives and deeds of remote predecessors, a tendency which increased in later times and led, as we shall see, to the elaboration of extravagant detail.

It is difficult not to associate the reference to a dream, or possibly to dream-divination, with the warning in which Enki reveals the purpose of the gods. For the later versions prepare us for a reference to a dream. If we take the line as describing Ziusudu's practice of dream-divination in general, "such as had not been before", he may have been represented as the first diviner of dreams, as Enmeduranki was held to be the first practitioner of divination in general. But it seems to me more probable that the reference is to a

121

particular dream, by means of which he obtained knowledge of the gods' intentions. On the rendering of this passage depends our interpretation of the whole of the Fourth Column, where the point will be further discussed. Meanwhile it may be noted that the conjuring "by the Name of Heaven and Earth", which we may assume is ascribed to Ziusudu, gains in significance if we may regard the setting of the myth as a magical incantation, an inference in support of which we shall note further evidence. For we are furnished at once with the grounds for its magical employment. If Ziusudu, through conjuring by the Name of Heaven and earth, could profit by the warning sent him and so escape the impending fate of mankind, the application of such a myth to the special needs of a Sumerian in peril or distress will be obvious. For should he, too, conjure by the Name of Heaven and Earth, he might look for a similar deliverance; and his recital of the myth itself would tend to clinch the magical effect of his own incantation.

The description of Ziusudu has also great interest in furnishing us with a close parallel to the piety of Noah in the Hebrew Versions. For in the Gilgamesh Epic and in Berossus this feature of the story is completely absent. We are there given no reason why Ut-napishtim was selected by Ea, nor Xisuthros by Kronos. For all that those versions tell us, the favour of each deity might have been conferred arbitrarily, and not in recognition of, or in response to, any particular quality or action on the part of its recipient. The Sumerian Version now restores the original setting of the story and incidentally proves that, in this particular, the Hebrew

Versions have not embroidered a simpler narrative for the purpose of edification, but have faithfully reproduced an original strand of the tradition.

IV. THE DREAM-WARNING

The top of the Fourth Column of the text follows immediately on the close of the Third Column, so that at this one point we have no great gap between the columns. But unfortunately the ends of all the lines in both columns are wanting, and the exact content of some phrases preserved and their relation to each other are consequently doubtful. This materially affects the interpretation of the passage as a whole, but the main thread of the narrative may be readily followed. Ziusudu is here warned that a flood is to be sent "to destroy the seed of mankind"; the doubt that exists concerns the manner in which the warning is conveyed. In the first line of the column, after a reference to "the gods", a building seems to be mentioned, and Ziusudu, standing beside it, apparently hears a voice, which bids him take his stand beside a wall and then conveys to him the warning of the coming flood. The destruction of mankind had been decreed in "the assembly (of the gods)" and would be carried out by the commands of Anu and Enlil. Before the text breaks off we again have a reference to the "kingdom" and "its rule", a further trace of the close association of the

123

Deluge with the dynastic succession in the early traditions of Sumer.

In the opening words of the warning to Ziusudu, with its prominent repetition of the word "wall", we must evidently trace some connexion with the puzzling words of Ea in the Gilgamesh Epic, when he begins his warning to Ut-napishtim. The warnings, as given in the two versions, are printed below in parallel columns for comparison.(1) The Gilgamesh Epic, after relating how the great gods in Shuruppak had decided to send a deluge, continues as follows in the right-hand column:

SUMERIAN VERSION SEMITIC VERSION

For (. . .) . . . the gods a Nin-igi-azag,(2) the god Ea,
. . . (. . .); sat with them,
Ziusudu standing at its side And he repeated their word to
heard (. . .): the house of reeds:
"At the wall on my left side take "Reed-hut, reed-hut! Wall,
thy stand and (. . .), wall!
At the wall I will speak a word O reed-hut, hear! O wall,
to thee (. . .). understand!
O my devout one . . . (. . .), Thou man of Shuruppak, son of
Ubar-Tutu,
By our hand(?) a flood(3) . . . Pull down thy house, build a
(. . .) will be (sent). ship,
To destroy the seed of mankind Leave thy possessions, take
(. . .) heed for thy life,
Is the decision, the word of the Abandon thy property, and save

124

assembly(4) (of the gods) thy life.
The commands of Anu (and) And bring living seed of every
En(lil . . .) kind into the ship.
Its kingdom, its rule (. . .) As for the ship, which thou
shalt build,
To his (. . .)" Of which the measurements
shall be carefully measured,
(. . .) Its breadth and length shall
correspond.
(. . .) In the deep shalt thou immerse
it."

(1) Col. IV, ll. 1 ff. are there compared with Gilg. Epic,
XI, ll. 19-31.

(2) Nin-igi-azag, "The Lord of Clear Vision", a title borne
by Enki, or Ea, as God of Wisdom.

(3) The Sumerian term *amaru*, here used for the flood and
rendered as "rain-storm" by Dr. Poebel, is explained in a
later syllabary as the equivalent of the Semitic-Babylonian
word *abûbu* (cf. Meissner, *S.A.I.*, No. 8909), the term
employed for the flood both in the early Semitic version of
the Atrakhasis story dated in Ammizaduga's reign and in the
Gilgamesh Epic. The word *abûbu* is often conventionally
rendered "deluge", but should be more accurately translated
"flood". It is true that the tempests of the Sumerian
Version probably imply rain; and in the Gilgamesh Epic
heavy

rain in the evening begins the flood and is followed at dawn by a thunderstorm and hurricane. But in itself the term *abûbu* implies flood, which could take place through a rise of the rivers unaccompanied by heavy local rain. The annual rainfall in Babylonia to-day is on an average only about 8 in., and there have been years in succession when the total rainfall has not exceeded 4 in.; and yet the *abûbu* is not a thing of the past.

(4) The word here rendered "assembly" is the Semitic loan-word *buhrum*, in Babylonian *puhrum*, the term employed for the "assembly" of the gods both in the Babylonian Creation Series and in the Gilgamesh Epic. Its employment in the Sumerian Version, in place of its Sumerian equivalent *ukkin*, is an interesting example of Semitic influence. Its occurrence does not necessarily imply the existence of a recognized Semitic Version at the period our text was inscribed. The substitution of *buhrum* for *ukkin* in the text may well date from the period of Hammurabi, when we may assume that the increased importance of the city-council was reflected in the general adoption of the Semitic term (cf. Poebel, *Hist. Texts*, p. 53).

In the Semitic Version Ut-napishtim, who tells the story in the first person, then says that he "understood", and that, after assuring Ea that he would carry out his commands, he asked how he was to explain his action to "the city, the people, and the elders"; and the god told him what to say.

Then follows an account of the building of the ship, introduced by the words "As soon as the dawn began to break". In the Sumerian Version the close of the warning, in which the ship was probably referred to, and the lines prescribing how Ziusudu carried out the divine instructions are not preserved.

It will be seen that in the passage quoted from the Semitic Version there is no direct mention of a dream; the god is represented at first as addressing his words to a "house of reeds" and a "wall", and then as speaking to Ut-napishtim himself. But in a later passage in the Epic, when Ea seeks to excuse his action to Enlil, he says that the gods' decision was revealed to Atrakhasis through a dream.(1) Dr. Poebel rightly compares the direct warning of Ut-napishtim by Ea in the passage quoted above with the equally direct warning Ziusudu receives in the Sumerian Version. But he would have us divorce the direct warning from the dream-warning, and he concludes that no less than three different versions of the story have been worked together in the Gilgamesh Epic. In the first, corresponding to that in our text, Ea communicates the gods' decision directly to Ut-napishtim; in the second he sends a dream from which Atrakhasis, "the Very Wise one", guesses the impending peril; while in the third he relates the plan to a wall, taking care that Ut-napishtim overhears him.(2) The version of Berossus, that Kronos himself appears to Xisuthros in a dream and warns him, is rejected by Dr. Poebel, who remarks that here the "original significance of the dream has already been obliterated". Consequently there seems to him to be "no

127

logical connexion" between the dreams or dream mentioned at the close of the Third Column and the communication of the plan of the gods at the beginning of the Fourth Column of our text.(3)

(1) Cf. l. 195 f.; "I did not divulge the decision of the great gods. I caused Atrakhasis to behold a dream and thus he heard the decision of the gods."

(2) Cf. Poebel, *Hist. Texts*, p. 51 f. With the god's apparent subterfuge in the third of these supposed versions Sir James Frazer (*Ancient Stories of a Great Flood*, p. 15) not inaptly compares the well-known story of King Midas's servant, who, unable to keep the secret of the king's deformity to himself, whispered it into a hole in the ground, with the result that the reeds which grew up there by their rustling in the wind proclaimed it to the world (Ovid, *Metamorphoses*, xi, 174 ff.).

(3) Op. cit., p. 51; cf. also Jastrow, *Heb. and Bab. Trad.*, p. 346.

So far from Berossus having missed the original significance of the narrative he relates, I think it can be shown that he reproduces very accurately the sense of our Sumerian text; and that the apparent discrepancies in the Semitic Version, and the puzzling references to a wall in both it and the Sumerian Version, are capable of a simple explanation. There appears to me no justification for splitting the Semitic narrative into the several versions suggested, since the assumption that the direct warning and

the dream-warning must be distinguished is really based on a misunderstanding of the character of Sumerian dreams by which important decisions of the gods in council were communicated to mankind. We fortunately possess an instructive Sumerian parallel to our passage. In it the will of the gods is revealed in a dream, which is not only described in full but is furnished with a detailed interpretation; and as it seems to clear up our difficulties, it may be well to summarize its main features.

The occasion of the dream in this case was not a coming deluge but a great dearth of water in the rivers, in consequence of which the crops had suffered and the country was threatened with famine. This occurred in the reign of Gudea, patesi of Lagash, who lived some centuries before our Sumerian document was inscribed. In his own inscription(1) he tells us that he was at a loss to know by what means he might restore prosperity to his country, when one night he had a dream; and it was in consequence of the dream that he eventually erected one of the most sumptuously appointed of Sumerian temples and thereby restored his land to prosperity. Before recounting his dream he describes how the gods themselves took counsel. On the day in which destinies were fixed in heaven and earth, Enlil, the chief of the gods, and Ningirsu, the city-god of Lagash, held converse; and Enlil, turning to Ningirsu, described the sad condition of Southern Babylonia, and remarked that "the decrees of the temple Eninnû should be made glorious in heaven and upon earth", or, in other words, that Ningirsu's city-temple must be rebuilt. Thereupon Ningirsu did not

129

communicate his orders directly to Gudea, but conveyed the will of the gods to him by means of a dream.

(1) See Thureau-Dangin, *Les inscriptions de Sumer et d'Akkad*, Cyl. A, pp. 134 ff., Germ. ed., pp. 88 ff.; and cf. King and Hall, *Eg. and West. Asia*, pp. 196 ff.

It will be noticed that we here have a very similar situation to that in the Deluge story. A conference of the gods has been held; a decision has been taken by the greatest god, Enlil; and, in consequence, another deity is anxious to inform a Sumerian ruler of that decision. The only difference is that here Enlil desires the communication to be made, while in the Deluge story it is made without his knowledge, and obviously against his wishes. So the fact that Ningirsu does not communicate directly with the patesi, but conveys his message by means of a dream, is particularly instructive. For here there can be no question of any subterfuge in the method employed, since Enlil was a consenting party.

The story goes on to relate that, while the patesi slept, a vision of the night came to him, and he beheld a man whose stature was so great that it equalled the heavens and the earth. By the diadem he wore upon his head Gudea knew that the figure must be a god. Beside the god was the divine eagle, the emblem of Lagash; his feet rested upon the whirlwind, and a lion crouched upon his right hand and upon his left. The figure spoke to the patesi, but he did not understand the meaning of the words. Then it seemed to Gudea that the Sun rose from the earth; and he beheld a woman holding in her hand a pure reed, and she carried also a tablet on which was a star of the heavens, and she seemed to take counsel with herself. While Gudea was gazing, he seemed to see a second man, who was like a warrior; and he carried a slab of lapis lazuli, on which he drew out the plan of a temple. Before the patesi himself it seemed that a fair cushion was placed, and upon the cushion was set a mould, and within the mould was a brick. And on the right hand the patesi beheld an ass that lay upon the ground. Such was the dream of Gudea, and he was troubled because he could not interpret it.(1)

(1) The resemblance its imagery bears to that of apocalyptic visions of a later period is interesting, as evidence of the latter's remote ancestry, and of the development in the use of primitive material to suit a completely changed political outlook. But those are points which do not concern our problem.

To cut the long story short, Gudea decided to seek the help of Ninâ, "the child of Eridu", who, as daughter of Enki, the God of Wisdom, could divine all the mysteries of the gods. But first of all by sacrifices and libations he secured the mediation of his own city-god and goddess, Ningirsu and Gatumdug; and then, repairing to Ninâ's temple, he recounted to her the details of his vision. When the patesi had finished, the goddess addressed him and said she would explain to him the meaning of his dream. Here, no doubt, we are to understand that she spoke through the mouth of her chief priest. And this was the interpretation of the dream. The man whose stature was so great, and whose head was that of a god, was the god Ningirsu, and the words which he uttered were an order to the patesi to rebuild the temple

131

Eninnû. The Sun which rose from the earth was the god Ningishzida, for like the Sun he goes forth from the earth. The maiden who held the pure reed and carried the tablet with the star was the goddess Nisaba; the star was the pure star of the temple's construction, which she proclaimed. The second man, who was like a warrior, was the god Nibub; and the plan of the temple which he drew was the plan of Eninnû; and the ass that lay upon the ground was the patesi himself.(1)

(1) The symbolism of the ass, as a beast of burden, was applicable to the patesi in his task of carrying out the building of the temple.

The essential feature of the vision is that the god himself appeared to the sleeper and delivered his message in words. That is precisely the manner in which Kronos warned Xisuthros of the coming Deluge in the version of Berossus; while in the Gilgamesh Epic the apparent contradiction between the direct warning and the dream-warning at once disappears. It is true that Gudea states that he did not understand the meaning of the god's message, and so required an interpretation; but he was equally at a loss as to the identity of the god who gave it, although Ningirsu was his own city-god and was accompanied by his own familiar city-emblem. We may thus assume that the god's words, as words, were equally intelligible to Gudea. But as they were uttered in a dream, it was necessary that the patesi, in view of his country's peril, should have divine assurance that they implied no other meaning. And in his case such assurance was the more essential, in view of the symbolism attaching to the other features of his vision. That this is sound reasoning is proved by a second vision vouchsafed to Gudea by Ningirsu. For the patesi, though he began to prepare for the building of the temple, was not content even with Ninâ's assurance. He offered a prayer to Ningirsu himself, saying that he wished to build the temple, but had received no sign that this was the will of the god; and he prayed for a sign. Then, as the patesi lay stretched upon the ground, the god again appeared to him and gave him detailed instructions, adding that he would grant the sign for which he asked. The sign was that he should feel his side touched as by a flame,(1) and thereby he should know that he was the man chosen by Ningirsu to carry out his commands. Here it is the sign which confirms the apparent meaning of the god's words. And Gudea was at last content and built the temple.(2)

(1) Cyl. A., col. xii, l. 10 f.; cf. Thureau-Dangin, op.
cit., p. 150 f., Germ. ed., p. 102 f. The word translated
"side" may also be rendered as "hand"; but "side" is the
more probable rendering of the two. The touching of
Gudea's
side (or hand) presents an interesting resemblance to the
touching of Jacob's thigh by the divine wrestler at Peniel
in Gen. xxxii. 24 ff. (J or JE). Given a belief in the
constant presence of the unseen and its frequent
manifestation, such a story as that of Peniel might well
arise from an unexplained injury to the sciatic muscle,
while more than one ailment of the heart or liver might
perhaps suggest the touch of a beckoning god. There is of

course no connexion between the Sumerian and Hebrew stories
beyond their common background. It may be added that those
critics who would reverse the *rôles* of Jacob and the wrestler miss the point of the Hebrew story.

(2) Even so, before starting on the work, he took the further precautions of ascertaining that the omens were favourable and of purifying his city from all malign influence.

We may conclude, then, that in the new Sumerian Version of the Deluge we have traced a logical connexion between the direct warning to Ziusudu in the Fourth Column of the text and the reference to a dream in the broken lines at the close of the Third Column. As in the Gilgamesh Epic and in Berossus, here too the god's warning is conveyed in a dream; and the accompanying reference to conjuring by the Name of Heaven and Earth probably represents the means by which Ziusudu was enabled to verify its apparent meaning. The assurance which Gudea obtained through the priest of Ninâ and the sign, the priest-king Ziusudu secured by his own act, in virtue of his piety and practice of divination. And his employment of the particular class of incantation referred to, that which conjures by the Name of Heaven and Earth, is singularly appropriate to the context. For by its use he was enabled to test the meaning of Enki's words, which related to the intentions of Anu and Enlil, the gods respectively of Heaven and of Earth. The symbolical setting of Gudea's vision also finds a parallel in the reed-house and wall of the Deluge story, though in the latter case we have not the benefit of interpretation by a goddess. In the Sumerian Version the wall is merely part of the vision and does not receive a direct address from the god. That appears as a later development in the Semitic Version, and it may perhaps have suggested the excuse, put in that version into the mouth of Ea, that he had not directly revealed the decision of the gods.(1)

(1) In that case the parallel suggested by Sir James Frazer
between the reed-house and wall of the Gilgamesh Epic,
now
regarded as a medium of communication, and the
whispering
reeds of the Midas story would still hold good.

The omission of any reference to a dream before the warning in the Gilgamesh Epic may be accounted for on the assumption that readers of the poem would naturally suppose that the usual method of divine warning was implied; and the text does indicate that the warning took place at night, for Gilgamesh proceeds to carry out the divine instructions at the break of day. The direct warning of the Hebrew Versions, on the other hand, does not carry this implication, since according to Hebrew ideas direct speech, as well as vision, was included among the methods by which the divine will could be conveyed to man.

V. THE FLOOD, THE ESCAPE OF THE GREAT BOAT, AND THE SACRIFICE TO THE SUN-GOD

The missing portion of the Fourth Column must have described Ziusudu's building of his great boat in order to escape the Deluge, for at the beginning of the Fifth Column we are in the middle of the Deluge itself. The column begins:

All the mighty wind-storms together blew,
 The flood ... raged.
 When for seven days, for seven nights,
 The flood had overwhelmed the land
 When the wind-storm had driven the great boat over the mighty
 waters,
 The Sun-god came forth, shedding light over heaven and earth.
 Ziusudu opened the opening of the great boat;
 The light of the hero, the Sun-god, (he) causes to enter into the
 interior(?) of the great boat.
 Ziusudu, the king,
 Bows himself down before the Sun-god;
 The king sacrifices an ox, a sheep he slaughters(?).

The connected text of the column then breaks off, only a sign or two remaining of the following half-dozen lines. It will be seen that in the eleven lines that are preserved we have several close parallels to the Babylonian Version and some equally striking differences. While attempting to define the latter, it will be well to point out how close the resemblances are, and at the same time to draw a comparison between the Sumerian and Babylonian Versions of this part of the story and the corresponding Hebrew accounts.

Here, as in the Babylonian Version, the Flood is accompanied by hurricanes of wind, though in the latter the description is worked up in considerable detail. We there read(1) that at the appointed time the ruler of the darkness at eventide sent a heavy rain. Ut-napishtim saw its beginning, but fearing to watch the storm, he entered the interior of the ship by Ea's instructions, closed the door, and handed over the direction of the vessel to the pilot Puzur-Amurri. Later a thunder-storm and hurricane added their terrors to the deluge. For at early dawn a black cloud came up from the horizon, Adad the Storm-god thundering in its midst, and his heralds, Nabû and Sharru, flying over mountain and plain. Nergal tore away the ship's anchor, while Ninib directed the storm; the Anunnaki carried their lightning-torches and lit up the land with their brightness; the whirlwind of the Storm-god reached the heavens, and all light was turned into darkness. The storm raged the whole day, covering mountain and people with water.(2) No man beheld his fellow; the gods themselves were afraid, so that they retreated into the highest heaven, where they crouched down, cowering like dogs. Then follows the lamentation of Ishtar, to which reference has already been made, the goddess reproaching herself for the part she had taken in the destruction of her people. This section of the Semitic narrative closes with the picture of the gods weeping with her, sitting bowed down with their lips pressed together. (1) Gilg. Epic, XI, ll. 90 ff.

(2) In the Atrakhasis version, dated in the reign of Ammizaduga, Col. I, l. 5, contains a reference to the "cry" of men when Adad the Storm-god, slays them with his flood.

It is probable that the Sumerian Version, in the missing portion of its Fourth Column, contained some account of Ziusudu's entry into his boat; and this may have been preceded, as in the Gilgamesh Epic, by a reference to "the living seed of every kind", or at any rate to "the four-legged creatures of the field", and to his personal possessions, with which we may assume he had previously loaded it. But in the Fifth Column we have no mention of the pilot or of any other companions who may have accompanied the king; and we shall see that the Sixth Column contains no reference to Ziusudu's wife. The description of the storm may have begun with the closing lines of the Fourth Column, though it is also quite possible that the first line of the Fifth Column actually begins the account. However that may be, and in spite of the poetic imagery of the Semitic Babylonian narrative, the general character of the catastrophe is the same in both versions.

We find an equally close parallel, between the Sumerian and Babylonian accounts, in the duration of the storm which accompanied the Flood, as will be seen by printing the two versions together:(3)

SUMERIAN VERSION	SEMITIC VERSION
When for seven days, for seven nights,	For six days and nights
The flood had overwhelmed the land,	The wind blew, the flood, tempest overwhelmed the land.
When the wind-storm had driven the great boat over the mighty waters,	When the seventh day drew near, the tempest, the flood, ceased from the battle
In which it had fought like a host.	
The Sun-god came forth shedding light over heaven and earth.	Then the sea rested and was still, and the wind-storm, the flood, ceased.

(3) Col. V, ll. 3-6 are here compared with Gilg. Epic, XI, ll. 128-32.

The two narratives do not precisely agree as to the duration of the storm, for while in the Sumerian account the storm lasts seven days and seven nights, in the Semitic-Babylonian Version it lasts only six days and nights, ceasing at dawn on the seventh day. The difference, however, is immaterial when we compare these estimates with those of the Hebrew Versions, the older of which speaks of forty days' rain, while the later version represents the Flood as rising for no less than a hundred and fifty days.

The close parallel between the Sumerian and Babylonian Versions is not, however, confined to subject-matter, but here, even extends to some of the words and phrases employed. It has already been noted that the Sumerian term employed for "flood" or "deluge" is the attested equivalent of the Semitic word; and it may now be added that the word which may be rendered "great boat" or "great ship" in the Sumerian text is the same word, though partly expressed by variant characters, which occurs in the early Semitic fragment of the Deluge story from Nippur.[1] In the Gilgamesh Epic, on the other hand, the ordinary ideogram for "vessel" or "ship"[2] is employed, though the great size of the vessel is there indicated, as in Berossus and the later Hebrew Version, by detailed measurements. Moreover, the Sumerian and Semitic verbs, which are employed in the parallel passages quoted above for the "overwhelming" of the land, are given as synonyms in a late syllabary, while in another explanatory text the Sumerian verb is explained as applying to the destructive action of a flood.[3] Such close linguistic parallels are instructive as furnishing additional proof, if it were needed, of the dependence of the Semitic-Babylonian and Assyrian Versions upon Sumerian originals.

(1) The Sumerian word is *(gish)ma-gur-gur*, corresponding to the term written in the early Semitic fragment, l. 8, as *(isu)ma-gur-gur*, which is probably to be read under its Semitized form *magurgurru*. In l. 6 of that fragment the vessel is referred to under the synonymous expression *(isu)elippu ra-be-tu*, "a great ship".

140

(2) i.e. (GISH)MA, the first element in the Sumerian word, read in Semitic Babylonian as *elippu*, "ship"; when employed in the early Semitic fragment it is qualified by the adj. *ra-be-tu*, "great". There is no justification for assuming, with Prof. Hilbrecht, that a measurement of the vessel was given in l. 7 of the early Semitic fragment.

(3) The Sumerian verb *ur*, which is employed in l. 2 of the Fifth Column in the expression *ba-an-da-ab-ur-ur*, translated as "raged", occurs again in l. 4 in the phrase *kalam-ma ba-ur-ra*, "had overwhelmed the land". That we are
justified in regarding the latter phrase as the original of the Semitic *i-sap-pan mâta* (Gilg. Epic, XI, l. 129) is proved by the equation Sum. *ur-ur* = Sem. *sa-pa-nu* (Rawlinson, *W.A.I.*, Vol. V, pl. 42, l. 54 c) and by the explanation Sum. *ur-ur* = Sem. *sa-ba-tu sa a-bu-bi*, i.e. "*ur-ur* = to smite, of a flood" (*Cun. Texts*, Pt. XII, pl. 50, Obv., l. 23); cf. Poebel, *Hist. Texts*, p. 54, n. 1.

It may be worth while to pause for a moment in our study of the text, in order to inquire what kind of boat it was in which Ziusudu escaped the Flood. It is only called "a great boat" or "a great ship" in the text, and this term, as we have noted, was taken over, semitized, and literally translated in an early Semitic-Babylonian Version. But the Gilgamesh Epic, representing the later Semitic-Babylonian Version, supplies fuller details, which have not, however, been satisfactorily explained. Either the obvious meaning of the description and figures there given has been ignored, or the measurements have been applied to a central structure placed upon a hull, much on the lines of a modern "house-boat" or the conventional Noah's ark.(1) For the latter interpretation the text itself affords no justification. The statement is definitely made that the length and breadth of the vessel itself are to be the same;(2) and a later passage gives ten *gar* for the height of its sides and ten *gar* for the breadth of its deck.(3) This description has been taken to imply a square box-like structure, which, in order to be seaworthy, must be placed on a conjectured hull.

(1) Cf., e.g., Jastrow, *Hebr. and Bab. Trad.*, p. 329.

(2) Gilg. Epic, XI, ll. 28-30.

(3) L. 58 f. The *gar* contained twelve cubits, so that the vessel would have measured 120 cubits each way; taking the
Babylonian cubit, on the basis of Gudea's scale, at 495 mm.
(cf. Thureau-Dangin, *Journal Asiatique*, Dix. Sér., t.
XIII, 1909, pp. 79 ff., 97), this would give a length,
breadth, and height of nearly 195 ft.

 I do not think it has been noted in this connexion that a vessel, approximately with the relative proportions of that described in the Gilgamesh Epic, is in constant use to-day on the lower Tigris and Euphrates. A *kuffah*,(1) the familiar pitched coracle of Baghdad, would provide an admirable model for the gigantic vessel in which Ut-napishtim rode out the Deluge. "Without either stem or stern, quite round like a shield"—so Herodotus described the *kuffah* of his day;2() so, too, is it represented on Assyrian slabs from Nineveh, where we see it employed for the transport of heavy building material;(3) its form and structure indeed suggest a prehistoric origin. The *kuffah* is one of those examples of perfect adjustment to conditions of use which cannot be improved. Any one who has travelled in one of these craft will agree that their storage capacity is immense, for their circular form and steeply curved side allow every inch of space to be utilized. It is almost impossible to upset them, and their only disadvantage is lack of speed. For their guidance all that is required is a steersman with a paddle, as indicated in the Epic. It is true that the larger kuffah of to-day tends to increase in diameter as compared to height, but that detail might well be ignored in picturing the monster vessel of Ut-napishtim. Its seven horizontal stages and their nine lateral divisions would have been structurally sound in supporting the vessel's sides; and the selection of the latter uneven number, though prompted doubtless by its sacred character, is only suitable to a circular craft in which the interior walls would radiate from the centre. The use of pitch and bitumen for smearing the vessel inside and out, though unusual even in Mesopotamian shipbuilding, is precisely the method employed in the *kuffah's* construction.

(1) Arab. *kuffah*, pl. *kufaf*; in addition to its common use for the Baghdad coracle, the word is also employed for a large basket.

(2) Herodotus, I, 194.

(3) The *kuffah* is formed of wicker-work coated with bitumen. Some of those represented on the Nineveh sculptures appear to be covered with skins; and Herodotus (I, 94) states that "the boats which come down the river to Babylon are circular and made of skins." But his further description shows that he is here referred to the *kelek* or skin-raft, with which he has combined a description of the *kuffah*. The late Sir Henry Rawlinson has never seen or heard of a skin-covered *kuffah* on either the Tigris or Euphrates, and there can be little doubt that bitumen was employed for their construction in antiquity, as it is to-day. These craft are often large enough to carry five or six horses and a dozen men.

We have no detailed description of Ziusudu's "great boat", beyond the fact that it was covered in and had an opening, or light-hole, which could be closed. But the form of Ut-napishtim's vessel was no doubt traditional, and we may picture that of Ziusudu as also of the *kuffah* type, though smaller and without its successor's elaborate internal structure. The gradual development of the huge coracle into a ship would have been encouraged by the Semitic use of the term "ship" to describe it; and the attempt to retain something of its original proportions resulted in producing the unwieldy ark of later tradition.(1)

(1) The description of the ark is not preserved from the earlier Hebrew Version (J), but the latter Hebrew Version (P), while increasing the length of the vessel, has considerably reduced its height and breadth. Its

measurements are there given (Gen. vi. 15) as 300 cubits in length, 50 cubits in breadth, and 30 cubits in height; taking the ordinary Hebrew cubit at about 18 in., this would give a length of about 450 ft., a breadth of about 75 ft., and a height of about 45 ft. The interior stories are necessarily reduced to three. The vessel in Berossus measures five stadia by two, and thus had a length of over three thousand feet and a breadth of more than twelve hundred.

We will now return to the text and resume the comparison we were making between it and the Gilgamesh Epic. In the latter no direct reference is made to the appearance of the Sun-god after the storm, nor is Ut-napishtim represented as praying to him. But the sequence of events in the Sumerian Version is very natural, and on that account alone, apart from other reasons, it may be held to represent the original form of the story. For the Sun-god would naturally reappear after the darkness of the storm had passed, and it would be equally natural that Ziusudu should address himself to the great light-god. Moreover, the Gilgamesh Epic still retains traces of the Sumerian Version, as will be seen from a comparison of their narratives,(1) the Semitic Version being quoted from the point where the hurricane ceased and the sea became still.

(1) Col. V, ll. 7-11 are here compared with Gilg. Epic, XI, ll. 133-9.

SUMERIAN VERSION SEMITIC VERSION

When I looked at the storm, the
uproar had ceased,
And all mankind was turned into
clay;
In place of fields there was a
swamp.

Ziusudu opened the opening of the great boat;	I opened the opening (lit. "hole"), and daylight fell upon my countenance.
The light of the hero, the Sun-god, (he) causes to enter into the interior(?) of the great boat.	
Ziusudu, the king, Bows himself down before the Sun-god;	I bowed myself down and sat down weeping;
The king sacrifices an ox, a sheep he slaughters(?).	Over my countenance flowed my tears.
I gazed upon the quarters (of the world)—all(?) was sea.	

It will be seen that in the Semitic Version the beams of the Sun-god have been reduced to "daylight", and Ziusudu's act of worship has become merely prostration in token of grief.

Both in the Gilgamesh Epic and in Berossus the sacrifice offered by the Deluge hero to the gods follows the episode of the birds, and it takes place on the top of the mountain after the landing from the vessel. It is hardly probable that two sacrifices were recounted in the Sumerian Version, one to

146

the Sun-god in the boat and another on the mountain after landing; and if we are right in identifying Ziusudu's recorded sacrifice with that of Ut-napishtim and Xisuthros, it would seem that, according to the Sumerian Version, no birds were sent out to test the abatement of the waters. This conclusion cannot be regarded as quite certain, inasmuch as the greater part of the Fifth Column is waning. We have, moreover, already seen reason to believe that the account on our tablet is epitomized, and that consequently the omission of any episode from our text does not necessarily imply its absence from the original Sumerian Version which it follows. But here at least it is clear that nothing can have been omitted between the opening of the light-hole and the sacrifice, for the one act is the natural sequence of the other. On the whole it seems preferable to assume that we have recovered a simpler form of the story.

As the storm itself is described in a few phrases, so the cessation of the flood may have been dismissed with equal brevity; the gradual abatement of the waters, as attested by the dove, the swallow, and the raven, may well be due to later elaboration or to combination with some variant account. Under its amended form the narrative leads naturally up to the landing on the mountain and the sacrifice of thanksgiving to the gods. In the Sumerian Version, on the other hand, Ziusudu regards himself as saved when he sees the Sun shining; he needs no further tests to assure himself that the danger is over, and his sacrifice too is one of gratitude for his escape. The disappearance of the Sun-god from the Semitic Version was thus a necessity, to avoid an

147

anti-climax; and the hero's attitude of worship had obviously to be translated into one of grief. An indication that the sacrifice was originally represented as having taken place on board the boat may be seen in the lines of the Gilgamesh Epic which recount how Enlil, after acquiescing in Ut-napishtim's survival of the Flood, went up into the ship and led him forth by the hand, although, in the preceding lines, he had already landed and had sacrificed upon the mountain. The two passages are hardly consistent as they stand, but they find a simple explanation of we regard the second of them as an unaltered survival from an earlier form of the story.

If the above line of reasoning be sound, it follows that, while the earlier Hebrew Version closely resembles the Gilgamesh Epic, the later Hebrew Version, by its omission of the birds, would offer a parallel to the Sumerian Version. But whether we may draw any conclusion from this apparent grouping of our authorities will be best dealt with when we have concluded our survey of the new evidence.

As we have seen, the text of the Fifth Column breaks off with Ziusudu's sacrifice to the Sun-god, after he had opened a light-hole in the boat and had seen by the god's beams that the storm was over. The missing portion of the Fifth Column must have included at least some account of the abatement of the waters, the stranding of the boat, and the manner in which Anu and Enlil became apprised of Ziusudu's escape, and consequently of the failure of their intention to annihilate mankind. For in the Sixth Column of the text we find these two deities reconciled to Ziusudu and bestowing

148

immortality upon him, as Enlil bestows immortality upon Ut-napishtim at the close of the Semitic Version. In the latter account, after the vessel had grounded on Mount Nisir and Ut-napishtim had tested the abatement of the waters by means of the birds, he brings all out from the ship and offers his libation and sacrifice upon the mountain, heaping up reed, cedar-wood, and myrtle beneath his seven sacrificial vessels. And it was by this act on his part that the gods first had knowledge of his escape. For they smelt the sweet savour of the sacrifice, and "gathered like flies over the sacrificer".(1)

(1) Gilg. Epic, XI, l. 162.

It is possible in our text that Ziusudu's sacrifice in the boat was also the means by which the gods became acquainted with his survival; and it seems obvious that the Sun-god, to whom it was offered, should have continued to play some part in the narrative, perhaps by assisting Ziusudu in propitiating Anu and Enlil. In the Semitic-Babylonian Version, the first deity to approach the sacrifice is Bêlit-ili or Ishtar, who is indignant with Enlil for what he has done. When Enlil himself approaches and sees the ship he is filled with anger against the gods, and, asking who has escaped, exclaims that no man must live in the destruction. Thereupon Ninib accuses Ea, who by his pleading succeeds in turning Enlil's purpose. He bids Enlil visit the sinner with his sin and lay his transgression on the transgressor; Enlil should not again send a deluge to destroy the whole of mankind, but should be content with less wholesale destruction, such as that wrought by wild beasts, famine, and

149

plague. Finally he confesses that it was he who warned Ziusudu of the gods' decision by sending him a dream. Enlil thereupon changes his intention, and going up into the ship, leads Ut-napishtim forth. Though Ea's intervention finds, of course, no parallel in either Hebrew version, the subject-matter of his speech is reflected in both. In the earlier Hebrew Version Yahweh smells the sweet savour of Noah's burnt offering and says in his heart he will no more destroy every living creature as he had done; while in the later Hebrew Version Elohim, after remembering Noah and causing the waters to abate, establishes his covenant to the same effect, and, as a sign of the covenant, sets his bow in the clouds.

In its treatment of the climax of the story we shall see that the Sumerian Version, at any rate in the form it has reached us, is on a lower ethical level than the Babylonian and Hebrew Versions. Ea's argument that the sinner should bear his own sin and the transgressor his own transgression in some measure forestalls that of Ezekiel;(1) and both the Hebrew Versions represent the saving of Noah as part of the divine intention from the beginning. But the Sumerian Version introduces the element of magic as the means by which man can bend the will of the gods to his own ends. How far the details of the Sumerian myth at this point resembled that of the Gilgamesh Epic it is impossible to say, but the general course of the story must have been the same. In the latter Enlil's anger is appeased, in the former that of Anu and Enlil; and it is legitimate to suppose that Enki, like

Ea, was Ziusudu's principal supporter, in view of the part he had already taken in ensuring his escape.

(1) Cf. Ezek. xviii, passim, esp. xviii. 20.

VI. THE PROPITIATION OF THE ANGRY GODS, AND ZIUSUDU'S IMMORTALITY

The presence of the puzzling lines, with which the Sixth Column of our text opens, was not explained by Dr. Poebel; indeed, they would be difficult to reconcile with his assumption that our text is an epic pure and simple. But if, as is suggested above, we are dealing with a myth in magical employment, they are quite capable of explanation. The problem these lines present will best be stated by giving a translation of the extant portion of the column, where they will be seen with their immediate context in relation to what follows them:

"By the Soul of Heaven, by the soul of Earth, shall ye conjure him,
That with you he may . . . !
Anu and Enlil by the Soul of Heaven, by the Soul of Earth, shall ye
conjure,
And with you will he . . . !

"The *niggilma* of the ground springs forth in abundance(?)!"
Ziusudu, the king,

Before Anu and Enlil bows himself down.
Life like (that of) a god he gives to him,
An eternal soul like (that of) a god he creates for him.
At that time Ziusudu, the king,
The name of the *niggilma* (named) "Preserver of the Seed of Mankind".

In a . . . land,(1) the land(1) of Dilmun(?), they caused him to dwell.

(1) Possibly to be translated "mountain". The rendering of the proper name as that of Dilmun is very uncertain. For the probable identification of Dilmun with the island of Bahrein in the Persian Gulf, cf. Rawlinson, *Journ. Roy. As. Soc.,* 1880, pp. 20 ff.; and see further, Meissner, *Orient. Lit-Zeit.,* XX. No. 7, col. 201 ff.

The first two lines of the column are probably part of the speech of some deity, who urges the necessity of invoking or conjuring Anu and Enlil "by the Soul of Heaven, by the Soul of Earth", in order to secure their support or approval. Now Anu and Enlil are the two great gods who had determined on mankind's destruction, and whose wrath at his own escape from death Ziusudu must placate. It is an obvious inference that conjuring "by the Soul of Heaven" and "by the Soul of Earth" is either the method by which Ziusudu has already succeeded in appeasing their anger, or the means by which he is here enjoined to attain that end. Against the latter alternative it is to be noted that the god is addressing more than one person; and, further, at Ziusudu is evidently already pardoned, for, so far from following the deity's advice, he immediately prostrates himself before Anu and Enlil and receives immortality. We may conjecture that at the close of the Fifth Column Ziusudu had already performed the invocation and thereby had appeased the divine wrath; and that the lines at the beginning of the Sixth Column point the moral of the story by enjoining on Ziusudu and his descendants, in other words on mankind, the advisability of employing this powerful incantation at their need. The speaker may perhaps have been one of Ziusudu's divine helpers—the Sun-god to whom he had sacrificed, or Enki who had saved him from the Flood. But it seems to me more probable that the words are uttered by Anu and Enlil themselves.(1) For thereby they would be represented as giving their own sanction to the formula, and as guaranteeing its magical efficacy. That the incantation, as addressed to Anu and Enlil, would be appropriate is obvious, since each would be magically approached through his own sphere of control.

(1) One of them may have been the speaker on behalf of both.

It is significant that at another critical point of the story we have already met with a reference to conjuring "by the Name of Heaven and Earth", the phrase occurring at the close of the Third Column after the reference to the dream or dreams. There, as we saw, we might possibly explain the passage as illustrating one aspect of Ziusudu's piety: he may have been represented as continually practising this class of divination, and in that case it would be natural enough that in the final crisis of the story he should have propitiated the gods he conjured by the same means. Or, as a more probable alternative, it was suggested that we might connect the line with Enki's warning, and assume that Ziusudu interpreted the dream-revelation of Anu and Enlil's purpose by means of the magical incantation which was peculiarly associated with them. On either alternative the phrase fits into the story itself, and there is no need to suppose that the narrative is interrupted, either in the Third or in the Sixth Column, by an address to the hearers of the myth, urging them to make the invocation on their own behalf.

On the other hand, it seems improbable that the lines in question formed part of the original myth; they may have been inserted to weld the myth more closely to the magic. Both incantation and epic may have originally existed independently, and, if so, their combination would have been suggested by their contents. For while the former is addressed to Anu and Enlil, in the latter these same gods play the dominant parts: they are the two chief creators, it is they who send the Flood, and it is their anger that must be appeased. If once combined, the further step of making the incantation the actual means by which Ziusudu achieved his own rescue and immortality would be a natural development. It may be added that the words would have been an equally appropriate addition if the incantation had not existed independently, but had been suggested by, and developed from, the myth.

In the third and eleventh lines of the column we have further references to the mysterious object, the creation of

154

which appears to have been recorded in the First Column of the text between man's creation and that of animals. The second sign of the group composing its name was not recognized by Dr. Poebel, but it is quite clearly written in two of the passages, and has been correctly identified by Professor Barton.(1) The Sumerian word is, in fact, to be read *nig-gil-ma*,(2) which, when preceded by the determinative for "pot", "jar", or "bowl", is given in a later syllabary as the equivalent of the Semitic word *mashkhalu*. Evidence that the word *mashkhalu* was actually employed to denote a jar or vessel of some sort is furnished by one of the Tel el-Amarna letters which refers to "one silver *mashkhalu*" and "one (or two) stone *mashkhalu*".(3) In our text the determinative is absent, and it is possible that the word is used in another sense. Professor Barton, in both passages in the Sixth Column, gives it the meaning "curse"; he interprets the lines as referring to the removal of a curse from the earth after the Flood, and he compares Gen. viii. 21, where Yahweh declares he will not again "curse the ground for man's sake". But this translation ignores the occurrence of the word in the First Column, where the creation of the *niggilma* is apparently recorded; and his rendering "the seed that was cursed" in l. 11 is not supported by the photographic reproduction of the text, which suggests that the first sign in the line is not that for "seed", but is the sign for "name", as correctly read by Dr. Poebel. In that passage the *niggilma* appears to be given by Ziusudu the name "Preserver of the Seed of Mankind", which we have already compared to the title bestowed on Uta-napishtim's ship, "Preserver of Life".

155

Like the ship, it must have played an important part in man's preservation, which would account not only for the honorific title but for the special record of its creation.

(1) See American Journal of Semitic Languages, Vol. XXXI, April 1915, p. 226.

(2) It is written nig-gil in the First Column.

(3) See Winckler, El-Amarna, pl. 35 f., No. 28, Obv., Col. II, l. 45, Rev., Col. I, l. 63, and Knudtzon, El-Am. Taf., pp. 112, 122; the vessels were presents from Amenophis IV to
Burnaburiash.

It we may connect the word with the magical colouring of the myth, we might perhaps retain its known meaning, "jar" or "bowl", and regard it as employed in the magical ceremony which must have formed part of the invocation "by the Soul of Heaven, by the Soul of Earth". But the accompanying references to the ground, to its production from the ground, and to its springing up, if the phrases may be so rendered, suggest rather some kind of plant;(1) and this, from its employment in magical rites, may also have given its name to a bowl or vessel which held it. A very similar plant was that found and lost by Gilgamesh, after his sojourn with Ut-napishtim; it too had potent magical power and bore a title descriptive of its peculiar virtue of transforming old age to youth. Should this suggestion prove to be correct, the three passages mentioning the *niggilma* must be classed with those in which the invocation is referred to, as ensuring the sanction of the myth to further elements in the magic. In accordance with this view, the fifth line in the Sixth Column is probably to be included in the divine speech, where a reference to the object employed in the ritual would not be out of place. But it is to be hoped that light will be thrown on this puzzling word by further study, and perhaps by new fragments of the text; meanwhile it would be hazardous to suggest a more definite rendering.

(1) The references to "the ground", or "the earth", also tend to connect it peculiarly with Enlil. Enlil's close association with the earth, which is, of course, independently attested, is explicitly referred to in the Babylonian Version (cf. Gilg. Epic. XI, ll. 39-42). Suggested reflections of this idea have long been traced in the Hebrew Versions; cf. Gen. viii. 21 (J), where Yahweh says he will not again curse the ground, and Gen. ix. 13 (P), where Elohim speaks of his covenant "between me and the earth".

With the sixth line of the column it is clear that the original narrative of the myth is resumed.(1) Ziusudu, the king, prostrates himself before Anu and Enlil, who bestow immortality upon him and cause him to dwell in a land, or mountain, the name of which may perhaps be read as Dilmun. The close parallelism between this portion of the text and the end of the myth in the Gilgamesh Epic will be seen from the following extracts,(2) the magical portions being omitted from the Sumerian Version:

157

(1) It will also be noted that with this line the text again falls naturally into couplets.

(2) Col. VI, ll. 6-9 and 12 are there compared with Gilg. Epic, XI, ll. 198-205.

SUMERIAN VERSION SEMITIC VERSION

Then Enlil went up into the
ship;
Ziusudu, the king, He took me by the hand and led
me forth.
Before Anu and Enlil bows himself He brought out my wife and
down. caused her to bow down at my
side;
He touched our brows, standing
between us and blessing us:
Life like (that of) a god he "Formerly was Ut-napishtim of
gives to him. mankind,
An eternal soul like (that of) a But now let Ut-napishtim be
god he creates for him. like the gods, even us!
And let Ut-napishtim dwell afar
off at the mouth of the
rivers!"
In a ... land, the land of(1) Then they took me and afar off,
Dilmun(?), they caused him to at the mouth of the rivers,
dwell. they caused me to dwell.

158

(1) Or, "On a mountain, the mountain of", &c.

The Sumerian Version thus apparently concludes with the familiar ending of the legend which we find in the Gilgamesh Epic and in Berossus, though it here occurs in an abbreviated form and with some variations in detail. In all three versions the prostration of the Deluge hero before the god is followed by the bestowal of immortality upon him, a fate which, according to Berossus, he shared with his wife, his daughter, and the steersman. The Gilgamesh Epic perhaps implies that Ut-napishtim's wife shared in his immortality, but the Sumerian Version mentions Ziusudu alone. In the Gilgamesh Epic Ut-napishtim is settled by the gods at the mouth of the rivers, that is to say at the head of the Persian Gulf, while according to a possible rendering of the Sumerian Version he is made to dwell on Dilmun, an island in the Gulf itself. The fact that Gilgamesh in the Epic has to cross the sea to reach Ut-napishtim may be cited in favour of the reading "Dilmun"; and the description of the sea as "the Waters of Death", if it implies more than the great danger of their passage, was probably a later development associated with Ut-napishtim's immortality. It may be added that in neither Hebrew version do we find any parallel to the concluding details of the original story, the Hebrew narratives being brought to an end with the blessing of Noah and the divine promise to, or covenant with, mankind.

Such then are the contents of our Sumerian document, and from the details which have been given it will have been seen that its story, so far as concerns the Deluge, is in essentials the same as that we already find in the Gilgamesh Epic. It is true that this earlier version has reached us in a magical setting, and to some extent in an abbreviated form. In the next lecture I shall have occasion to refer to another early mythological text from Nippur, which was thought by its first interpreter to include a second Sumerian Version of the Deluge legend. That suggestion has not been substantiated, though we shall see that the contents of the document are of a very interesting character. But in view of the discussion that has taken place in the United States over the interpretation of the second text, and of the doubts that have subsequently been expressed in some quarters as to the recent discovery of any new form of the Deluge legend, it may be well to formulate briefly the proof that in the inscription published by Dr. Poebel an early Sumerian Version of the Deluge story has actually been recovered. Any one who has followed the detailed analysis of the new text which has been attempted in the preceding paragraphs will, I venture to think, agree that the following conclusions may be drawn:

(i) The points of general resemblance presented by the narrative to that in the Gilgamesh Epic are sufficiently close in themselves to show that we are dealing with a Sumerian Version of that story. And this conclusion is further supported (a) by the occurrence throughout the text of the attested Sumerian equivalent of the Semitic word, employed in the Babylonian Versions, for the "Flood" or "Deluge", and (b) by the use of precisely the same term for the hero's "great boat", which is already familiar to us from an early Babylonian Version.

(ii) The close correspondence in language between portions of the Sumerian legend and the Gilgamesh Epic suggest that the one version was ultimately derived from the other. And this conclusion in its turn is confirmed (a) by the identity in meaning of the Sumerian and Babylonian names for the Deluge hero, which are actually found equated in a late explanatory text, and (b) by small points of difference in the Babylonian form of the story which correspond to later political and religious developments and suggest the work of Semitic redactors.

The cumulative effect of such general and detailed evidence is overwhelming, and we may dismiss all doubts as to the validity of Dr. Poebel's claim. We have indeed recovered a very early, and in some of its features a very primitive, form of the Deluge narrative which till now has reached us only in Semitic and Greek renderings; and the stream of tradition has been tapped at a point far above any at which we have hitherto approached it. What evidence, we may ask, does this early Sumerian Version offer with regard to the origin and literary history of the Hebrew Versions?

The general dependence of the biblical Versions upon the Babylonian legend as a whole has long been recognized, and needs no further demonstration; and it has already been observed that the parallelisms with the version in the Gilgamesh Epic are on the whole more detailed and striking in the earlier than in the later Hebrew Version.(1) In the course of our analysis of the Sumerian text its more striking points of agreement or divergence, in relation to the Hebrew Versions, were noted under the different sections of its narrative. It was also obvious that, in many features in which the Hebrew Versions differ from the Gilgamesh Epic, the latter finds Sumerian support. These facts confirm the conclusion, which we should naturally base on grounds of historical probability, that while the Semitic-Babylonian Versions were derived from Sumer, the Hebrew accounts were equally clearly derived from Babylon. But there are one or two pieces of evidence which are apparently at variance with this conclusion, and these call for some explanation.

(1) For details see especially Skinner, *Genesis*, pp. 177 ff.

Not too much significance should be attached to the apparent omission of the episode of the birds from the Sumerian narrative, in which it would agree with the later as against the earlier Hebrew Version; for, apart from its epitomized character, there is so much missing from the text that the absence of this episode cannot be regarded as established with certainty. And in any case it could be balanced by the Sumerian order of Creation of men before animals, which agrees with the earlier Hebrew Version against the later. But there is one very striking point in which our new Sumerian text agrees with both the Hebrew Versions as against the Gilgamesh Epic and Berossus; and that is in the character of Ziusudu, which presents so close a parallel to the piety of Noah. As we have already seen, the latter is due to no Hebrew idealization of the story, but represents a genuine strand of the original tradition, which

162

is completely absent from the Babylonian Versions. But the Babylonian Versions are the media through which it has generally been assumed that the tradition of the Deluge reached the Hebrews. What explanation have we of this fact?

This grouping of Sumerian and Hebrew authorities, against the extant sources from Babylon, is emphasized by the general framework of the Sumerian story. For the literary connexion which we have in Genesis between the Creation and the Deluge narratives has hitherto found no parallel in the cuneiform texts. In Babylon and Assyria the myth of Creation and the Deluge legend have been divorced. From the one a complete epic has been evolved in accordance with the tenets of Babylonian theology, the Creation myth being combined in the process with other myths of a somewhat analogous character. The Deluge legend has survived as an isolated story in more than one setting, the principal Semitic Version being recounted to the national hero Gilgamesh, towards the close of the composite epic of his adventures which grew up around the nucleus of his name. It is one of the chief surprises of the newly discovered Sumerian Version that the Hebrew connexion of the narratives is seen to be on the lines of very primitive tradition. Noah's reputation for piety does not stand alone. His line of descent from Adam, and the thread of narrative connecting the creation of the world with its partial destruction by the Deluge, already appear in Sumerian form at a time when the city of Babylon itself had not secured its later power. How then are we to account for this correspondence of Sumerian and Hebrew traditions, on points completely wanting in our intermediate authorities, from which, however, other evidence suggests that the Hebrew narratives were derived?

At the risk of anticipating some of the conclusions to be drawn in the next lecture, it may be well to define an answer now. It is possible that those who still accept the traditional authorship of the Pentateuch may be inclined to see in this correspondence of Hebrew and Sumerian ideas a confirmation of their own hypothesis. But it should be pointed out at once that this is not an inevitable deduction from the evidence. Indeed, it is directly contradicted by the rest of the evidence we have summarized, while it would leave completely unexplained some significant features of the problem. It is true that certain important details of the Sumerian tradition, while not affecting Babylon and Assyria, have left their stamp upon the Hebrew narratives; but that is not an exhaustive statement of the case. For we have also seen that a more complete survival of Sumerian tradition has taken place in the history of Berossus. There we traced the same general framework of the narratives, with a far closer correspondence in detail. The kingly rank of Ziusudu is in complete harmony with the Berossian conception of a series of supreme Antediluvian rulers, and the names of two of the Antediluvian cites are among those of their newly recovered Sumerian prototypes. There can thus be no suggestion that the Greek reproductions of the Sumerian tradition were in their turn due to Hebrew influence. On the contrary we have in them a parallel case of survival in a far more complete form.

The inference we may obviously draw is that the Sumerian narrative continued in existence, in a literary form that closely resembled the original version, into the later historical periods. In this there would be nothing to surprise us, when we recall the careful preservation and study of ancient Sumerian religious texts by the later Semitic priesthood of the country. Each ancient cult-centre in Babylonia continued to cling to its own local traditions, and the Sumerian desire for their preservation, which was inherited by their Semitic guardians, was in great measure unaffected by political occurrences elsewhere. Hence it was that Ashur-bani-pal, when forming his library at Nineveh, was able to draw upon so rich a store of the more ancient literary texts of Babylonia. The Sumerian Version of the Deluge and of Antediluvian history may well have survived in a less epitomized form than that in which we have recovered it; and, like other ancient texts, it was probably provided with a Semitic translation. Indeed its literary study and reproduction may have continued without interruption in Babylon itself. But even if Sumerian tradition died out in the capital under the influence of the Babylonian priesthood, its re-introduction may well have taken place in Neo-Babylonian times. Perhaps the antiquarian researches of Nabonidus were characteristic of his period; and in any case the collection of his country's gods into the capital must have been accompanied by a renewed interest in the more ancient versions of the past with which their cults were peculiarly associated. In the extant summary from Berossus we may possibly see evidence of a subsequent attempt to combine

165

with these more ancient traditions the continued religious dominance of Marduk and of Babylon.

Our conclusion, that the Sumerian form of the tradition did not die out, leaves the question as to the periods during which Babylonian influence may have acted upon Hebrew tradition in great measure unaffected; and we may therefore postpone its further consideration to the next lecture. To-day the only question that remains to be considered concerns the effect of our new evidence upon the wider problem of Deluge stories as a whole. What light does it throw on the general character of Deluge stories and their suggested Egyptian origin?

One thing that strikes me forcibly in reading this early text is the complete absence of any trace or indication of astrological *motif*. It is true that Ziusudu sacrifices to the Sun-god; but the episode is inherent in the story, the appearance of the Sun after the storm following the natural sequence of events and furnishing assurance to the king of his eventual survival. To identify the worshipper with his god and to transfer Ziusudu's material craft to the heavens is surely without justification from the simple narrative. We have here no prototype of Ra sailing the heavenly ocean. And the destructive flood itself is not only of an equally material and mundane character, but is in complete harmony with its Babylonian setting.

In the matter of floods the Tigris and Euphrates present a striking contrast to the Nile. It is true that the life-blood of each country is its river-water, but the conditions of its use are very different, and in Mesopotamia it becomes a curse

166

when out of control. In both countries the river-water must be used for maturing the crops. But while the rains of Abyssinia cause the Nile to rise between August and October, thus securing both summer and winter crops, the melting snows of Armenia and the Taurus flood the Mesopotamian rivers between March and May. In Egypt the Nile flood is gentle; it is never abrupt, and the river gives ample warning of its rise and fall. It contains just enough sediment to enrich the land without choking the canals; and the water, after filling its historic basins, may when necessary be discharged into the falling river in November. Thus Egypt receives a full and regular supply of water, and there is no difficulty in disposing of any surplus. The growth in such a country of a legend of world-wide destruction by flood is inconceivable.

In Mesopotamia, on the other hand, the floods, which come too late for the winter crops, are followed by the rainless summer months; and not only must the flood-water be controlled, but some portion of it must be detained artificially, if it is to be of use during the burning months of July, August, and September, when the rivers are at their lowest. Moreover, heavy rain in April and a warm south wind melting the snow in the hills may bring down such floods that the channels cannot contain them; the dams are then breached and the country is laid waste. Here there is first too much water and then too little.

The great danger from flood in Babylonia, both in its range of action and in its destructive effect, is due to the strangely flat character of the Tigris and Euphrates delta.(1) Hence after a severe breach in the Tigris or Euphrates, the river after inundating the country may make itself a new channel miles away from the old one. To mitigate the danger, the floods may be dealt with in two ways—by a multiplication of canals to spread the water, and by providing escapes for it into depressions in the surrounding desert, which in their turn become centres of fertility. Both methods were employed in antiquity; and it may be added that in any scheme for the future prosperity of the country they must be employed again, of course with the increased efficiency of modern apparatus.(2) But while the Babylonians succeeded in controlling the Euphrates, the Tigris was never really tamed,(3) and whenever it burst its right bank the southern plains were devastated. We could not have more suitable soil for the growth of a Deluge story.

(1) Baghdad, though 300 miles by crow-fly from the sea and 500 by river, is only 120 ft. above sea-level.

(2) The Babylonians controlled the Euphrates, and at the same time provided against its time of "low supply", by escapes into two depressions in the western desert to the NW. of Babylon, known to-day as the Habbânîyah and Abu Dîs depressions, which lie S. of the modern town of Ramâdi and N. of Kerbela. That these depressions were actually used as reservoirs in antiquity is proved by the presence along their edges of thick beds of Euphrates shells. In addition to canals and escapes, the Babylonian system included well-constructed dikes protected by brushwood. By cutting an eight-mile channel through a low hill between the

Habbânîyah
and Abu Dîs depressions and by building a short dam 50 ft.
high across the latter's narrow outlet, Sir William
Willcocks estimates that a reservoir could be obtained
holding eighteen milliards of tons of water. See his work
The Irrigations of Mesopotamia (E. and F. N. Spon, 1911),
Geographical Journal, Vol. XL, No. 2 (Aug., 1912), pp. 129
ff., and the articles in *The Near East* cited on p. 97, n.
1, and p. 98, n. 2. Sir William Willcocks's volume and
subsequent papers form the best introduction to the study
of
Babylonian Deluge tradition on its material side.

(3) Their works carried out on the Tigris were effective for
irrigation; but the Babylonians never succeeded in
controlling its floods as they did those of the Euphrates. A
massive earthen dam, the remains of which are still known
as
"Nimrod's Dam", was thrown across the Tigris above the
point
where it entered its delta; this served to turn the river
over hard conglomerate rock and kept it at a high level so
that it could irrigate the country on both banks. Above the
dam were the heads of the later Nahrwân Canal, a great
stream 400 ft. wide and 17 ft. deep, which supplied the
country east of the river. The Nâr Sharri or "King's Canal",
the Nahar Malkha of the Greeks and the Nahr el-Malik of the
Arabs, protected the right bank of the Tigris by its own
high artificial banks, which can still be traced for

hundreds of miles; but it took its supply from the Euphrates at Sippar, where the ground is some 25 ft. higher than on the Tigris. The Tigris usually flooded its left bank; it was the right bank which was protected, and a breach here meant
disaster. Cf. Willcocks, op. cit., and *The Near East*, Sept. 29, 1916 (Vol. XI, No. 282), p. 522.

It was only by constant and unremitting attention that disaster from flood could be averted; and the difficulties of the problem were and are increased by the fact that the flood-water of the Mesopotamian rivers contains five times as much sediment as the Nile. In fact, one of the most pressing of the problems the Sumerian and early Babylonian engineers had to solve was the keeping of the canals free from silt.(1) What the floods, if left unchecked, may do in Mesopotamia, is well illustrated by the decay of the ancient canal-system, which has been the immediate cause of the country's present state of sordid desolation. That the decay was gradual was not the fault of the rivers, but was due to the sound principles on which the old system of control had been evolved through many centuries of labour. At the time of the Moslem conquest the system had already begun to fail. In the fifth century there had been bad floods; but worse came in A.D. 629, when both rivers burst their banks and played havoc with the dikes and embankments. It is related that the Sassanian king Parwiz, the contemporary of Mohammed, crucified in one day forty canal-workers at a certain breach, and yet was unable to master the flood.(2) All repairs were suspended during the anarchy of the Moslem invasion. As a consequence the Tigris left its old bed for the Shatt el-Hai at Kût, and pouring its own and its tributaries' waters into the Euphrates formed the Great Euphrates Swamp, two hundred miles long and fifty broad. But even then what was left of the old system was sufficient to support the splendour of the Eastern Caliphate.

(1) Cf. *Letters of Hammurabi*, Vol. III, pp. xxxvi ff.; it was the duty of every village or town upon the banks of the main canals in Babylonia to keep its own section clear of silt, and of course it was also responsible for its own smaller irrigation-channels. While the invention of the system of basin-irrigation was practically forced on Egypt, the extraordinary fertility of Babylonia was won in the teeth of nature by the system of perennial irrigation, or irrigation all the year round. In Babylonia the water was led into small fields of two or three acres, while the Nile valley was irrigated in great basins each containing some thirty to forty thousand acres. The Babylonian method gives far more profitable results, and Sir William Willcocks points out that Egypt to-day is gradually abandoning its own system and adopting that of its ancient rival; see *The Near East*, Sept. 29, 1916, p. 521.

(2) See Le Strange, *The Lands of the Eastern Caliphate*, p. 27.

The second great blow to the system followed the Mongol conquest, when the Nahrwân Canal, to the east of the Tigris, had its head swept away by flood and the area it had irrigated became desert. Then, in about the fifteenth century, the Tigris returned to its old course; the Shatt el-Hai shrank, and much of the Great Swamp dried up into the desert it is to-day.(1) Things became worse during the centuries of Turkish misrule. But the silting up of the Hillah, or main, branch of the Euphrates about 1865, and the transference of a great part of its stream into the Hindîyah Canal, caused even the Turks to take action. They constructed the old Hindîyah Barrage in 1890, but it gave way in 1903 and the state of things was even worse than before; for the Hillah branch then dried entirely.(2)

(1) This illustrates the damage the Tigris itself is capable of inflicting on the country. It may be added that Sir William Willcocks proposes to control the Tigris floods by an escape into the Tharthâr depression, a great salt pan at the tail of Wadi Tharthâr, which lies 14 ft. below sea level and is 200 ft. lower than the flood-level of the Tigris some thirty-two miles away. The escape would leave the Tigris to the S. of Sâmarra, the proposed Beled Barrage being built below it and up-stream of "Nimrod's Dam". The Tharthâr escape would drain into the Euphrates, and the latter's Habbânîyah escape would receive any surplus water from the
Tigris, a second barrage being thrown across the Euphrates up-stream of Fallûjah, where there is an outcrop of limestone near the head of the Sakhlawîyah Canal. The Tharthâr depression, besides disposing of the Tigris flood-water, would thus probably feed the Euphrates; and a second
barrage on the Tigris, to be built at Kût, would supply

water to the Shatt el-Hai. When the country is freed from danger of flood, the Baghdad Railway could be run through the cultivated land instead of through the eastern desert; see Willcocks, *The Near East*, Oct. 6, 1916 (Vol. XI, No. 283), p. 545 f.

(2) It was then that Sir William Willcocks designed the new Hindîyah Barrage, which was completed in 1913. The Hindîyah
branch, to-day the main stream of the Euphrates, is the old low-lying Pallacopas Canal, which branched westward above
Babylon and discharged its waters into the western marshes.
In antiquity the head of this branch had to be opened in high floods and then closed again immediately after the flood to keep the main stream full past Babylon, which entailed the employment of an enormous number of men. Alexander the Great's first work in Babylonia was cutting a new head for the Pallacopas in solid ground, for hitherto it had been in sandy soil; and it was while reclaiming the marshes farther down-stream that he contracted the fever that killed him.

From this brief sketch of progressive disaster during the later historical period, the inevitable effect of neglected silt and flood, it will be gathered that the two great rivers of Mesopotamia present a very strong contrast to the Nile. For during the same period of misgovernment and neglect in Egypt the Nile did not turn its valley and delta into a desert.

On the Tigris and Euphrates, during ages when the earliest dwellers on their banks were struggling to make effective their first efforts at control, the waters must often have regained the upper hand. Under such conditions the story of a great flood in the past would not be likely to die out in the future; the tradition would tend to gather illustrative detail suggested by later experience. Our new text reveals the Deluge tradition in Mesopotamia at an early stage of its development, and incidentally shows us that there is no need to postulate for its origin any convulsion of nature or even a series of seismic shocks accompanied by cyclone in the Persian Gulf.

If this had been the only version of the story that had come down to us, we should hardly have regarded it as a record of world-wide catastrophe. It is true the gods' intention is to destroy mankind, but the scene throughout is laid in Southern Babylonia. After seven days' storm, the Sun comes out, and the vessel with the pious priest-king and his domestic animals on board grounds, apparently still in Babylonia, and not on any distant mountain, such as Mt. Nisir or the great mass of Ararat in Armenia. These are obviously details which tellers of the story have added as it passed down to later generations. When it was carried still farther afield, into the area of the Eastern Mediterranean, it was again adapted to local conditions. Thus Apollodorus makes Deucalion land upon Parnassus,(1) and the pseudo-Lucian relates how he founded the temple of Derketo at Hierapolis in Syria beside the hole in the earth which swallowed up the Flood.(2) To the Sumerians who first told the story, the great Flood appeared to have destroyed mankind, for Southern Babylonia was for them the world. Later peoples who heard it have fitted the story to their own geographical horizon, and in all good faith and by a purely logical process the mountain-tops are represented as submerged, and the ship, or ark, or chest, is made to come to ground on the highest peak known to the story-teller and his hearers. But in its early Sumerian form it is just a simple tradition of some great inundation, which overwhelmed the plain of Southern Babylonia and was peculiarly disastrous in its effects. And so its memory survived in the picture of Ziusudu's solitary coracle upon the face of the waters, which, seen through the mists of the Deluge tradition, has given us the Noah's ark of our nursery days.

(1) Hesiod is our earliest authority for the Deucalion Flood story. For its probable Babylonian origin, cf. Farnell, *Greece and Babylon* (1911), p. 184.

(2) *De Syria dea*, 12 f.

Thus the Babylonian, Hebrew, and Greek Deluge stories resolve themselves, not into a nature myth, but into an early legend, which has the basis of historical fact in the Euphrates Valley. And it is probable that we may explain after a similar fashion the occurrence of tales of a like character at least in some other parts of the world. Among races dwelling in low-lying or well-watered districts it would be surprising if we did not find independent stories of past floods from which few inhabitants of the land escaped. It is only in hilly countries such as Palestine, where for the great part of the year water is scarce and precious, that we are forced to deduce borrowing; and there is no doubt that both the Babylonian and the biblical stories have been responsible for some at any rate of the scattered tales. But there is no need to adopt the theory of a single source for all of them, whether in Babylonia or, still less, in Egypt.(1)

(1) This argument is taken from an article I published in Professor Headlam's *Church Quarterly Review*, Jan., 1916, pp. 280 ff., containing an account of Dr. Poebel's discovery.

I should like to add, with regard to this reading of our new evidence, that I am very glad to know Sir James Frazer holds a very similar opinion. For, as you are doubtless all aware, Sir James is at present collecting Flood stories from all over the world, and is supplementing from a wider range the collections already made by Lenormant, Andree, Winternitz, and Gerland. When his work is complete it will be possible to conjecture with far greater confidence how particular traditions or groups of tradition arose, and to what extent transmission has taken place. Meanwhile, in his recent Huxley Memorial Lecture,(1) he has suggested a third possibility as to the way Deluge stories may have arisen.

(1) Sir J. G. Frazer, *Ancient Stories of a Great Flood* (the Huxley Memorial Lecture, 1916), Roy. Anthrop. Inst., 1916.

Stated briefly, it is that a Deluge story may arise as a popular explanation of some striking natural feature in a country, although to the scientific eye the feature in question is due to causes other than catastrophic flood. And he worked out the suggestion in the case of the Greek traditions of a great deluge, associated with the names of Deucalion and Dardanus. Deucalion's deluge, in its later forms at any rate, is obviously coloured by Semitic tradition; but both Greek stories, in their origin, Sir James Frazer would trace to local conditions—the one suggested by the Gorge of Tempe in Thessaly, the other explaining the existence of the Bosphorus and Dardanelles. As he pointed out, they would be instances, not of genuine historical traditions, but of what Sir James Tyler calls "observation myths". A third story of a great flood, regarded in Greek tradition as the earliest of the three, he would explain by an extraordinary inundation of the Copaic Lake in Boeotia, which to this day is liable to great fluctuations of level. His new theory applies only to the other two traditions. For in them no historical kernel is presupposed, though gradual erosion by water is not excluded as a cause of the surface features which may have suggested the myths.

This valuable theory thus opens up a third possibility for our analysis. It may also, of course, be used in combination, if in any particular instance we have reason to believe that transmission, in some vague form, may already have taken place. And it would with all deference suggest the possibility that, in view of other evidence, this may have occurred in the case of the Greek traditions. With regard to the theory itself we may confidently expect that further examples will be found in its illustration and support. Meanwhile in the new Sumerian Version I think we may conclude that we have recovered beyond any doubt the origin of the Babylonian

177

and Hebrew traditions and of the large group of stories to which they in their turn have given rise.

LECTURE III — CREATION AND THE DRAGON MYTH; AND THE PROBLEM OF BABYLONIAN PARALLELS IN HEBREW TRADITION

In our discussion of the new Sumerian version of the Deluge story we came to the conclusion that it gave no support to any theory which would trace all such tales to a single origin, whether in Egypt or in Babylonia. In spite of strong astrological elements in both the Egyptian and Babylonian religious systems, we saw grounds for regarding the astrological tinge of much ancient mythology as a later embellishment and not as primitive material. And so far as our new version of the Deluge story was concerned, it resolved itself into a legend, which had a basis of historical fact in the Euphrates Valley. It will be obvious that the same class of explanation cannot be applied to narratives of the Creation of the World. For there we are dealing, not with legends, but with myths, that is, stories exclusively about the gods. But where an examination of their earlier forms is possible, it would seem to show that many of these tales also, in their origin, are not to be interpreted as nature myths, and that none arose as mere reflections of the solar system. In their more primitive and simpler aspects they seem in many cases to have been suggested by very human and terrestrial experience. To-day we will examine the Egyptian, Sumerian, and Babylonian myths of Creation, and, after we have noted the more striking features of our new material, we will consider the problem of foreign influences upon Hebrew traditions concerning the origin and early history of the world.

In Egypt, as until recently in Babylonia, we have to depend for our knowledge of Creation myths on documents of a comparatively late period. Moreover, Egyptian religious literature as a whole is textually corrupt, and in consequence it is often difficult to determine the original significance of its allusions. Thanks to the funerary inscriptions and that great body of magical formulae and ritual known as "The Chapters of Coming forth by Day", we are very fully informed on the Egyptian doctrines as to the future state of the dead. The Egyptian's intense interest in his own remote future, amounting almost to an obsession, may perhaps in part account for the comparatively meagre space in the extant literature which is occupied by myths relating solely to the past. And it is significant that the one cycle of myth, of which we are fully informed in its latest stage of development, should be that which gave its sanction to the hope of a future existence for man. The fact that Herodotus, though he claims a knowledge of the sufferings or "Mysteries" of Osiris, should deliberately refrain from describing them or from even uttering the name,(1) suggests that in his time at any rate some sections of the mythology had begun to acquire an esoteric character. There is no doubt that at all periods myth played an important part in the ritual of feast-days. But mythological references in the earlier texts are often obscure; and the late form in which a few of the stories have come to us is obviously artificial. The tradition, for example, which relates how mankind came from the tears which issued from Ra's eye undoubtedly arose from a play upon words.

(1) Herodotus, II, 171.

On the other hand, traces of myth, scattered in the religious literature of Egypt, may perhaps in some measure betray their relative age by the conceptions of the universe which underlie them. The Egyptian idea that the sky was a heavenly ocean, which is not unlike conceptions current among the Semitic Babylonians and Hebrews, presupposes some thought and reflection. In Egypt it may well have been evolved from the probably earlier but analogous idea of the river in heaven, which the Sun traversed daily in his boats. Such a river was clearly suggested by the Nile; and its world-embracing character is reminiscent of a time when through communication was regularly established, at least as far south as Elephantine. Possibly in an earlier period the long narrow valley, or even a section of it, may have suggested the figure of a man lying prone upon his back. Such was Keb, the Earth-god, whose counterpart in the sky was the goddess Nut, her feet and hands resting at the limits of the world and her curved body forming the vault of heaven. Perhaps still more primitive, and dating from a pastoral age, may be the notion that the sky was a great cow, her body, speckled with stars, alone visible from the earth beneath. Reference has already been made to the dominant influence of the Sun in Egyptian religion, and it is not surprising that he should so often appear as the first of created beings. His orb itself, or later the god in youthful human form, might be pictured as emerging from a lotus on the primaeval waters, or from a

181

marsh-bird's egg, a conception which influenced the later Phoenician cosmogeny. The Scarabaeus, or great dung-feeding beetle of Egypt, rolling the ball before it in which it lays its eggs, is an obvious theme for the early myth-maker. And it was natural that the Beetle of Khepera should have been identified with the Sun at his rising, as the Hawk of Ra represented his noonday flight, and the aged form of Attun his setting in the west. But in all these varied conceptions and explanations of the universe it is difficult to determine how far the poetical imagery of later periods has transformed the original myths which may lie behind them.

As the Egyptian Creator the claims of Ra, the Sun-god of Heliopolis, early superseded those of other deities. On the other hand, Ptah of Memphis, who for long ages had been merely the god of architects and craftsmen, became under the Empire the architect of the universe and is pictured as a potter moulding the world-egg. A short poem by a priest of Ptah, which has come down to us from that period, exhibits an attempt to develop this idea on philosophical lines.(1) Its author represents all gods and living creatures as proceeding directly from the mind and thought of Ptah. But this movement, which was more notably reflected in Akhenaton's religious revolution, died out in political disaster, and the original materialistic interpretation of the myths was restored with the cult of Amen. How materialistic this could be is well illustrated by two earlier members of the XVIIIth Dynasty, who have left us vivid representations of the potter's wheel employed in the process of man's creation. When the famous Hatshepsut, after the return of her expedition to Punt in the ninth year of her young consort Thothmes III, decided to build her temple at Deir el-Bahari in the necropolis of Western Thebes, she sought to emphasize her claim to the throne of Egypt by recording her own divine origin upon its walls. We have already noted the Egyptians' belief in the solar parentage of their legitimate rulers, a myth that goes back at least to the Old Kingdom and may have had its origin in prehistoric times. With the rise of Thebes, Amen inherited the prerogatives of Ra; and so Hatshepsut seeks to show, on the north side of the retaining wall of her temple's Upper Platform, that she was the daughter of Amen himself, "the great God, Lord of the sky, Lord of the Thrones of the Two Lands, who resides at Thebes". The myth was no invention of her own, for obviously it must have followed traditional lines, and though it is only employed to exhibit the divine creation of a single personage, it as obviously reflects the procedure and methods of a general Creation myth.

(1) See Breasted, *Zeitschrift fur Aegyptische Sprache*, XXXIX, pp. 39 ff., and *History of Egypt*, pp. 356 ff.

This series of sculptures shared the deliberate mutilation that all her records suffered at the hands of Thothmes III after her death, but enough of the scenes and their accompanying text has survived to render the detailed interpretation of the myth quite certain.(1) Here, as in a general Creation myth, Amen's first act is to summon the great gods in council, in order to announce to them the future birth of the great princess. Of the twelve gods who attend, the first is Menthu, a form of the Sun-god and closely associated with Amen.(2) But the second deity is Atum, the great god of Heliopolis, and he is followed by his cycle of deities—Shu, "the son of Ra"; Tefnut, "the Lady of the sky"; Keb, "the Father of the Gods"; Nut, "the Mother of the Gods"; Osiris, Isis, Nephthys, Set, Horus, and Hathor. We are here in the presence of cosmic deities, as befits a projected act of creation. The subsequent scenes exhibit the Egyptian's literal interpretation of the myth, which necessitates the god's bodily presence and personal participation. Thoth mentions to Amen the name of queen Aahmes as the future mother of Hatshepsut, and we later see Amen himself, in the form of her husband, Aa-kheperka-Ra (Thothmes I), sitting with Aahmes and giving her the Ankh, or sign of Life, which she receives in her hand and inhales through her nostrils.(3) God and queen are seated on thrones above a couch, and are supported by two goddesses. After leaving the queen, Amen calls on Khnum or Khnemu, the flat-horned ram-god, who in texts of all periods is referred to as the "builder" of gods and men;(4) and he instructs him to create the body of his future daughter and that of her *Ka*, or "double", which would be united to her from birth.

(1) See Naville, *Deir el-Bahari*, Pt. II, pp. 12 ff., plates xlvi ff.

(2) See Budge, *Gods of the Egyptians*, Vol. II, pp. 23 ff. His chief cult-centre was Hermonthis, but here as elsewhere he is given his usual title "Lord of Thebes".

(3) Pl. xlvii. Similar scenes are presented in the "birth-

184

temples" at Denderah, Edfu, Philae, Esneh, and Luxor; see Naville, op. cit., p. 14.

(4) Cf. Budge, op. cit., Vol. II, p. 50.

The scene in the series, which is of greatest interest in the present connexion, is that representing Khnum at his work of creation. He is seated before a potter's wheel which he works with his foot,(1) and on the revolving table he is fashioning two children with his hands, the baby princess and her "double". It was always Hatshepsut's desire to be represented as a man, and so both the children are boys.(2) As yet they are lifeless, but the symbol of Life will be held to their nostrils by Heqet, the divine Potter's wife, whose frog-head typifies birth and fertility. When Amenophis III copied Hatshepsut's sculptures for his own series at Luxor, he assigned this duty to the greater goddess Hathor, perhaps the most powerful of the cosmic goddesses and the mother of the world. The subsequent scenes at Deir el-Bahari include the leading of queen Aahmes by Khnum and Heqet to the birth-chamber; the great birth scene where the queen is attended by the goddesses Nephthys and Isis, a number of divine nurses and midwives holding several of the "doubles" of the baby, and favourable genii, in human form or with the heads of crocodiles, jackals, and hawks, representing the four cardinal points and all bearing the gift of life; the presentation of the young child by the goddess Hathor to Amen, who is well pleased at the sight of his daughter; and the divine suckling of Hatshepsut and her "doubles". But these episodes do not concern us, as of course they merely

185

reflect the procedure following a royal birth. But Khnum's part in the princess's origin stands on a different plane, for it illustrates the Egyptian myth of Creation by the divine Potter, who may take the form of either Khnum or Ptah. Monsieur Naville points out the extraordinary resemblance in detail which Hatshepsut's myth of divine paternity bears to the Greek legend of Zeus and Alkmene, where the god takes the form of Amphitryon, Alkmene's husband, exactly as Amen appears to the queen;(3) and it may be added that the Egyptian origin of the Greek story was traditionally recognized in the ancestry ascribed to the human couple.(4)

(1) This detail is not clearly preserved at Deir el-Bahari; but it is quite clear in the scene on the west wall of the "Birth-room" in the Temple at Luxor, which Amenophis III evidently copied from that of Hatshepsut.

(2) In the similar scene at Luxor, where the future Amenophis III is represented on the Creator's wheel, the sculptor has distinguished the human child from its spiritual "double" by the quaint device of putting its finger in its mouth.

(3) See Naville, op. cit., p. 12.

(4) Cf., e.g., Herodotus, II, 43.

The only complete Egyptian Creation myth yet recovered is preserved in a late papyrus in the British Museum, which was published some years ago by Dr. Budge.(1) It occurs under two separate versions embedded in "The Book of the

Overthrowing of Apep, the Enemy of Ra". Here Ra, who utters the myth under his late title of Neb-er-tcher, "Lord to the utmost limit", is self-created as Khepera from Nu, the primaeval water; and then follow successive generations of divine pairs, male and female, such as we find at the beginning of the Semitic-Babylonian Creation Series.(2) Though the papyrus was written as late as the year 311 B.C., the myth is undoubtedly early. For the first two divine pairs Shu and Tefnut, Keb and Nut, and four of the latter pairs' five children, Osiris and Isis, Set and Nephthys, form with the Sun-god himself the Greater Ennead of Heliopolis, which exerted so wide an influence on Egyptian religious speculation. The Ennead combined the older solar elements with the cult of Osiris, and this is indicated in the myth by a break in the successive generations, Nut bringing forth at a single birth the five chief gods of the Osiris cycle, Osiris himself and his son Horus, with Set, Isis, and Nephthys. Thus we may see in the myth an early example of that religious syncretism which is so characteristic of later Egyptian belief.

(1) See *Archaeologia*, Vol. LII (1891). Dr. Budge published a new edition of the whole papyrus in *Egyptian Hieratic Papyri in the British Museum* (1910), and the two versions of the Creation myth are given together in his *Gods of the Egyptians*, Vol. I (1904), Chap. VIII, pp. 308 ff., and more recently in his *Egyptian Literature*, Vol. I, "Legends of the Gods" (1912), pp. 2 ff. An account of the papyrus is included in the Introduction to "Legends of the Gods", pp. xiii ff.

(2) In *Gods of the Egyptians*, Vol. I, Chap. VII, pp. 288 ff., Dr. Budge gives a detailed comparison of the Egyptian pairs of primaeval deities with the very similar couples of the Babylonian myth.

The only parallel this Egyptian myth of Creation presents to the Hebrew cosmogony is in its picture of the primaeval water, corresponding to the watery chaos of Genesis i. But the resemblance is of a very general character, and includes no etymological equivalence such as we find when we compare the Hebrew account with the principal Semitic-Babylonian Creation narrative.(1) The application of the Ankh, the Egyptian sign for Life, to the nostrils of a newly-created being is no true parallel to the breathing into man's nostrils of the breath of life in the earlier Hebrew Version,(2) except in the sense that each process was suggested by our common human anatomy. We should naturally expect to find some Hebrew parallel to the Egyptian idea of Creation as the work of a potter with his clay, for that figure appears in most ancient mythologies. The Hebrews indeed used the conception as a metaphor or parable,(3) and it also underlies their earlier picture of man's creation. I have not touched on the grosser Egyptian conceptions concerning the origin of the universe, which we may probably connect with African ideas; but those I have referred to will serve to demonstrate the complete absence of any feature that presents a detailed resemblance of the Hebrew tradition.

(1) For the wide diffusion, in the myths of remote peoples, of a vague theory that would trace all created things to a watery origin, see Farnell, *Greece and Babylon*, p. 180.

188

(2) Gen. ii. 7 (J).

(3) Cf., e.g., Isaiah xxix. 16, xlv. 9; and Jeremiah xviii. 2f.

When we turn to Babylonia, we find there also evidence of conflicting ideas, the product of different and to some extent competing religious centres. But in contrast to the rather confused condition of Egyptian mythology, the Semitic Creation myth of the city of Babylon, thanks to the latter's continued political ascendancy, succeeded in winning a dominant place in the national literature. This is the version in which so many points of resemblance to the first chapter of Genesis have long been recognized, especially in the succession of creative acts and their relative order. In the Semitic-Babylonian Version the creation of the world is represented as the result of conflict, the emergence of order out of chaos, a result that is only attained by the personal triumph of the Creator. But this underlying dualism does not appear in the more primitive Sumerian Version we have now recovered. It will be remembered that in the second lecture I gave some account of the myth, which occurs in an epitomized form as an introduction to the Sumerian Version of the Deluge, the two narratives being recorded in the same document and connected with one another by a description of the Antediluvian cities. We there saw that Creation is ascribed to the three greatest gods of the Sumerian pantheon, Anu, Enlil, and Enki, assisted by the goddess Ninkharsagga.

It is significant that in the Sumerian version no less than four deities are represented as taking part in the Creation. For in this we may see some indication of the period to which its composition must be assigned. Their association in the text suggests that the claims of local gods had already begun to compete with one another as a result of political combination between the cities of their cults. To the same general period we must also assign the compilation of the Sumerian Dynastic record, for that presupposes the existence of a supreme ruler among the Sumerian city-states. This form of political constitution must undoubtedly have been the result of a long process of development, and the fact that its existence should be regarded as dating from the Creation of the world indicates a comparatively developed stage of the tradition. But behind the combination of cities and their gods we may conjecturally trace anterior stages of development, when each local deity and his human representative seemed to their own adherents the sole objects for worship and allegiance. And even after the demands of other centres had been conceded, no deity ever quite gave up his local claims.

Enlil, the second of the four Sumerian creating deities, eventually ousted his rivals. It has indeed long been recognized that the *rôle* played by Marduk in the Babylonian Version of Creation had been borrowed from Enlil of Nippur; and in the Atrakhasis legend Enlil himself appears as the ultimate ruler of the world and the other gods figure as "his sons". Anu, who heads the list and plays with Enlil the leading part in the Sumerian narrative, was clearly his chief rival. And though we possess no detailed account of Anu's creative work, the persistent ascription to him of the creation of heaven, and his familiar title, "the Father of the Gods", suggest that he once possessed a corresponding body of myth in Eanna, his temple at Erech. Enki, the third of the creating gods, was naturally credited, as God of Wisdom, with special creative activities, and fortunately in his case we have some independent evidence of the varied forms these could assume.

According to one tradition that has come down to us,(1) after Anu had made the heavens, Enki created Apsû or the Deep, his own dwelling-place. Then taking from it a piece of clay(2) he proceeded to create the Brick-god, and reeds and forests for the supply of building material. From the same clay he continued to form other deities and materials, including the Carpenter-god; the Smith-god; Arazu, a patron deity of building; and mountains and seas for all that they produced; the Goldsmith-god, the Stone-cutter-god, and kindred deities, together with their rich products for offerings; the Grain-deities, Ashnan and Lakhar; Siris, a Wine-god; Ningishzida and Ninsar, a Garden-god, for the sake of the rich offerings they could make; and a deity described as "the High priest of the great gods," to lay down necessary ordinances and commands. Then he created "the King", for the equipment probably of a particular temple, and finally men, that they might practise the cult in the temple so elaborately prepared.

(1) See Weissbach, *Babylonische Miscellen*, pp. 32 ff.

(2) One of the titles of Enki was "the Potter"; cf. *Cun. Texts* in the Brit. Mus., Pt. XXIV, pl. 14 f., ll. 41, 43.

It will be seen from this summary of Enki's creative activities, that the text from which it is taken is not a general Creation myth, but in all probability the introductory paragraph of a composition which celebrated the building or restoration of a particular temple; and the latter's foundation is represented, on henotheistic lines, as the main object of creation. Composed with that special purpose, its narrative is not to be regarded as an exhaustive account of the creation of the world. The incidents are eclective, and only such gods and materials are mentioned as would have been required for the building and adornment of the temple and for the provision of its offerings and cult. But even so its mythological background is instructive. For while Anu's creation of heaven is postulated as the necessary precedent of Enki's activities, the latter creates the Deep, vegetation, mountains, seas, and mankind. Moreover, in his character as God of Wisdom, he is not only the teacher but the creator of those deities who were patrons of man's own constructive work. From such evidence we may infer that in his temple at Eridu, now covered by the mounds of Abu Shahrain in the extreme south of Babylonia, and regarded in early Sumerian tradition as the first city in the world, Enki himself was once celebrated as the sole creator of the universe.

The combination of the three gods Anu, Enlil, and Enki, is persistent in the tradition; for not only were they the great gods of the universe, representing respectively heaven, earth, and the watery abyss, but they later shared the

192

heavenly sphere between them. It is in their astrological character that we find them again in creative activity, though without the co-operation of any goddess, when they appear as creators of the great light-gods and as founders of time divisions, the day and the month. This Sumerian myth, though it reaches us only in an extract or summary in a Neo-Babylonian schoolboy's exercise,(1) may well date from a comparatively early period, but probably from a time when the "Ways" of Anu, Enlil, and Enki had already been fixed in heaven and their later astrological characters had crystallized.

(1) See *The Seven Tablets of Creation*, Vol. I, pp. 124 ff.
The tablet gives extracts from two very similar Sumerian and
Semitic texts. In both of them Anu, Enlil, and Enki appear
as creators "through their sure counsel". In the Sumerian
extract they create the Moon and ordain its monthly course,
while in the Semitic text, after establishing heaven and
earth, they create in addition to the New Moon the bright
Day, so that "men beheld the Sun-god in the Gate of his
going forth".

The idea that a goddess should take part with a god in man's creation is already a familiar feature of Babylonian mythology. Thus the goddess Aruru, in co-operation with Marduk, might be credited with the creation of the human race,(1) as she might also be pictured creating on her own initiative an individual hero such as Enkidu of the Gilgamesh Epic. The *rôle* of mother of mankind was also shared, as we have seen, by the Semitic Ishtar. And though the old

193

Sumerian goddess, Ninkharsagga, the "Lady of the Mountains", appears in our Sumerian text for the first time in the character of creatress, some of the titles we know she enjoyed, under her synonyms in the great God List of Babylonia, already reflected her cosmic activities.(2) For she was known as

"The Builder of that which has Breath",
"The Carpenter of Mankind",
"The Carpenter of the Heart",
"The Coppersmith of the Gods",
"The Coppersmith of the Land", and
"The Lady Potter".

(1) Op. cit., p. 134 f.

(2) Cf. *Cun. Texts in the Brit. Mus.*, Pt. XXIV, pl. 12, ll. 32, 26, 27, 25, 24, 23, and Poebel, *Hist. Texts*, p. 34.

In the myth we are not told her method of creation, but from the above titles it is clear that in her own cycle of tradition Ninkhasagga was conceived as fashioning men not only from clay but also from wood, and perhaps as employing metal for the manufacture of her other works of creation. Moreover, in the great God List, where she is referred to under her title Makh, Ninkhasagga is associated with Anu, Enlil, and Enki; she there appears, with her dependent deities, after Enlil and before Enki. We thus have definite proof that her association with the three chief Sumerian gods was widely recognized in the early Sumerian period and dictated her position in the classified pantheon of Babylonia. Apart from this evidence, the important rank assigned her in the historical and legal records and in votive inscriptions,(1) especially in the early period and in Southern Babylonia, accords fully with the part she here plays in the Sumerian Creation myth. Eannatum and Gudea of Lagash both place her immediately after Anu and Enlil, giving her precedence over Enki; and even in the Kassite Kudurru inscriptions of the thirteenth and twelfth centuries, where she is referred to, she takes rank after Enki and before the other gods. In Sumer she was known as "the Mother of the Gods", and she was credited with the power of transferring the kingdom and royal insignia from one king to his successor.

(1) See especially, Poebel, op. cit., pp. 24 ff.

Her supreme position as a goddess is attested by the relative insignificance of her husband Dunpae, whom she completely overshadows, in which respect she presents a contrast to the goddess Ninlil, Enlil's female counterpart. The early clay figurines found at Nippur and on other sites, representing a goddess suckling a child and clasping one of her breasts, may well be regarded as representing Ninkharsagga and not Ninlil. Her sanctuaries were at Kesh and Adab, both in the south, and this fact sufficiently explains her comparative want of influence in Akkad, where the Semitic Ishtar took her place. She does indeed appear in the north during the Sargonic period under her own name, though later she survives in her synonyms of Ninmakh, "the Sublime Lady", and Nintu, "the Lady of Child-bearing". It is under the latter title that Hammurabi refers to her in his Code of Laws, where she is tenth in a series of eleven deities. But as Goddess of Birth she retained only a pale reflection of her original cosmic character, and her functions were gradually specialized.(1)

(1) Cf. Poebel, op. cit., p. 33. It is possible that, under one of her later synonyms, we should identify her, as Dr. Poebel suggests, with the Mylitta of Herodotus.

From a consideration of their characters, as revealed by independent sources of evidence, we thus obtain the reason for the co-operation of four deities in the Sumerian Creation. In fact the new text illustrates a well-known principle in the development of myth, the reconciliation of the rival claims of deities, whose cults, once isolated, had been brought from political causes into contact with each other. In this aspect myth is the medium through which a working pantheon is evolved. Naturally all the deities concerned cannot continue to play their original parts in detail. In the Babylonian Epic of Creation, where a single deity, and not a very prominent one, was to be raised to pre-eminent rank, the problem was simple enough. He could retain his own qualities and achievements while borrowing those of any former rival. In the Sumerian text we have the result of a far more delicate process of adjustment, and it is possible that the brevity of the text is here not entirely due to compression of a longer narrative, but may in part be regarded as evidence of early combination. As a result of the association of several competing deities in the work of creation, a tendency may be traced to avoid discrimination between rival claims. Thus it is that the assembled gods, the pantheon as a whole, are regarded as collectively responsible for the creation of the universe. It may be added that this use of *ilâni*, "the gods", forms an interesting linguistic parallel to the plural of the Hebrew divine title Elohim.

It will be remembered that in the Sumerian Version the account of Creation is not given in full, only such episodes being included as were directly related to the Deluge story. No doubt the selection of men and animals was suggested by their subsequent rescue from the Flood; and emphasis was purposely laid on the creation of the *niggilma* because of the part it played in securing mankind's survival. Even so, we noted one striking parallel between the Sumerian Version and that of the Semitic Babylonians, in the reason both give for man's creation. But in the former there is no attempt to explain how the universe itself had come into being, and the existence of the earth is presupposed at the moment when Anu, Enlil, Enki, and Ninkharsagga undertake the creation of man. The Semitic-Babylonian Version, on the other hand, is mainly occupied with events that led up to the acts of creation, and it concerns our problem to inquire how far those episodes were of Semitic and how far of Sumerian origin. A further question arises as to whether some strands of the narrative may not at one time have existed in Sumerian form independently of the Creation myth.

The statement is sometimes made that there is no reason to assume a Sumerian original for the Semitic-Babylonian Version, as recorded on "the Seven Tablets of Creation";(1) and this remark, though true of that version as a whole, needs some qualification. The composite nature of the poem has long been recognized, and an analysis of the text has shown that no less than five principal strands have been combined for its formation. These consist of (i) The Birth of the Gods; (ii) The Legend of Ea and Apsû; (iii) The principal Dragon Myth; (iv) The actual account of Creation; and (v) the Hymn to Marduk under his fifty titles.(2) The Assyrian commentaries to the Hymn, from which considerable portions of its text are restored, quote throughout a Sumerian original, and explain it word for word by the phrases of the Semitic Version;(3) so that for one out of the Seven Tablets a Semitic origin is at once disproved. Moreover, the majority of the fifty titles, even in the forms in which they have reached us in the Semitic text, are demonstrably Sumerian, and since many of them celebrate details of their owner's creative work, a Sumerian original for other parts of the version is implied. Enlil and Ea are both represented as bestowing their own names upon Marduk,(4) and we may assume that many of the fifty titles were originally borne by Enlil as a Sumerian Creator.(5) Thus some portions of the actual account of Creation were probably derived from a Sumerian original in which "Father Enlil" figured as the hero.

(1) Cf., e.g., Jastrow, *Journ. of the Amer. Or. Soc.*, Vol. XXXVI (1916), p. 279.

(2) See *The Seven Tablets of Creation*, Vol. I, pp. lxvi ff.; and cf. Skinner, *Genesis*, pp. 43 ff.

(3) Cf. *Sev. Tabl.*, Vol. I, pp. 157 ff.

(4) Cf. Tabl. VII, ll. 116 ff.

(5) The number fifty was suggested by an ideogram employed
for Enlil's name.

For what then were the Semitic Babylonians themselves responsible? It seems to me that, in the "Seven Tablets", we may credit them with considerable ingenuity in the combination of existing myths, but not with their invention. The whole poem in its present form is a glorification of Marduk, the god of Babylon, who is to be given pre-eminent rank among the gods to correspond with the political position recently attained by his city. It would have been quite out of keeping with the national thought to make a break in the tradition, and such a course would not have served the purpose of the Babylonian priesthood, which was to obtain recognition of their claims by the older cult-centres in the country. Hence they chose and combined the more important existing myths, only making such alterations as would fit them to their new hero. Babylon herself had won her position by her own exertions; and it would be a natural idea to give Marduk his opportunity of becoming Creator of the world as the result of successful conflict. A combination of the Dragon myth with the myth of Creation would have admirably served their purpose; and this is what we find in the Semitic poem. But even that combination may not have been their own invention; for, though, as we shall see, the idea of conflict had no part in the earlier forms of the Sumerian Creation myth, its combination with the Dragon *motif* may have characterized the local Sumerian Version of Nippur. How mechanical was the Babylonian redactors' method of glorifying Marduk is seen in their use of the description of Tiamat and her monster brood, whom Marduk is made to conquer. To impress the hearers of the poem with his prowess, this is repeated at length no less than four times, one god carrying the news of her revolt to another.

Direct proof of the manner in which the later redactors have been obliged to modify the original Sumerian Creation myth, in consequence of their incorporation of other elements, may be seen in the Sixth Tablet of the poem, where Marduk states the reason for man's creation. In the second lecture we noted how the very words of the principal Sumerian Creator were put into Marduk's mouth; but the rest of the Semitic god's speech finds no equivalent in the Sumerian Version and was evidently inserted in order to reconcile the narrative with its later ingredients. This will best be seen by printing the two passages in parallel columns:(1)

(1) The extract from the Sumerian Version, which occurs in the lower part of the First Column, is here compared with the Semitic-Babylonian Creation Series, Tablet VI, ll. 6-10 (see *Seven Tablets*, Vol. I, pp. 86 ff.). The comparison is justified whether we regard the Sumerian speech as a direct preliminary to man's creation, or as a reassertion of his duty after his rescue from destruction by the Flood.

SUMERIAN VERSION	SEMITIC VERSION
"The people will I cause to . . .	"I will make man, that man may
in their settlements, (. . .).	
Cities . . . shall (man) build,	I will create man who shall
in their protection will I cause	inhabit (. . .),
him to rest,	
That he may lay the brick of our	That the service of the gods may
house in a clean spot,	be established, and that
(their) shrines (may be	
built).	
That in a clean spot he may	But I will alter the ways of the
establish our . . . !"	gods, and I will change (their paths);
	Together shall they be
	oppressed, and unto evil shall
	(they . . .)!"

The welding of incongruous elements is very apparent in the Semitic Version. For the statement that man will be created in order that the gods may have worshippers is at once followed by the announcement that the gods themselves must be punished and their "ways" changed. In the Sumerian Version the gods are united and all are naturally regarded as worthy of man's worship. The Sumerian Creator makes no distinctions; he refers to "our houses", or temples, that shall be established. But in the later version divine conflict has been introduced, and the future

201

head of the pantheon has conquered and humiliated the revolting deities. Their "ways" must therefore be altered before they are fit to receive the worship which was accorded them by right in the simpler Sumerian tradition. In spite of the epitomized character of the Sumerian Version, a comparison of these passages suggests very forcibly that the Semitic-Babylonian myth of Creation is based upon a simpler Sumerian story, which has been elaborated to reconcile it with the Dragon myth.

The Semitic poem itself also supplies evidence of the independent existence of the Dragon myth apart from the process of Creation, for the story of Ea and Apsû, which it incorporates, is merely the local Dragon myth of Eridu. Its inclusion in the story is again simply a tribute to Marduk; for though Ea, now become Marduk's father, could conquer Apsû, he was afraid of Tiamat, "and turned back".(1) The original Eridu myth no doubt represented Enki as conquering the watery Abyss, which became his home; but there is nothing to connect this tradition with his early creative activities. We have long possessed part of another local version of the Dragon myth, which describes the conquest of a dragon by some deity other than Marduk; and the fight is there described as taking place, not before Creation, but at a time when men existed and cities had been built.(2) Men and gods were equally terrified at the monster's appearance, and it was to deliver the land from his clutches that one of the gods went out and slew him. Tradition delighted to dwell on the dragon's enormous size and terrible appearance. In this version he is described as fifty *bêru*(3) in length and one in height; his mouth measured six cubits and the circuit of his ears twelve; he dragged himself along in the water, which he lashed with his tail; and, when slain, his blood flowed for three years, three months, a day and a night. From this description we can see he was given the body of an enormous serpent.(4)

(1) Tabl. III, l. 53, &c. In the story of Bel and the Dragon, the third of the apocryphal additions to Daniel, we have direct evidence of the late survival of the Dragon *motif* apart from any trace of the Creation myth; in this connexion see Charles, *Apocrypha and Pseudopigrapha*, Vol. I (1913), p. 653 f.

(2) See *Seven Tablets*, Vol. I, pp. 116 ff., lxviii f. The text is preserved on an Assyrian tablet made for the library of Ashur-bani-pal.

(3) The *bêru* was the space that could be covered in two hours' travelling.

(4) The Babylonian Dragon has progeny in the later apocalyptic literature, where we find very similar descriptions of the creatures' size. Among them we may perhaps include the dragon in the Apocalypse of Baruch, who,
according to the Slavonic Version, apparently every day drinks a cubit's depth from the sea, and yet the sea does not sink because of the three hundred and sixty rivers that flow into it (cf. James, "Apocrypha Anecdota", Second

Series, in Armitage Robinson's *Texts and Studies*, V, No. 1, pp. lix ff.). But Egypt's Dragon *motif* was even more prolific, and the *Pistis Sophia* undoubtedly suggested descriptions of the Serpent, especially in connexion with Hades.

A further version of the Dragon myth has now been identified on one of the tablets recovered during the recent excavations at Ashur,(1) and in it the dragon is not entirely of serpent form, but is a true dragon with legs. Like the one just described, he is a male monster. The description occurs as part of a myth, of which the text is so badly preserved that only the contents of one column can be made out with any certainty. In it a god, whose name is wanting, announces the presence of the dragon: "In the water he lies and I (. . .)!" Thereupon a second god cries successively to Aruru, the mother-goddess, and to Pallil, another deity, for help in his predicament. And then follows the description of the dragon:

In the sea was the Serpent cre(ated).
Sixty *bêru* is his length;
Thirty *bêru* high is his he(ad).(2)
For half (a *bêru*) each stretches the surface of his ey(es);(3)
For twenty *bêru* go (his feet).(4)
He devours fish, the creatures (of the sea),
He devours birds, the creatures (of the heaven),
He devours wild asses, the creatures (of the field),
He devours men,(5) to the peoples (he . . .).

(1) For the text, see Ebeling, *Assurtexte* I, No. 6; it is translated by him in *Orient. Lit.-Zeit.*, Vol. XIX, No. 4

(April, 1916).

(2) The line reads: *30 bêru sa-ka-a ri-(sa-a-su)*. Dr. Ebeling renders *ri-sa-a* as "heads" (Köpfe), implying that the dragon had more than one head. It may be pointed out that, if we could accept this translation, we should have an interesting parallel to the description of some of the primaeval monsters, preserved from Berossus, as {soma men ekhontas en, kephalas de duo}. But the common word for "head" is *kakkadu*, and there can be little doubt that *rîsâ* is here used in its ordinary sense of "head, summit, top" when applied to a high building.

(3) The line reads: *a-na 1/2 ta-am la-bu-na li-bit ên(a-su)*. Dr. Ebeling translates, "auf je eine Hälfte ist ein Ziegel (ihrer) Auge(n) gelegt". But *libittu* is clearly used here, not with its ordinary meaning of "brick", which yields a strange rendering, but in its special sense, when applied to large buildings, of "foundation, floor-space, area", i.e. "surface". Dr. Ebeling reads *ênâ-su* at the end of the line, but the sign is broken; perhaps the traces may prove to be those of *uznâ su*, "his ears", in which case *li-bit uz(nâ-su)* might be rendered either as "surface of his ears", or as "base (lit. foundation) of his ears".

(4) i.e. the length of his pace was twenty *bêru*.

(5) Lit. "the black-headed".

The text here breaks off, at the moment when Pallil, whose help against the dragon had been invoked, begins to speak. Let us hope we shall recover the continuation of the narrative and learn what became of this carnivorous monster.

There are ample grounds, then, for assuming the independent existence of the Babylonian Dragon-myth, and though both the versions recovered have come to us in Semitic form, there is no doubt that the myth itself existed among the Sumerians. The dragon *motif* is constantly recurring in descriptions of Sumerian temple-decoration, and the twin dragons of Ningishzida on Gudea's libation-vase, carved in green steatite and inlaid with shell, are a notable product of Sumerian art.(1) The very names borne by Tiamat's brood of monsters in the "Seven Tablets" are stamped in most cases with their Sumerian descent, and Kingu, whom she appointed as her champion in place of Apsû, is equally Sumerian. It would be strange indeed if the Sumerians had not evolved a Dragon myth,(2) for the Dragon combat is the most obvious of nature myths and is found in most mythologies of Europe and the Near East. The trailing storm-clouds suggest his serpent form, his fiery tongue is seen in the forked lightning, and, though he may darken the world for a time, the Sun-god will always be victorious. In Egypt the myth of "the Overthrowing of Apep, the enemy of Ra" presents a close parallel to that of Tiamat;(3) but of all Eastern mythologies that of the Chinese has inspired in art the most beautiful treatment of the Dragon, who, however, under his varied forms was for them

206

essentially beneficent. Doubtless the Semites of Babylonia had their own versions of the Dragon combat, both before and after their arrival on the Euphrates, but the particular version which the priests of Babylon wove into their epic is not one of them.

(1) See E. de Sarzec, *Découvertes en Chaldée*, pl. xliv, Fig. 2, and Heuzey, *Catalogue des antiquités chaldéennes*, p. 281.

(2) In his very interesting study of "Sumerian and Akkadian Views of Beginnings", contributed to the *Journ. of the Amer. Or. Soc.*, Vol. XXXVI (1916), pp. 274 ff., Professor Jastrow suggests that the Dragon combat in the Semitic-Babylonian Creation poem is of Semitic not Sumerian origin. He does not examine the evidence of the poem itself in detail, but bases the suggestion mainly on the two hypotheses, that the Dragon combat of the poem was suggested by the winter storms and floods of the Euphrates Valley, and that the Sumerians came from a mountain region where water was not plentiful. If we grant both assumptions, the suggested conclusion does not seem to me necessarily to follow, in view of the evidence we now possess as to the remote date of the Sumerian settlement in the Euphrates Valley. Some evidence may still be held to point to a mountain home for the proto-Sumerians, such as the name of their early goddess Ninkharsagga, "the Lady of the

Mountains". But, as we must now regard Babylonia itself as the cradle of their civilization, other data tend to lose something of their apparent significance. It is true that the same Sumerian sign means "land" and "mountain"; but it may have been difficult to obtain an intelligible profile for "land" without adopting a mountain form. Such a name as Ekur, the "Mountain House" of Nippur, may perhaps indicate size, not origin; and Enki's association with metal-working may be merely due to his character as God of Wisdom, and is not appropriate solely "to a god whose home is in the mountains where metals are found" (op. cit., p. 295). It should be added that Professor Jastrow's theory of the Dragon combat is bound up with his view of the origin of an interesting Sumerian "myth of beginnings", to which reference is made later.

(3) Cf. Budge, *Gods of the Egyptians*, Vol. I, pp. 324 ff. The inclusion of the two versions of the Egyptian Creation myth, recording the Birth of the Gods in the "Book of Overthrowing Apep", does not present a very close parallel to the combination of Creation and Dragon myths in the Semitic-Babylonian poem, for in the Egyptian work the two myths are not really combined, the Creation Versions being inserted in the middle of the spells against Apep, without any attempt at assimilation (see Budge, *Egyptian Literature*, Vol. I, p. xvi).

We have thus traced four out of the five strands which form the Semitic-Babylonian poem of Creation to a Sumerian ancestry. And we now come back to the first of the strands, the Birth of the Gods, from which our discussion started. For if this too should prove to be Sumerian, it would help to fill in the gap in our Sumerian Creation myth, and might furnish us with some idea of the Sumerian view of "beginnings", which preceded the acts of creation by the great gods. It will be remembered that the poem opens with the description of a time when heaven and earth did not exist, no field or marsh even had been created, and the universe consisted only of the primaeval water-gods, Apsû, Mummu, and Tiamat, whose waters were mingled together. Then follows the successive generation of two pairs of deities, Lakhmu and Lakhamu, and Anshar and Kishar, long ages separating the two generations from each other and from the birth of the great gods which subsequently takes place. In the summary of the myth which is given by Damascius(1) the names of the various deities accurately correspond to those in the opening lines of the poem; but he makes some notable additions, as will be seen from the following table:

DAMASCUS "SEVEN TABLETS" I

{'Apason—-Tauthe} Apsû—-Tiamat
|
{Moumis} Mummu
{Lakhos—-Lakhe}(2) Lakhmu—-Lakhamu
{'Assoros—-Kissare} Anshar—-Kishar
{'Anos, 'Illinos, 'Aos} Anu, ( ), Nudimmud (= Ea)

{'Aos—-Dauke}
|
{Belos}

(1) *Quaestiones de primis principiis*, cap. 125; ed. Kopp, p. 384.

(2) Emended from the reading {Dakhen kai Dakhon} of the text.

In the passage of the poem which describes the birth of the great gods after the last pair of primaeval deities, mention is duly made of Anu and Nudimmud (the latter a title of Ea), corresponding to the {'Anos} and {'Aos} of Damascius; and there appears to be no reference to Enlil, the original of {'Illinos}. It is just possible that his name occurred at the end of one of the broken lines, and, if so, we should have a complete parallel to Damascius. But the traces are not in favour of the restoration;(1) and the omission of Enlil's name from this part of the poem may be readily explained as a further tribute to Marduk, who definitely usurps his place throughout the subsequent narrative. Anu and Ea had both to be mentioned because of the parts they play in the Epic, but Enlil's only recorded appearance is in the final assembly of the gods, where he bestows his own name "the Lord of the World"(2) upon Marduk. The evidence of Damascius suggests that Enlil's name was here retained, between those of Anu and Ea, in other versions of the poem. But the occurrence of the name in any version is in itself evidence of the antiquity of this strand of the narrative. It is a legitimate inference that the myth of the Birth of the Gods goes back to a time at least before the rise of Babylon, and is presumably of Sumerian origin.

(1) Anu and Nudimmud are each mentioned for the first time at the beginning of a line, and the three lines following the reference to Nudimmud are entirely occupied with descriptions of his wisdom and power. It is also probable that the three preceding lines (ll. 14-16), all of which refer to Anu by name, were entirely occupied with his description. But it is only in ll. 13-16 that any reference to Enlil can have occurred, and the traces preserved of their second halves do not suggestion the restoration.

(2) Cf. Tabl. VII, . 116.

Further evidence of this may be seen in the fact that Anu, Enlil, and Ea (i.e. Enki), who are here created together, are the three great gods of the Sumerian Version of Creation; it is they who create mankind with the help of the goddess Ninkharsagga, and in the fuller version of that myth we should naturally expect to find some account of their own origin. The reference in Damascius to Marduk ({Belos}) as the son of Ea and Damkina ({Dauke}) is also of interest in this connexion, as it exhibits a goddess in close connexion with one of the three great gods, much as we find Ninkharsagga associated with them in the Sumerian Version.(1) Before leaving the names, it may be added that, of the primaeval deities, Anshar and Kishar are obviously Sumerian in form.

(1) Damkina was the later wife of Ea or Enki; and Ninkharsagga is associated with Enki, as his consort, in another Sumerian myth.

It may be noted that the character of Apsû and Tiamat in this portion of the poem(1) is quite at variance with their later actions. Their revolt at the ordered "way" of the gods was a necessary preliminary to the incorporation of the Dragon myths, in which Ea and Marduk are the heroes. Here they appear as entirely beneficent gods of the primaeval water, undisturbed by storms, in whose quiet depths the equally beneficent deities Lakhmu and Lakhamu, Anshar and Kishar, were generated.(2) This interpretation, by the way, suggests a more satisfactory restoration for the close of the ninth line of the poem than any that has yet been proposed. That line is usually taken to imply that the gods were created "in the midst of (heaven)", but I think the following rendering, in connexion with ll. 1-5, gives better sense:

When in the height heaven was not named,
And the earth beneath did not bear a name,
And the primaeval Apsû who begat them,(3)
And Mummu, and Tiamat who bore them(3) all,—
Their waters were mingled together,
. . .
. . .
. . .
Then were created the gods in the midst of (their waters),(4)
Lakhmu and Lakhamu were called into being . . .

(1) Tabl. I, ll. 1-21.

(2) We may perhaps see a survival of Tiamat's original character in her control of the Tablets of Fate. The poem does not represent her as seizing them in any successful fight; they appear to be already hers to bestow on Kingu, though in the later mythology they are "not his by right" (cf. Tabl. I, ll. 137 ff., and Tabl. IV, l. 121).

(3) i.e. the gods.

(4) The ninth line is preserved only on a Neo-Babylonian duplicate (*Seven Tablets*, Vol. II, pl. i). I suggested the restoration *ki-rib s(a-ma-mi)*, "in the midst of heaven", as possible, since the traces of the first sign in the last word of the line seemed to be those of the Neo-Babylonian form of *sa*. The restoration appeared at the time not altogether satisfactory in view of the first line of the poem, and it could only be justified by supposing that *samâmu*, or "heaven", was already vaguely conceived as in existence (op. cit., Vol. I, p. 3, n. 14). But the traces of the sign, as I have given them (op. cit., Vol. II, pl. i), may also possibly be those of the Neo-Babylonian form of the sign *me*; and I would now restore the end of the line in the Neo-Babylonian tablet as *ki-rib m(e-e-su-nu)*, "in the midst of (their waters)", corresponding to the form *mu-u-su-nu* in l. 5 of this duplicate. In the Assyrian Version *mé(pl)-su-nu* would be read in both lines. It will be

213

possible to verify the new reading, by a re-examination of the traces on the tablet, when the British Museum collections again become available for study after the war.

If the ninth line of the poem be restored as suggested, its account of the Birth of the Gods will be found to correspond accurately with the summary from Berossus, who, in explaining the myth, refers to the Babylonian belief that the universe consisted at first of moisture in which living creatures, such as he had already described, were generated.(1) The primaeval waters are originally the source of life, not of destruction, and it is in them that the gods are born, as in Egyptian mythology; there Nu, the primaeval water-god from whom Ra was self-created, never ceased to be the Sun-god's supporter. The change in the Babylonian conception was obviously introduced by the combination of the Dragon myth with that of Creation, a combination that in Egypt would never have been justified by the gentle Nile. From a study of some aspects of the names at the beginning of the Babylonian poem we have already seen reason to suspect that its version of the Birth of the Gods goes back to Sumerian times, and it is pertinent to ask whether we have any further evidence that in Sumerian belief water was the origin of all things.

(1) {ugrou gar ontos tou pantos kai zoon en auto gegennemenon (toionde) ktl}. His creatures of the primaeval
water were killed by the light; and terrestrial animals were then created which could bear (i.e. breathe and exist in) the air.

For many years we have possessed a Sumerian myth of Creation, which has come to us on a late Babylonian tablet as the introductory section of an incantation. It is provided with a Semitic translation, and to judge from its record of the building of Babylon and Egasila, Marduk's temple, and its identification of Marduk himself with the Creator, it has clearly undergone some editing at the hands of the Babylonian priests. Moreover, the occurrence of various episodes out of their logical order, and the fact that the text records twice over the creation of swamps and marshes, reeds and trees or forests, animals and cities, indicate that two Sumerian myths have been combined. Thus we have no guarantee that the other cities referred to by name in the text, Nippur, Erech, and Eridu, are mentioned in any significant connexion with each other.(1) Of the actual cause of Creation the text appears to give two versions also, one in its present form impersonal, and the other carried out by a god. But these two accounts are quite unlike the authorized version of Babylon, and we may confidently regard them as representing genuine Sumerian myths. The text resembles other early accounts of Creation by introducing its narrative with a series of negative statements, which serve to indicate the preceding non-existence of the world, as will be seen from the following extract:(2)

No city had been created, no creature had been made,
Nippur had not been created, Ekur had not been built,
Erech had not been created, Eanna had not been built,
Apsû had not been created, Eridu had not been built,
Of the holy house, the house of the gods, the habitation had

not

been created.

All lands(3) were sea.

At the time when a channel (was formed) in the midst of the sea,

Then was Eridu created, Esagila built, etc.

Here we have the definite statement that before Creation all the world was sea. And it is important to note that the primaeval water is not personified; the ordinary Sumerian word for "sea" is employed, which the Semitic translator has faithfully rendered in his version of the text.(4) The reference to a channel in the sea, as the cause of Creation, seems at first sight a little obscure; but the word implies a "drain" or "water-channel", not a current of the sea itself, and the reference may be explained as suggested by the drainage of a flood-area. No doubt the phrase was elaborated in the original myth, and it is possible that what appears to be a second version of Creation later on in the text is really part of the more detailed narrative of the first myth. There the Creator himself is named. He is the Sumerian god Gilimma, and in the Semitic translation Marduk's name is substituted. To the following couplet, which describes Gilimma's method of creation, is appended a further extract from a later portion of the text, there evidently displaced, giving additional details of the Creator's work:

Gilimma bound reeds in the face of the waters,

He formed soil and poured it out beside the reeds.(5)

(He)(6) filled in a dike by the side of the sea,

(He . . .) a swamp, he formed a marsh.
(. . .), he brought into existence,
(Reeds he form)ed,(7) trees he created.

(1) The composite nature of the text is discussed by
Professor Jastrow in his *Hebrew and Babylonian Traditions*,
pp. 89 ff.; and in his paper in the *Journ. Amer. Or. Soc.*,
Vol. XXXVI (1916), pp. 279 ff.; he has analysed it into two
main versions, which he suggests originated in Eridu and
Nippur respectively. The evidence of the text does not
appear to me to support the view that any reference to a
watery chaos preceding Creation must necessarily be of
Semitic origin. For the literature of the text (first
published by Pinches, *Journ. Roy. Asiat. Soc.*, Vol. XXIII,
pp. 393 ff.), see *Sev. Tabl.*, Vol. I, p. 130.

(2) Obv., ll. 5-12.

(3) Sum. *nigin-kur-kur-ra-ge*, Sem. *nap-har ma-ta-a-tu*,
lit. "all lands", i.e. Sumerian and Babylonian expressions
for "the world".

(4) Sum. *a-ab-ba*, "sea", is here rendered by *tâmtum*, not
by its personified equivalent Tiamat.

(5) The suggestion has been made that *amu*, the word in the
Semitic version here translated "reeds", should be
connected
with *ammatu*, the word used for "earth" or "dry land" in

the Babylonian Creation Series, Tabl. I, l. 2, and given some such meaning as "expanse". The couplet is thus explained to mean that the god made an expanse on the face of the waters, and then poured out dust "on the expanse". But the Semitic version in l. 18 reads *itti ami*, "beside the *a.*", not *ina ami*, "on the *a.*"; and in any case there does not seem much significance in the act of pouring out specially created dust on or beside land already formed. The Sumerian word translated by *amu* is written *gi-dir*, with the element *gi*, "reed", in l. 17, and though in the following line it is written under its variant form *a-dir* without *gi*, the equation *gi-a-dir* = *amu* is elsewhere attested (cf. Delitzsch, *Handwörterbuch*, p. 77). In favour of regarding *amu* as some sort of reed, here used collectively, it may be pointed out that the Sumerian verb in l. 17 is *kesda*, "to bind", accurately rendered by *rakasu* in the Semitic version. Assuming that l. 34 belongs to the same account, the creation of reeds in general beside trees, after dry land is formed, would not of course be at variance with the god's use of some sort of reed in his first act of creation. He creates the reed-bundles, as he creates the soil, both of which go to form the first dike; the reed-beds, like the other vegetation, spring up from the ground when it appears.

(6) The Semitic version here reads "the lord Marduk"; the corresponding name in the Sumerian text is not preserved.

218

(7) The line is restored from l. 2 o the obverse of the text.

Here the Sumerian Creator is pictured as forming dry land from the primaeval water in much the same way as the early cultivator in the Euphrates Valley procured the rich fields for his crops. The existence of the earth is here not really presupposed. All the world was sea until the god created land out of the waters by the only practical method that was possible in Mesopotamia.

In another Sumerian myth, which has been recovered on one of the early tablets from Nippur, we have a rather different picture of beginnings. For there, though water is the source of life, the existence of the land is presupposed. But it is bare and desolate, as in the Mesopotamian season of "low water". The underlying idea is suggestive of a period when some progress in systematic irrigation had already been made, and the filling of the dry canals and subsequent irrigation of the parched ground by the rising flood of Enki was not dreaded but eagerly desired. The myth is only one of several that have been combined to form the introductory sections of an incantation; but in all of them Enki, the god of the deep water, plays the leading part, though associated with different consorts.(1) The incantation is directed against various diseases, and the recitation of the closing mythical section was evidently intended to enlist the aid of special gods in combating them. The creation of these deities is recited under set formulae in a sort of refrain, and the divine name assigned to each bears a magical connexion with the sickness he or she is intended to dispel.(2)

219

(1) See Langdon, Univ. of Penns. Mus. Publ., Bab. Sect., Vol. X, No. 1 (1915), pl. i f., pp. 69 ff.; *Journ. Amer. Or. Soc.*, Vol. XXXVI (1916), pp. 140 ff.; cf. Prince, *Journ. Amer. Or. Soc.*, Vol. XXXVI, pp. 90 ff.; Jastrow, *Journ. Amer. Or. Soc.*, Vol. XXXVI, pp. 122 ff., and in particular his detailed study of the text in *Amer. Journ. Semit. Lang.*, Vol. XXXIII, pp. 91 ff. Dr. Langdon's first description of the text, in *Proc. Soc. Bibl. Arch.*, Vol. XXXVI (1914), pp. 188 ff., was based on a comparatively small fragment only; and on his completion of the text from other fragments in Pennsylvania. Professor Sayce at once realized that the preliminary diagnosis of a Deluge myth could not be sustained (cf. *Expos. Times*, Nov., 1915, pp. 88 ff.). He, Professor Prince, and Professor Jastrow independently showed that the action of Enki in the myth in sending water on the land was not punitive but beneficent; and the preceding section, in which animals are described as

not performing their usual activities, was shown independently by Professor Prince and Professor Jastrow to have reference, not to their different nature in an ideal existence in Paradise, but, on familiar lines, to their non-existence in a desolate land. It may be added that Professor Barton and Dr. Peters agree generally with Professor Prince and Professor Jastrow in their interpretation of the text, which excludes the suggested biblical parallels; and I understand from Dr. Langdon that he very rightly recognizes

that the text is not a Deluge myth. It is a subject for

220

congratulation that the discussion has materially increased our knowledge of this difficult composition.

(2) Cf. Col. VI, ll. 24 ff.; thus *Ab*-u was created for the sickness of the cow (*ab*); Nin-*tul* for that of the flock (u-*tul*); Nin-*ka*-u-tu and Nin-*ka*-si for that of the mouth (*ka*); Na-zi for that of the *na-zi* (meaning uncertain); *Da zi*-ma for that of the *da-zi* (meaning uncertain); Nin-*til* for that of *til* (life); the name of the eighth and last deity is imperfectly preserved.

We have already noted examples of a similar use of myth in magic, which was common to both Egypt and Babylonia; and to illustrate its employment against disease, as in the Nippur document, it will suffice to cite a well-known magical cure for the toothache which was adopted in Babylon.(1) There toothache was believed to be caused by the gnawing of a worm in the gum, and a myth was used in the incantation to relieve it. The worm's origin is traced from Anu, the god of heaven, through a descending scale of creation; Anu, the heavens, the earth, rivers, canals and marshes are represented as each giving rise to the next in order, until finally the marshes produce the worm. The myth then relates how the worm, on being offered tempting food by Ea in answer to her prayer, asked to be allowed to drink the blood of the teeth, and the incantation closes by invoking the curse of Ea because of the worm's misguided choice. It is clear that power over the worm was obtained by a recital of her creation and of her subsequent ingratitude, which led to her present occupation and the curse under which she laboured. When the myth and invocation had been recited three times over the proper mixture of beer, a plant, and oil, and the mixture had been applied to the offending tooth, the worm would fall under the spell of the curse and the patient would at once gain relief. The example is instructive, as the connexion of ideas is quite clear. In the Nippur document the recital of the creation of the eight deities evidently ensured their presence, and a demonstration of the mystic bond between their names and the corresponding diseases rendered the working of their powers effective. Our knowledge of a good many other myths is due solely to their magical employment.

(1) See Thompson, *Devils and Evil Spirits of Babylonia*, Vol. II, pp. 160 ff.; for a number of other examples, see Jastrow, *J.A.O.S.*, Vol. XXXVI, p. 279, n. 7.

Perhaps the most interesting section of the new text is one in which divine instructions are given in the use of plants, the fruit or roots of which may be eaten. Here Usmû, a messenger from Enki, God of the Deep, names eight such plants by Enki's orders, thereby determining the character of each. As Professor Jastrow has pointed out, the passage forcibly recalls the story from Berossus, concerning the mythical creature Oannes, who came up from the Erythraean Sea, where it borders upon Babylonia, to instruct mankind in all things, including "seeds and the gathering of fruits".(1) But the only part of the text that concerns us here is the introductory section, where the life-giving flood, by which the dry fields are irrigated, is pictured as following the union of the water-deities, Enki and Ninella.(2) Professor Jastrow is right in emphasizing the complete absence of any conflict in this Sumerian myth of beginnings; but, as with the other Sumerian Versions we have examined, it seems to me there is no need to seek its origin elsewhere than in the Euphrates Valley.

(1) Cf. Jastrow, *J.A.O.S.*, Vol. XXXVI, p. 127, and *A.J.S.L.*, Vol. XXXIII, p. 134 f. It may be added that the divine naming of the plants also presents a faint parallel to the naming of the beasts and birds by man himself in Gen. ii. 19 f.

(2) Professor Jastrow (*A.J.S.L.*, Vol. XXXIII, p. 115) compares similar myths collected by Sir James Frazer (*Magic Art*, Vol. II, chap. xi and chap. xii, § 2). He also notes the parallel the irrigation myth presents to the mist (or flood) of the earlier Hebrew Version (Gen. ii. 5 f). But Enki, like Ea, was no rain-god; he had his dwellings in the Euphrates and the Deep.

Even in later periods, when the Sumerian myths of Creation had been superseded by that of Babylon, the Euphrates never ceased to be regarded as the source of life and the creator of all things. And this is well brought out in the following introductory lines of a Semitic incantation, of which we possess two Neo-Babylonian copies:(1)

O thou River, who didst create all things,
When the great gods dug thee out,
They set prosperity upon thy banks,

Within thee Ea, King of the Deep, created his dwelling.
The Flood they sent not before thou wert!

Here the river as creator is sharply distinguished from the Flood; and we may conclude that the water of the Euphrates Valley impressed the early Sumerians, as later the Semites, with its creative as well as with its destructive power. The reappearance of the fertile soil, after the receding inundation, doubtless suggested the idea of creation out of water, and the stream's slow but automatic fall would furnish a model for the age-long evolution of primaeval deities. When a god's active and artificial creation of the earth must be portrayed, it would have been natural for the primitive Sumerian to picture the Creator working as he himself would work when he reclaimed a field from flood. We are thus shown the old Sumerian god Gilimma piling reed-bundles in the water and heaping up soil beside them, till the ground within his dikes dries off and produces luxuriant vegetation. But here there is a hint of struggle in the process, and we perceive in it the myth-redactor's opportunity to weave in the Dragon *motif*. No such excuse is afforded by the other Sumerian myth, which pictures the life-producing inundation as the gift of the two deities of the Deep and the product of their union.

But in their other aspect the rivers of Mesopotamia could be terrible; and the Dragon *motif* itself, on the Tigris and Euphrates, drew its imagery as much from flood as from storm. When therefore a single deity must be made to appear, not only as Creator, but also as the champion of his divine allies and the conqueror of other gods, it was inevitable that the myths attaching to the waters under their two aspects should be combined. This may already have taken place at Nippur, when Enlil became the head of the pantheon; but the existence of his myth is conjectural.(1) In a later age we can trace the process in the light of history and of existing texts. There Marduk, identified wholly as the Sun-god, conquers the once featureless primaeval water, which in the process of redaction has now become the Dragon of flood and storm.

(1) The aspect of Enlil as the Creator of Vegetation is emphasized in Tablet VII of the Babylonian poem of Creation.
It is significant that his first title, Asara, should be interpreted as "Bestower of planting", "Founder of sowing", "Creator of grain and plants", "He who caused the green herb
to spring up" (cf. *Seven Tablets*, Vol. I, p. 92 f.). These opening phrases, by which the god is hailed, strike the key-note of the whole composition. It is true that, as Sukh-kur, he is "Destroyer of the foe"; but the great majority of the titles and their Semitic glosses refer to creative activities, not to the Dragon myth.

Thus the dualism which is so characteristic a feature of the Semitic-Babylonian system, though absent from the earliest Sumerian ideas of Creation, was inherent in the nature of the local rivers, whose varied aspects gave rise to or coloured separate myths. Its presence in the later mythology may be traced as a reflection of political development, at first probably among the warring cities of Sumer, but certainly later in the Semitic triumph at Babylon. It was but to be expected that the conqueror, whether Sumerian or Semite, should represent his own god's victory as the establishment of order out of chaos. But this would be particularly in harmony with the character of the Semitic Babylonians of the First Dynasty, whose genius for method and organization produced alike Hammurabi's Code of Laws and the straight streets of the capital.

We have thus been able to trace the various strands of the Semitic-Babylonian poem of Creation to Sumerian origins; and in the second lecture we arrived at a very similar conclusion with regard to the Semitic-Babylonian Version of the Deluge preserved in the Epic of Gilgamesh. We there saw that the literary structure of the Sumerian Version, in which Creation and Deluge are combined, must have survived under some form into the Neo-Babylonian period, since it was reproduced by Berossus. And we noted the fact that the same arrangement in Genesis did not therefore prove that the Hebrew accounts go back directly to early Sumerian originals. In fact, the structural resemblance presented by Genesis can only be regarded as an additional proof that the Sumerian originals continued to be studied and translated by the Semitic priesthood, although they had long been superseded officially by their later descendants, the Semitic epics. A detailed comparison of the Creation and Deluge narratives in the various versions at once discloses the fact that the connexion between those of the Semitic Babylonians and the Hebrews is far closer and more striking than that which can be traced when the latter are placed beside the

Sumerian originals. We may therefore regard it as certain that the Hebrews derived their knowledge of Sumerian tradition, not directly from the Sumerians themselves, but through Semitic channels from Babylon.

It will be unnecessary here to go in detail through the points of resemblance that are admitted to exist between the Hebrew account of Creation in the first chapter of Genesis and that preserved in the "Seven Tablets".(1) It will suffice to emphasize two of them, which gain in significance through our newly acquired knowledge of early Sumerian beliefs. It must be admitted that, on first reading the poem, one is struck more by the differences than by the parallels; but that is due to the polytheistic basis of the poem, which attracts attention when compared with the severe and dignified monotheism of the Hebrew writer. And if allowance be made for the change in theological standpoint, the material points of resemblance are seen to be very marked. The outline or general course of events is the same. In both we have an abyss of waters at the beginning denoted by almost the same Semitic word, the Hebrew *tehôm*, translated "the deep" in Gen. i. 2, being the equivalent of the Semitic-Babylonian *Tiamat*, the monster of storm and flood who presents so striking a contrast to the Sumerian primaeval water.(2) The second act of Creation in the Hebrew narrative is that of a "firmament", which divided the waters under it from those above.(3) But this, as we have seen, has no parallel in the early Sumerian conception until it was combined with the Dragon combat in the form in which we find it in the Babylonian poem. There the body of Tiamat is divided by

227

Marduk, and from one half of her he constructs a covering or dome for heaven, that is to say a "firmament", to keep her upper waters in place. These will suffice as text passages, since they serve to point out quite clearly the Semitic source to which all the other detailed points of Hebrew resemblance may be traced.

(1) See *Seven Tablets*, Vol. I, pp. lxxxi ff., and Skinner, *Genesis*, pp. 45 ff.

(2) The invariable use of the Hebrew word *tehôm* without the article, except in two passages in the plural, proves that it is a proper name (cf. Skinner, op. cit., p. 17); and its correspondence with *Tiamat* makes the resemblance of the versions far more significant than if their parallelism were confined solely to ideas.

(3) Gen. i. 6-8.

In the case of the Deluge traditions, so conclusive a demonstration is not possible, since we have no similar criterion to apply. And on one point, as we saw, the Hebrew Versions preserve an original Sumerian strand of the narrative that was not woven into the Gilgamesh Epic, where there is no parallel to the piety of Noah. But from the detailed description that was given in the second lecture, it will have been noted that the Sumerian account is on the whole far simpler and more primitive than the other versions. It is only in the Babylonian Epic, for example, that the later Hebrew writer finds material from which to construct the ark, while the sweet savour of Ut-napishtim's sacrifice, and possibly his sending forth of the birds, though reproduced in the earlier Hebrew Version, find no parallels in the Sumerian account.(1) As to the general character of the Flood, there is no direct reference to rain in the Sumerian Version, though its presence is probably implied in the storm. The heavy rain of the Babylonian Epic has been increased to forty days of rain in the earlier Hebrew Version, which would be suitable to a country where local rain was the sole cause of flood. But the later Hebrew writer's addition of "the fountains of the deep" to "the windows of heaven" certainly suggests a more intimate knowledge of Mesopotamia, where some contributary cause other than local rain must be sought for the sudden and overwhelming catastrophes of which the rivers are capable.

(1) For detailed lists of the points of agreement presented by the Hebrew Versions J and P to the account in the Gilgamesh Epic, see Skinner, op. cit., p. 177 f.; Driver, *Genesis*, p. 106 f.; and Gordon, *Early Traditions of Genesis* (1907), pp. 38 ff.

Thus, viewed from a purely literary standpoint, we are now enabled to trace back to a primitive age the ancestry of the traditions, which, under a very different aspect, eventually found their way into Hebrew literature. And in the process we may note the changes they underwent as they passed from one race to another. The result of such literary analysis and comparison, so far from discrediting the narratives in Genesis, throws into still stronger relief the moral grandeur of the Hebrew text.

We come then to the question, at what periods and by what process did the Hebrews become acquainted with Babylonian ideas? The tendency of the purely literary school of critics has been to explain the process by the direct use of Babylonian documents wholly within exilic times. If the Creation and Deluge narratives stood alone, a case might perhaps be made out for confining Babylonian influence to this late period. It is true that during the Captivity the Jews were directly exposed to such influence. They had the life and civilization of their captors immediately before their eyes, and it would have been only natural for the more learned among the Hebrew scribes and priests to interest themselves in the ancient literature of their new home. And any previous familiarity with the myths of Babylonia would undoubtedly have been increased by actual residence in the country. We may perhaps see a result of such acquaintance with Babylonian literature, after Jehoiachin's deportation, in an interesting literary parallel that has been pointed out between Ezek. xiv. 12-20 and a speech in the Babylonian account of the Deluge in the Gilgamesh Epic, XI, ii. 180-194.(1) The passage in Ezekiel occurs within chaps. i-xxiv, which correspond to the prophet's first period and consist in the main of his utterances in exile before the fall of Jerusalem. It forms, in fact, the introduction to the prophet's announcement of the coming of "four sore judgements upon Jerusalem", from which there "shall be left a remnant that shall be carried forth".(2) But in consequence, here and there, of traces of a later point of view, it is generally admitted that many of the chapters in this section may have been considerably amplified and altered by Ezekiel himself in the course of writing. And if we may regard the literary parallel that has been pointed out as anything more than fortuitous, it is open to us to assume that chap. xiv may have been worked up by Ezekiel many years after his prophetic call at Tel-abib.

(1) See Daiches, "Ezekiel and the Babylonian Account of the Deluge", in the *Jewish Quarterly Review*, April 1905. It has of course long been recognized that Ezekiel, in announcing the punishment of the king of Egypt in xxxii. 2 ff., uses imagery which strongly recalls the Babylonian Creation myth. For he compares Pharaoh to a sea-monster over
whom Yahweh will throw his net (as Marduk had thrown his
over Tiamat); cf. Loisy, *Les mythes babyloniens et les premiers chaptires de la Genèse* (1901), p. 87.

(2) Ezek. xiv. 21 f.

In the passage of the Babylonian Epic, Enlil had already sent the Flood and had destroyed the good with the wicked. Ea thereupon remonstrates with him, and he urges that in future the sinner only should be made to suffer for his sin; and, instead of again causing a flood, let there be discrimination in the divine punishments sent on men or lands. While the flood made the escape of the deserving impossible, other forms of punishment would affect the guilty only. In Ezekiel the subject is the same, but the point of view is different. The land the prophet has in his mind in

231

verse 13 is evidently Judah, and his desire is to explain why it will suffer although not all its inhabitants deserved to share its fate. The discrimination, which Ea urges, Ezekiel asserts will be made; but the sinner must bear his own sin, and the righteous, however eminent, can only save themselves by their righteousness. The general principle propounded in the Epic is here applied to a special case. But the parallelism between the passages lies not only in the general principle but also in the literary setting. This will best be brought out by printing the passages in parallel columns.

Gilg. Epic, XI, 180-194 Ezek. xiv. 12-20

Ea opened his mouth and spake, And the word of the Lord came
He said to the warrior Enlil; unto me, saying,
Thou director of the gods! O Son of man, when a land sinneth
warrior! against me by committing a
Why didst thou not take counsel trespass, and I stretch out
but didst cause a flood? mine hand upon it, and break
On the transgressor lay his the staff of the bread
transgression! thereof, and send *famine* Be merciful, so that
(all) be not upon it, and cut off from it
destroyed! Have patience, so man and beast; though these
that (all) be not (cut off)! three men, Noah, Daniel, and
Instead of causing a flood, Job, were in it, they should
Let *lions*(1) come and diminish deliver but their own souls by

232

mankind! their righteousness, saith the
Instead of causing a flood, Lord God.
Let *leopards*(1) come and If I cause *noisome beasts* to
diminish mankind! pass through the land, and
Instead of causing a flood, they spoil it, so that it be
Let *famine* be caused and let it desolate, that no man may
pass
  smite the land! through because of the beasts;
Instead of causing a flood, though these three men were in
Let the *Plague-god* come and it, as I live, saith the Lord
(slay) mankind! God, they shall deliver
neither sons nor daughters;
they only shall be delivered,
but the land shall be
desolate.
Or if I bring a *sword* upon
that land, and say, Sword, go
through the land; so that I
cut off from it man and beast;
though these three men were in
it, as I live, saith the Lord
God, they shall deliver
neither sons nor daughters,
but they only shall be
delivered themselves.
Or if I send a *pestilence* into
that land, and pour out my
fury upon it in blood, to cut
off from it man and beast;

though Noah, Daniel, and Job,
were in it, as I live, saith
the Lord God, they shall
deliver neither son nor
daughter; they shall but
deliver their own souls by
their righteousness.

(1) Both Babylonian words are in the singular, but probably used collectively, as is the case with their Hebrew equivalent in Ezek. xiv. 15.

It will be seen that, of the four kinds of divine punishment mentioned, three accurately correspond in both compositions. Famine and pestilence occur in both, while the lions and leopards of the Epic find an equivalent in "noisome beasts". The sword is not referred to in the Epic, but as this had already threatened Jerusalem at the time of the prophecy's utterance its inclusion by Ezekiel was inevitable. Moreover, the fact that Noah should be named in the refrain, as the first of the three proverbial examples of righteousness, shows that Ezekiel had the Deluge in his mind, and increases the significance of the underlying parallel between his argument and that of the Babylonian poet.(1) It may be added that Ezekiel has thrown his prophecy into poetical form, and the metre of the two passages in the Babylonian and Hebrew is, as Dr. Daiches points out, not dissimilar.

(1) This suggestion is in some measure confirmed by the *Biblical Antiquities of Philo*, ascribed by Dr. James to

the closing years of the first century A.D.; for its writer, in his account of the Flood, has actually used Ezek. xiv. 12 ff. in order to elaborate the divine speech in Gen. viii. 21 f. This will be seen from the following extract, in which the passage interpolated between verses 21 and 22 of Gen. viii is enclosed within brackets: "And God said: I will not again curse the earth for man's sake, for the guise of man's heart hath left off (sic) from his youth. And therefore I will not again destroy together all living as I have done. (But it shall be, when the dwellers upon earth have sinned, I will judge them by *famine* or by the *sword* or by fire or by *pestilence* (lit. death), and there shall be earthquakes, and they shall be scattered into places not inhabited (or, the places of their habitation shall be scattered). But I will not again spoil the earth with the water of a flood, and) in all the days of the earth seed time and harvest, cold and heat, summer and autumn, day and night shall not cease . . ."; see James, *The Biblical Antiquities of Philo*, p. 81, iii. 9. Here wild beasts are omitted, and fire, earthquakes, and exile are added; but famine, sword, and pestilence are prominent, and the whole passage is clearly suggested by Ezekiel. As a result of the combination, we have in the *Biblical Antiquities* a complete parallel to the passage in the Gilgamesh Epic.

It may of course be urged that wild beasts, famine, and pestilence are such obvious forms of divine punishment that their enumeration by both writers is merely due to chance. But the parallelism should be considered with the other

235

possible points of connexion, namely, the fact that each writer is dealing with discrimination in divine punishments of a wholesale character, and that while the one is inspired by the Babylonian tradition of the Flood, the other takes the hero of the Hebrew Flood story as the first of his selected types of righteousness. It is possible that Ezekiel may have heard the Babylonian Version recited after his arrival on the Chebar. And assuming that some form of the story had long been a cherished tradition of the Hebrews themselves, we could understand his intense interest in finding it confirmed by the Babylonians, who would show him where their Flood had taken place. To a man of his temperament, the one passage in the Babylonian poem that would have made a special appeal would have been that quoted above, where the poet urges that divine vengeance should be combined with mercy, and that all, righteous and wicked alike, should not again be destroyed. A problem continually in Ezekiel's thoughts was this very question of wholesale divine punishment, as exemplified in the case of Judah; and it would not have been unlikely that the literary structure of the Babylonian extract may have influenced the form in which he embodied his own conclusions.

But even if we regard this suggestion as unproved or improbable, Ezekiel's reference to Noah surely presupposes that at least some version of the Flood story was familiar to the Hebrews before the Captivity. And this conclusion is confirmed by other Babylonian parallels in the early chapters of Genesis, in which oral tradition rather than documentary borrowing must have played the leading

236

part.(1) Thus Babylonian parallels may be cited for many features in the story of Paradise,(2) though no equivalent of the story itself has been recovered. In the legend of Adapa, for example, wisdom and immortality are the prerogative of the gods, and the winning of immortality by man is bound up with eating the Food of Life and drinking the Water of Life; here too man is left with the gift of wisdom, but immortality is withheld. And the association of winged guardians with the Sacred Tree in Babylonian art is at least suggestive of the Cherubim and the Tree of Life. The very side of Eden has now been identified in Southern Babylonia by means of an old boundary-stone acquired by the British Museum a year or two ago.(3)

(1) See Loisy, *Les mythes babyloniens*, pp. 10 ff., and cf. S. Reinach, *Cultes, Mythes et Religions*, t. II, pp. 386 ff.

(2) Cf. especially Skinner, *Genesis*, pp. 90 ff. For the latest discussion of the Serpent and the Tree of Life, suggested by Dr. Skinner's summary of the evidence, see Frazer in *Essays and Studies presented to William Ridgeway* (1913), pp. 413 ff.

(3) See *Babylonian Boundary Stones in the British Museum* (1912), pp. 76 ff., and cf. *Geographical Journal*, Vol. XL, No. 2 (Aug., 1912), p. 147. For the latest review of the evidence relating to the site of Paradise, see Boissier, "La situation du paradis terrestre", in *Le Globe*, t. LV, Mémoires (Geneva, 1916).

But I need not now detain you by going over this familiar ground. Such possible echoes from Babylon seem to suggest pre-exilic influence rather than late borrowing, and they surely justify us in inquiring to what periods of direct or indirect contact, earlier than the Captivity, the resemblances between Hebrew and Babylonian ideas may be traced. One point, which we may regard as definitely settled by our new material, is that these stories of the Creation and of the early history of the world were not of Semitic origin. It is no longer possible to regard the Hebrew and Babylonian Versions as descended from common Semitic originals. For we have now recovered some of those originals, and they are not Semitic but Sumerian. The question thus resolves itself into an inquiry as to periods during which the Hebrews may have come into direct or indirect contact with Babylonia.

There are three pre-exilic periods at which it has been suggested the Hebrews, or the ancestors of the race, may have acquired a knowledge of Babylonian traditions. The earliest of these is the age of the patriarchs, the traditional ancestors of the Hebrew nation. The second period is that of the settlement in Canaan, which we may put from 1200 B.C. to the establishment of David's kingdom at about 1000 B.C. The third period is that of the later Judaean monarch, from 734 B.C. to 586 B.C., the date of the fall of Jerusalem; and in this last period there are two reigns of special importance in this connexion, those of Ahaz (734-720 B.C.) and Manasseh (693-638 B.C.).

With regard to the earliest of these periods, those who support the Mosaic authorship of the Pentateuch may quite consistently assume that Abraham heard the legends in Ur of the Chaldees. And a simple retention of the traditional view seems to me a far preferable attitude to any elaborate attempt at rationalizing it. It is admitted that Arabia was the cradle of the Semitic race; and the most natural line of advance from Arabia to Aram and thence to Palestine would be up the Euphrates Valley. Some writers therefore assume that nomad tribes, personified in the traditional figure of Abraham, may have camped for a time in the neighbourhood of Ur and Babylon; and that they may have carried the Babylonian stories with them in their wanderings, and continued to preserve them during their long subsequent history. But, even granting that such nomads would have taken any interest in traditions of settled folk, this view hardly commends itself. For stories received from foreign sources become more and more transformed in the course of centuries.(1) The vivid Babylonian colouring of the Genesis narratives cannot be reconciled with this explanation of their source.

(1) This objection would not of course apply to M. Naville's suggested solution, that cuneiform tablets formed the medium
of transmission. But its author himself adds that he does not deny its conjectural character; see *The Text of the Old Testament* (Schweich Lectures, 1915), p. 32.

A far greater number of writers hold that it was after their arrival in Palestine that the Hebrew patriarchs came into contact with Babylonian culture. It is true that from an early period Syria was the scene of Babylonian invasions, and in the first lecture we noted some newly recovered evidence upon this point. Moreover, the dynasty to which Hammurabi belonged came originally from the north-eastern border of Canaan and Hammurabi himself exercised authority in the west. Thus a plausible case could be made out by exponents of this theory, especially as many parallels were noted between the Mosaic legislation and that contained in Hammurabi's Code. But it is now generally recognized that the features common to both the Hebrew and the Babylonian legal systems may be paralleled to-day in the Semitic East and elsewhere,(1) and cannot therefore be cited as evidence of cultural contact. Thus the hypothesis that the Hebrew patriarchs were subjects of Babylon in Palestine is not required as an explanation of the facts; and our first period still stands or falls by the question of the Mosaic authorship of the Pentateuch, which must be decided on quite other grounds. Those who do not accept the traditional view will probably be content to rule this first period out.

(1) See Cook, *The Laws of Moses and the Code of Hammurabi*, p. 281 f.; Driver, *Genesis*, p. xxxvi f.; and cf. Johns, *The Laws of Babylonia and the Laws of the Hebrew Peoples* (Schweich Lectures, 1912), pp. 50 ff.

During the second period, that of the settlement in Canaan, the Hebrews came into contact with a people who had used the Babylonian language as the common medium of communication throughout the Near East. It is an interesting fact that among the numerous letters found at Tell el-Amarna were two texts of quite a different character. These were legends, both in the form of school exercises, which had been written out for practice in the Babylonian tongue. One of them was the legend of Adapa, in which we noted just now a distant resemblance to the Hebrew story of Paradise. It seems to me we are here standing on rather firmer ground; and provisionally we might place the beginning of our process after the time of Hebrew contact with the Canaanites.

Under the earlier Hebrew monarchy there was no fresh influx of Babylonian culture into Palestine. That does not occur till our last main period, the later Judaean monarchy, when, in consequence of the westward advance of Assyria, the civilization of Babylon was once more carried among the petty Syrian states. Israel was first drawn into the circle of Assyrian influence, when Arab fought as the ally of Benhadad of Damascus at the battle of Karkar in 854 B.C.; and from that date onward the nation was menaced by the invading power. In 734 B.C., at the invitation of Ahaz of Judah, Tiglath-Pileser IV definitely intervened in the affairs of Israel. For Ahaz purchased his help against the allied armies of Israel and Syria in the Syro-Ephraimitish war. Tiglath-pileser threw his forces against Damascus and Israel, and Ahaz became his vassal.(1) To this period, when Ahaz, like Panammu II, "ran at the wheel of his lord, the king of Assyria", we may ascribe the first marked invasion of Assyrian influence over Judah. Traces of it may be seen in the altar which Ahaz caused to be erected in Jerusalem after the pattern of the Assyrian altar at Damascus.(2) We saw in the first lecture, in the monuments we have recovered of Panammu I and of Bar-rekub, how the life of another small

Syrian state was inevitably changed and thrown into new channels by the presence of Tiglath-pileser and his armies in the West.

(1) 2 Kings xvi. 7 ff.

(2) 2 Kings xvi. 10 ff.

Hezekiah's resistance checked the action of Assyrian influence on Judah for a time. But it was intensified under his son Manasseh, when Judah again became tributary to Assyria, and in the house of the Lord altars were built to all the host of heaven.(1) Towards the close of his long reign Manasseh himself was summoned by Ashur-bani-pal to Babylon.(2) So when in the year 586 B.C. the Jewish exiles came to Babylon they could not have found in its mythology an entirely new and unfamiliar subject. They must have recognized several of its stories as akin to those they had assimilated and now regarded as their own. And this would naturally have inclined them to further study and comparison.

(1) 2 Kings xxi. 5.

(2) Cf. 2 Chron. xxxiii. 11 ff.

The answer I have outlined to this problem is the one that appears to me most probable, but I do not suggest that it is the only possible one that can be given. What I do suggest is that the Hebrews must have gained some acquaintance with the legends of Babylon in pre-exilic times. And it depends on our reading of the evidence into which of the three main periods the beginning of the process may be traced.

So much, then, for the influence of Babylon. We have seen that no similar problem arises with regard to the legends of Egypt. At first sight this may seem strange, for Egypt lay nearer than Babylon to Palestine, and political and commercial intercourse was at least as close. We have already noted how Egypt influenced Semitic art, and how she offered an ideal, on the material side of her existence, which was readily adopted by her smaller neighbours. Moreover, the Joseph traditions in Genesis give a remarkably accurate picture of ancient Egyptian life; and even the Egyptian proper names embedded in that narrative may be paralleled with native Egyptian names than that to which the traditions refer. Why then is it that the actual myths and legends of Egypt concerning the origin of the world and its civilization should have failed to impress the Hebrew mind, which, on the other hand, was so responsive to those of Babylon?

One obvious answer would be, that it was Nebuchadnezzar II, and not Necho, who carried the Jews captive. And we may readily admit that the Captivity must have tended to perpetuate and intensify the effects of any Babylonian influence that may have previously been felt. But I think there is a wider and in that sense a better answer than that.

I do not propose to embark at this late hour on what ethnologists know as the "Hamitic" problem. But it is a fact that many striking parallels to Egyptian religious belief and practice have been traced among races of the Sudan and East Africa. These are perhaps in part to be explained as the result of contact and cultural inheritance. But at the same time they are evidence of an African, but non-Negroid, substratum in the religion of ancient Egypt. In spite of his proto-Semitic strain, the ancient Egyptian himself never became a Semite. The Nile Valley, at any rate until the Moslem conquest, was stronger than its invaders; it received and moulded them to its own ideal. This quality was shared in some degree by the Euphrates Valley. But Babylonia was not endowed with Egypt's isolation; she was always open on the south and west to the Arabian nomad, who at a far earlier period sealed her Semitic type.

To such racial division and affinity I think we may confidently trace the influence exerted by Egypt and Babylon respectively upon Hebrew tradition.

APPENDIX I

COMPARATIVE TABLE OF THE SUMERIAN, SEMITIC-BABYLONIAN,
HELLENISTIC, AND HEBREW VERSIONS OF CREATION,
ANTEDILUVIAN HISTORY, AND THE DELUGE

N.B.—Parallels with the new Sumerian Version are in upper-case.

Sumerian Version. Seven Tablets Gilgamesh Epic, XI
Berossus('Damscius) Earlier Heb. (J) Later Heb. (P)
(No heaven or earth No heaven or earth Darkness and water
Creation of earth Earth without form

First Creation from Primaeval water- (Primaeval water- and
heaven and void; darkness
primaeval water gods: Apsû-Tiamat, gods: {'Apason- No
plant or herb on face of *tehôm*,
without conflict; Mummu Tauthe}, {Moumis} Ground
watered by the primaeval water
cf. Later Sum. Ver. Generation of: Generation of: mist (or
flood) Divine spirit moving
Lakhmu-Lakhamu {Lakhos-Lakhe} (cf. Sumerian (hovering,
brooding)
Anshar-Kishar {'Assoros-Kissare} irrigation myth of upon
face of waters
Creation)

The great gods: Birth of great gods: Birth of great gods:
ANU, ENLIL, ENKI, ANU, Nudimmud (=EA) {'Anos, 'Illinos,
and Ninkharsagga, Apsû and Tiamat 'Aos, 'Aois-Lauke,
creating deities revolt Belos)
Conquest of Tiamat Conquest of {'Omorka}, Creation of light
by Marduk as Sun- or {Thamte}, by
god {Belos}
Creation of covering Creation of heaven and Creation of
firmament,
for heaven from earth from two halves or heaven, to divide
half of Tiamat's of body of Thamte waters; followed by
body, to keep her emergence of land
waters in place Creation of vegetation
Creation of luminaries Creation of luminaries Creation of
luminaries

(Creation of (probable order) Creation of animals
vegetation)

REASON FOR MAN'S REASON FOR MAN'S
CREATION: worship of CREATION: worship of
gods gods
Creation of MAN Creation of MAN from Creation of MAN
from Creation of MAN from Creation of MAN in
Creator's blood and Creator's blood and dust and Creator's
image of Creator, to
from bone from earth breath of life have dominion
Creation of ANIMALS (Creation of animals) Creation of
ANIMALS Creation of vegetation
Hymn on Seventh Tablet able to bear the air ANIMALS, and
woman Rest on Seventh Day

Creation of KINGDOM 10 Antediluvian KINGS The line of
Cain Antediluvian
5 ANTEDILUVIAN CITIES: Antediluvian city: 3
ANTEDILUVIAN CITIES: The Nephilim (cf. patriarchs (cf.
Eridu, Bad.., LARAK, SHURUPPAK Babylon, SIPPAR,
Sumerian Dynastic Sumerian Dynastic
SIPPAR, SHURUPPAK LARANKHA List) List)

Gods decree MANKIND'S Gods decree flood, Destruction of
MAN Destruction of all
destruction by flood, goddess ISHTAR decreed, because of
flesh decreed, because
NINTU protesting protesting his wickedness of its

246

corruption

ZIUSUDU, hero of UT-NAPISHTIM, hero {Xisouthros} Noah,
hero of Deluge Noah, hero of Deluge
Deluge, KING and of Deluge (=Khasisatra), hero
priest of Deluge, KING

Ziusudu's PIETY Noah's FAVOUR Noah's RIGHTEOUSNESS

WARNING of Ziusudu by WARNING of Ut-nap- WARNING of
Xisuthros WARNING of Noah, and
Enki in DREAM ishtim by Ea in DREAM by Kronos in DREAM
instructions for ark

Ziusudu's vessel a SHIP: 120x120x120 Size of SHIP: 5x2
Instructions to enter Size of ARK: 300x50x30
HUGE SHIP cubits; 7 stories; 9 stadia ark cubits; 3 stories
divisions

All kinds of animals All kinds of animals 7(x2) clean, 2
unclean 2 of all animals

Flood and STORM for 7 FLOOD from heavy rain FLOOD
FLOOD from rain for 40 FLOOD; founts. of deep
days and STORM for 6 days days and rain, 150 days

Ship on Mt. Nisir Ark on Ararat

Abatement of waters Abatement of waters Abatement of

waters Abatement of waters
tested by birds tested by birds tested by birds through
drying wind

SACRIFICE to Sun-god SACRIFICE with sweet SACRIFICE to
gods, SACRIFICE with sweet Landing from ark (after
in ship savour on mountain after landing and savour after
landing year (+10 days))
paying adoration to
EARTH

Anu and Enlil appeased Ea's protest to ENLIL APOTHEOSIS
of X., Divine promise to Noah Divine covenant not
(by "Heaven and Earth") IMMORTALITY of Ut-nap- wife,
daughter, and not again to curse again to destroy EARTH
IMMORTALITY of Ziusudu ishtim and his wife pilot the
GROUND by flood; bow as sign
APPENDIX II

THE ANTEDILUVIAN KINGS OF BEROSSUS AND
THE SUMERIAN DYNASTIC LIST

It may be of assistance to the reader to repeat in tabular
form the
equivalents to the mythical kings of Berossus which are
briefly
discussed in Lecture I. In the following table the two new
equations,
obtained from the earliest section of the Sumerian Dynastic
List, are in

248

upper-case.(1) The established equations to other names are in normal
case, while those for which we should possibly seek other equivalents
are enclosed within brackets.(2) Aruru has not been included as a
possible equivalent for {'Aloros}.(3)

1. {'Aloros}
2. {'Alaparos (? 'Adaparos)}, *Alaporus*, *Alapaurus* (Adapa)
3. {'Amelon, 'Amillaros}, *Almelon* (Amêlu)
4. {'Ammenon} ENMENUNNA
5. {Megalaros, Megalanos}, *Amegalarus* 6. {Daonos, Daos} ETANA
7. {Euedorakhos, Euedoreskhos}, *Edoranchus* Enmeduranki
8. {'Amemphinos}, *Amemphsinus* (Amêl-Sin)
9. {'Otiartes (? 'Opartes)} (Ubar-Tutu)
10. {Xisouthros, Sisouthros, Sisithros} Khasisatra, Atrakhasis(4)

(1) For the royal names of Berossus, see *Euseb. chron. lib. pri.*, ed. Schoene, cols. 7 f., 31 ff. The latinized variants correspond to forms in the Armenian translation of Eusebius.

(2) For the principal discussions of equivalents, see Hommel, *Proc. Soc. Bibl. Arch.*, Vol. XV (1893), pp. 243 ff., and *Die altorientalischen Denkmäler und das Alte Testament* (1902), pp. 23 ff.; Zimmern, *Die Keilinschriften und das Alte Testament*, 3rd ed. (1902), pp. 531 ff.; and

cf. Lenormant, *Les origines de l'histoire*, I (1880), pp.
214 ff. See also Driver, *Genesis*, 10th ed. (1916), p. 80
f.; Skinner, *Genesis*, p. 137 f.; Ball, *Genesis*, p. 50;
and Gordon, *Early Traditions of Genesis*, pp. 46 ff.

(3) There is a suggested equation of Lal-ur-alimma with
{'Aloros}.

(4) The hundred and twenty "sars", or 432,000 years
assigned
by Berossus for the duration of the Antediluvian dynasty,
are distributed as follows among the ten kings; the numbers
are given below first in "sars", followed by their
equivalents in years within brackets: 1. Ten "sars"
(36,000); 2. Three (10,800); 3. Thirteen (46,800); 4. Twelve
(43,200); 5. Eighteen (64,800); 6. Ten (36,000); 7. Eighteen
(64,800); 8. Ten (36,000); 9. Eight (28,800); 10. Eighteen
(64,800).
For comparison with Berossus it may be useful to abstract
from the
Sumerian Dynastic List the royal names occurring in the
earliest
extant dynasties. They are given below with variant forms
from
duplicate copies of the list, and against each is added the
number of
years its owner is recorded to have ruled. The figures giving
the
total duration of each dynasty, either in the summaries or

under the
separate reigns, are sometimes not completely preserved; in such cases
an x is added to the total of the figures still legible. Except in those cases referred to in the foot-notes, all the names are written
in the Sumerian lists without the determinative for "god".

KINGDOM OF KISH
(23 kings; 18,000 + x years, 3 months, 3 days)

...(1)
8. (...) 900(?) years
9. Galumum, Kalumum 900 "
10. Zugagib, Zugakib 830 "
11. Arpi, Arpiu, Arbum 720 "
12. Etana(2) 635 (or 625) years
13. Pili...(3) 410 years
14. Enmenunna, Enmennunna(4) 611 "
15. Melamkish 900 "
16. Barsalnunna 1,200 "
17. Mesza(...) (...) "
...(5)
22.... 900 years
23.... 625 "

KINGDOM OF EANNA (ERECH)(6)
(About 10-12 kings; 2,171 + x years)

1. Meskingasher 325 years
2. Enmerkar 420 "
3. Lugalbanda(7) 1,200 "
4. Dumuzi(8) (i.e. Tammuz) 100 "
5. Gishbilgames(9) (i.e. Gilgamesh) 126 (or 186) years
6. (...)lugal (...) years
...(10)

KINGDOM OF UR
(4 kings; 171 years)

1. Mesannipada 80 years
2. Meskiagnunna 30 "
3. Elu(...) 25 "
4. Balu(...) 36 "

KINGDOM OF AWAN
(3 kings; 356 years)
...(11)

(1) Gap of seven, or possibly eight, names.

(2) The name Etana is written in the lists with and without the determinative for "god".

(3) The reading of the last sign in the name is unknown. A variant form of the name possibly begins with Bali.

(4) This form is given on a fragment of a late Assyrian copy

of the list; cf. *Studies in Eastern History*, Vol. III, p. 143.

(5) Gap of four, or possibly three, names.

(6) Eanna was the great temple of Erech. In the Second Column of the list "the kingdom" is recorded to have passed from Kish to Eanna, but the latter name does not occur in the summary.

(7) The name Lugalbanda is written in the lists with and without the determinative for "god".

(8) The name Dumuzi is written in the list with the determinative for "god".

(9) The name Gishbilgames is written in the list with the determinative for "god".

(10) Gap of about four, five, or six kings.

(11) Wanting.

At this point a great gap occurs in our principal list. The names of some of the missing "kingdoms" may be inferred from the summaries, but their relative order is uncertain. Of two of them we know the duration, a second Kingdom of Ur containing four kings and lasting for a hundred and eight years, and another kingdom, the name of which is not preserved, consisting of only one king who ruled for seven years. The dynastic succession only again becomes assured with the opening of the Dynastic chronicle published by Père Scheil and recently acquired by the British Museum. It will be noted that with the Kingdom of Ur the separate reigns last for decades and not hundreds of years each, so that we here seem to approach genuine tradition, though the Kingdom of Awan makes a partial reversion to myth so far as its duration is concerned. The two suggested equations with Antediluvian kings of Berossus both occur in the earliest Kingdom of Kish and lie well within the Sumerian mythical period. The second of the rulers concerned, Enmenunna (Ammenon), is placed in Sumerian tradition several thousand years before the reputed succession of the gods Lugalbanda and Tammuz and of the national hero Gilgamesh to the throne of Erech. In the first lecture some remarkable points of general resemblance have already been pointed out between Hebrew and Sumerian traditions of these early ages of the world.

CONTENTS